M4S

Past Tense

Also by Catherine Aird

Past Tense

A Sloan and Crosby Mystery

CATHERINE AIRD

Minotaur Books ❦ New York

PAST TENSE. Copyright © 2010 by Catherine Aird. All rights reserved. Printed in the United States of America. For information, address St. Martin's Press, 175 Fifth Avenue, New York, N.Y. 10010.

www.minotaurbooks.com

Library of Congress Cataloging-in-Publication Data

Aird, Catherine.
    Past tense : a Sloan and Crosby mystery / Catherine Aird.—1st U.S. ed.
      p. cm.
    ISBN 978-0-312-67291-1
    1. Sloan, C. D. (Fictitious character)—Fiction. 2. Crosby, Detective Constable W. (Fictitious character)—Fiction. 3. Murder—Investigation—Fiction. 4. Police—Great Britain—Fiction. I. Title.
    PR6051.I65P35 2011
    823'.914—dc22

2010042896

First published in Great Britain by Allison & Busby Limited

First U.S. Edition: March 2011

10 9 8 7 6 5 4 3 2 1

For Rosie, Andrew, Joseph and Tristram
with love

CATHERINE AIRD is the author of more than twenty crime novels and story collections, most of which feature Detective Chief Inspector CD Sloan. She holds an honorary MA from the University of Kent and was made an MBE. Her other works include *Hole in One* and *Losing Ground*. Apart from writing the successful *Chronicles of Calleshire*, she has also written and edited a series of village histories and is active in village life. She lives in Kent.

Past Tense

CATHERINE AIRD

CHAPTER ONE

'Certainly, madam,' said the man in the black jacket and striped trousers, pen and notepad at the ready. 'Now, how many would that be for?'

'I don't know exactly,' muttered Janet, 'so I can't tell you.' She hated being addressed as 'madam'. What she liked to be called by all and sundry was the friendly, familiar-sounding 'Jan' or even her proper Christian name of 'Janet', and after that – if the worst came to the worst – 'Mrs Wakefield': certainly not by anything as formal as 'madam'.

This man was definitely not 'all and sundry'. He was, in fact, the manager of the very grand hotel in whose lobby they were now sitting. His pen was still hovering above the paper while he waited politely for her to continue.

'It's for after a funeral, you see,' Janet said awkwardly. She had already felt quite intimidated enough by the splendour of the Almstone Towers Hotel without having to explain that she didn't even know who – let alone how many people – would be coming.

'I quite understand, madam,' he said as a uniformed hotel minion approached their table with a tray of coffee. 'A wake.'

It wasn't a word she liked. Actually it was one she had been avoiding ever since Bill's Great-Aunt Josephine had died, preferring instead 'bereavement reception' or, even better, just 'a gathering'.

'That's right,' she said.

'And would that be after a burial or a cremation?' he enquired.

'What difference does that make?' she asked curiously.

'Timing,' replied the manager promptly. 'Cremations tend to run to time and, of course, we know exactly how long it takes for the mourners to get here from the Calleford crematorium. It's a little different with a church service and burial.'

The word 'mourners' was another one that Janet Wakefield didn't really like using. After all, she could scarcely be described as a mourner for some old lady whom she had never even seen, let alone known. Her husband, Bill, had just described his Great-Aunt Josephine Short vaguely as one of his late mother's many aunts whom he hadn't known either. He'd rather thought that his Great-Aunt Josephine had fallen out with the rest of her family years ago but he wasn't really sure. And, of course, his own mother – Janet's mother-in-law, that is – had died before Bill and Janet had been married and so wasn't around any more to ask.

'A church service is more difficult, then, is it?' she asked, searching around in her mind for something neutral to say.

'Oh, no, madam, but the actual burial afterwards, as

opposed to cremation, takes longer and can sometimes delay the arrival of the...er...family here.'

'The funeral is at the church at Damory Regis,' she said, reaching for the coffee pot, and adding firmly, 'to be followed by interment in the churchyard there.' Why 'interment' was a less emotive word than 'burial' she didn't know but it was.

'Allow me, madam,' said the manager, deftly picking up the coffee pot ahead of her with one hand and arranging the cups with the other. 'Black or white?'

'White, please.' Janet subsided back in her chair – an elegant affair in the French Empire style but more comfortable than it looked – and determinedly carried on speaking while he poured. 'I've just made the arrangements with the vicar there.'

'That would be Reverend Mr Tompkinson,' said the major-domo smoothly.

'That's right,' she agreed, adding the vicar's Christian name in an attempt at introducing a little informality into the proceedings. 'Derek Tompkinson.'

'Just so,' said the manager.

Janet decided that this man was pretty nearly as formal as the registrar of deaths had been and that had been bad enough. Especially when it transpired that she hadn't brought with her all the documents that the registrar had wanted. Her stammered explanation that they – she – hadn't visited the deceased's room at the nursing home yet and so didn't have what was wanted to hand was accepted with the proviso that she would do so and go back to the registrar with them as speedily as possible.

Bill and Janet Wakefield hadn't even known that Miss Josephine Eleanor Short was a resident in the Berebury Nursing Home in the town, let alone ill and dying in the place, until

the matron there had rung to say that a Mr William Wakefield
of Bill and Janet's address was down in their records as their
late resident's next of kin, and what did he want doing about
the funeral?

Actually Mr William Wakefield wasn't there and therefore
wasn't able to do anything at all about the funeral of the
late Miss Josephine Short anyway; moreover Mr William
Wakefield's employers, having sent him out to South America
on their behalf only a few months earlier, were unlikely to
countenance his return to England until the job in hand had
been completed – and there was no gainsaying them. Not with
the Wakefields' mortgage. This was why Bill's wife Janet had
found herself for the first time in her short life having to make
all the necessary arrangements for a funeral.

And she wasn't sure that she was making a very good job of
it even though Mrs Linda Luxton, the matron of the Berebury
Nursing Home, had helped a lot by indicating that Messrs
Morton & Son, Funeral Directors, had already been selected
by the deceased for the job. Janet knew even less about
undertakers than she did about wakes, her connection with
them until now being limited to something about them that
used to be chanted in the school playground – 'First they take
you under and then they take' – and to children's autograph
books signed 'Yours until the undertaker undertakes to take
you under'.

Fortunately Tod Morton, that young sprig of the firm of
Morton & Son, Funeral Directors Ltd, of Berebury, had been
even more helpful than the matron of the home.

'Josephine Eleanor Short, did you say?' he had asked. 'Ah,
yes. I think you'll find she had a funeral plan with us. That
helps a lot.'

Janet Wakefield hadn't liked to admit that she hadn't known what a funeral plan was. 'The hymns and things she wanted, you mean?' she had asked vaguely.

'No, no,' Tod Morton had said. 'I mean that Miss Short had already paid for her funeral and instructed us in what she had wanted carrying out. What, when and where, you might say.'

That had completely confounded Janet Wakefield.

'Service at St Nicholas Church at Damory Regis and burial in the churchyard there, followed by a decent send-off at the Almstone Towers Hotel,' explained Tod cheerfully. 'Oh, and no flowers.'

'No flowers?' she had echoed weakly. Sending a wreath was the one thing she had thought would be easy.

'No flowers,' said the young undertaker. 'Donations instead.'

'Who to?' Janet Wakefield had her own pet charity and if…

'The Rowlettian Society.'

'I've never heard of them.'

'Nor me,' said Tod Morton frankly, 'but I've got their address filed with her funeral plan. All you have to do is to add their name to the notice for the newspapers, together with our name and address, and the donations can come to us in the first instance. Then I'll list them for you and send the money on to the Rowlettian Society, whoever they are. That is what is usual.'

This had served to remind her that the newspapers were something else she had to worry about. Or, rather, what to say in the obituary notice to be published in them.

'Just put the name of the deceased and her age and where she died,' advised Tod easily. 'Unless you know what she did before she retired…'

'We don't,' she said with absolute truth. 'That's the trouble. We don't know anything about her at all.'

'Then you can go straight to putting in the bit about the date of the funeral and saying where it will be.' Tod Morton paused and then added, 'If I were you, Mrs Wakefield, I shouldn't say in the paper that there's a bunfight afterwards at the Almstone Towers. You never know who'll turn up just because of that – they do you very well there, you know.'

'We don't know who'll turn up – full stop,' she had said rather tartly. 'Maybe nobody at all.'

'You never can tell,' said the young undertaker wisely. 'Funerals are funny things. There are always people who haven't visited the deceased in years who'll come to his or her funeral.'

'Adding hypocrisy to neglect,' said Janet crisply.

'Could be,' he said pacifically.

'And there will always be those who should be there and aren't, I suppose,' suggested Janet, even though she had no idea at all who should be at Bill's Great-Aunt Josephine's funeral but weren't going to be there. Surely there must be some of them, too...

Tod Morton shook his head. 'They usually come as well. In our experience, Mrs Wakefield, apologies for absence aren't often the order of the day.'

'So what about hymns and things, then?' Janet had asked, leaving this thorny subject alone.

'That's Reverend Tompkinson's department, not mine,' said Tod Morton. 'You'll have to ask him.'

So Janet Wakefield had duly made her way to the vicarage at Damory Regis.

'Ah, yes,' said Derek Tompkinson, the clergyman there.

'I've had a note of the date and time of the service from the undertaker's but I needed to see you, Mrs Wakefield, about what to say about your...er...late aunt.'

'My husband's great-aunt,' she corrected him, adding shortly, 'and he's upcountry in Brazil without mobile reception. Not that he knows any more about her than I do. That's for sure.'

'I see,' said the vicar pensively. 'So there's no one you know of at all who would like to give the address at the service?'

She shook her head. 'No one.'

'Tell me, did she not have any favourite visitors at the nursing home?'

'I asked,' said Janet. 'According to the matron there she didn't have any visitors at all in the time that she had been in there bar one – an old gentleman – whom she wouldn't see anyway. Apparently she wasn't much of a letter writer and had no correspondence to speak of either but did do some telephoning until she got too deaf. Bad eyesight, too, they thought.'

'Strange,' mused Derek Tompkinson, 'very strange. By the way, do you happen to know why the burial is to be here in Damory Regis?' He frowned. 'You see, Short is not a familiar name in this village and nobody at all in the parish seems to have known anyone called Josephine Short.'

'I don't know anything about anything,' said Janet flatly. 'That's the whole trouble.'

'I did take the liberty of consulting my fellow cleric on the matter.' The vicar gave a little cough. 'He's the one in whose parish the Berebury Nursing Home is and who visits there regularly. That was to see if he had any suggestions on the matter, but it turns out that he had never seen her there.' He amended this. 'Or rather, that Miss Short had never asked to see him. Nursing homes have to be very tactful about that sort of thing, you know.'

Janet Wakefield had said that she could see that they would have to be. 'It would be a bit of a reminder of the Grim Reaper, wouldn't it?'

'Quite so,' said the vicar of Damory Regis, leaving Janet not entirely sure whether he liked her use of the expression.

'So we're back to hymns and things,' she said a trifle ungraciously. 'I suppose we ought to have "Abide with Me".'

'A lot of people do,' said Derek Tompkinson.

'And "The Day Thou Gavest, Lord, is Ended",' she said. This suggestion had come from her best friend, Dawn, enrolled to give advice over a cup of coffee.

'Very popular,' said the vicar.

'Well, if we don't know anything about her,' said Janet astringently, 'we can hardly have "For All the Saints", can we?'

The vicar had smiled gently at this. 'There is no reason why you shouldn't, if you want to. We are all equal in death, you know. The trappings of this world fall away. All is forgiven.'

Janet had flushed, unsure of her ground at that point. 'Anyway, there's no way we can have that one about promising to serve thee to the end if we don't know what she believed in.'

'You may have whatever you wish, Mrs Wakefield.'

'What about "All Things Bright and Beautiful"?' she said suddenly, watching his face. It was one hymn she and Dawn had both remembered from their childhood.

'You may have whatever you wish,' the vicar repeated.

'At least,' she said, feeling somehow defeated, 'we can't

have that one that begins "O Love that will not let me go", because she wasn't married.'

Derek Tompkinson, at first tempted to go into the theology of this, said instead, 'Might I suggest you have "Father, Hear the Prayer We Offer"?'

In the end Janet settled for that and 'Dear Lord and Father of Mankind'.

'And the readings, Mrs Wakefield?'

Janet gave in and said she would leave these to the vicar.

'And as for the address,' he said, 'might I suggest you have a word with her solicitor? He may well know more about her than we do. He might even be prevailed upon to say a few words himself.'

'Her solicitors are Puckle, Puckle & Nunnery in Berebury High Street.' Janet knew that because she had been told it was they who had been seeing to the fees at the nursing home. 'I understand that Simon Puckle's the member of the firm who looked after her affairs.'

The vicar had nodded at that. 'Try him,' he had advised. 'He's a helpful sort of chap.'

So Janet had dutifully made an appointment with Simon Puckle at the firm's offices in Berebury High Street.

'Give the funeral address?' said Simon Puckle. 'I'm very sorry, Mrs Wakefield, but I really don't know a great deal about the late Miss Short. Certainly not enough to deliver the eulogy.'

'I see,' said Janet, mentally chalking up someone else who wasn't ever going to call her Jan.

Simon Puckle hastened on. 'She was indeed a client of ours but only since she came as a resident near here in the Berebury Nursing Home. I was given to understand that she used to live over Calleford way before she went into the home, so she wasn't exactly local to Berebury and I don't know her past history at all.'

'Would there be any clues in her will?' asked Janet. She hadn't herself come across any will of Great-Aunt Josephine's so far. 'That's if you've got it here?'

'We have indeed got her will here, Mrs Wakefield, but there is a caveat attached to it that it isn't to be read until after the funeral.'

The images of a last will and testament solemnly being read by an elderly solicitor to the assembled family in the library came, as far as Janet was concerned, straight from Hollywood.

'Uncommon but not unknown,' added Simon Puckle.

'Is that because it's got something in it saying that if someone didn't turn up for the funeral they mightn't get anything?' suggested Janet. She wasn't sure if that came from Hollywood, too, or from fiction borrowed from the library shelves labelled 'Romance'.

'That could be one reason, although,' the solicitor paused and went on carefully, 'I would expect any professional adviser to have counselled against making any such...er...unusual provision.' He hesitated before adding, 'Especially one that could conceivably lead to difficulties. So, Mrs Wakefield, I must remind you, would be the...er...premature disposition of any of the possessions in her room.'

'There's not many of them, I can tell you,' responded Janet smartly.

'The very old don't need a lot,' murmured the solicitor, a veteran in these matters.

'So we won't know anything at all, then, until after the

funeral,' concluded Janet, aware that he hadn't said whether or not the firm of Puckle, Puckle & Nunnery had actually drawn up the aforementioned will. She sighed. 'There's so much we don't know about Bill's Great-Aunt Josephine.'

It was only at the funeral itself, though, that she began to realise quite how much that lack of knowledge amounted to. Resolutely heading for her place in the front pew as the chief mourner, Janet, who had dressed carefully in an ambiguous mixture of mauve, black, green and cream, had dutifully followed Tod Morton and the coffin into the church at Damory Regis.

The first thing of which she was aware was the odd assortment of people in the congregation. This was something she hadn't expected. Certainly the notice of the death of Josephine Short and the time and place of the funeral had been well published to the wider world but no one had been in touch with her. Firmly occupying the pew behind the one reserved for the family was a cohort from the Berebury Nursing Home led by the matron, Mrs Linda Luxton, and on the other side of the church she spotted Simon Puckle, the solicitor.

Further back were a couple of women obviously so familiar with the church and its ritual that they exuded the feeling of being regular members of the congregation. And on the opposite side of the aisle were two men and some women, who might or might not have come from the Rowlettian Society. Scattered about the church were several other men, mostly oldish, and some more women – only one young, her auburn hair standing out in a sea of grey heads. At the back, handing out service books, hovered a churchwarden and a sidesman.

Ahead of her now and after the organ voluntary had come to a stop, the vicar, robed in full canonicals, was pronouncing the words '"We brought nothing into this world, and it is certain that we can carry nothing out...'"

Janet Wakefield had no quarrel with these sentiments as far as the late Josephine Short was concerned. Detailed examination of the bedroom in the nursing home had been singularly unrevealing, her possessions there few and far between. Certainly there was everything present in the room that one bedridden old lady could or would possibly need, but nothing whatsoever to shed light on the personality of that same old lady – not even anything about the Rowlettian Society. There were some rather worn black and white photographs in a torn brown envelope in a bottom drawer but they had had no names on them that had meant anything to her and Janet had left them where they were.

As the vicar began the Sentences '"I know that my Redeemer liveth...",' and while the coffin was being set upon the waiting trestles, Janet Wakefield sat herself down in the right-hand front pew and picked up the prayer book there.

Her solitary splendour in that pew, though, was not destined to last long. Seconds after she was seated, a tall youngish man wearing a dark suit and a black tie slid into the pew in which she was sitting. He sat down beside her, bowed his head, and gave every appearance of entering into silent prayer. '"Whom I shall see for myself and shall mine eyes behold, and not another",' finished the Reverend Derek Tompkinson, reaching his stall after first reverencing the altar and turning to face the congregation. Janet cast a covert glance in the direction of the newcomer but was little the wiser after that beyond being aware that the man's suit was of a light wool and had been cut in a slightly un-English way.

'The first hymn,' announced the vicar, 'is "Father, Hear the

Prayer We Offer" which is number 172 in the green book...'
Under cover of the general rustling of activity, caused by the
taking up of hymn books and the searching for the right page
and the starting up of the organ again, the newcomer leant
over towards Janet and whispered in her ear, 'Phew! That was
a near thing. Just made it in time, thank goodness. Mother
always said I'd be late for my own funeral but if I was late for
Granny's there'd be big trouble. Well, I'm not, am I?'

CHAPTER TWO

Sheila, Mrs Linda Luxton's deputy at the Berebury Nursing Home, in St Clement's Row, took a deep breath and carefully counted to three before she spoke. They had learnt the hard way at the Home that, while people who wanted to become resident there queued up for a bed in the place, good care staff were very much more difficult to come by and keep.

Ellen Steele was good care staff in the sense that she had an idle, no-good husband, a heavy drinker to boot, and an even more ne'er-do-well son, who was forever in trouble, and thus she could not easily afford to leave the employment there.

'Smashed, you say?' said the deputy matron, playing for time.

'Smashed into little pieces,' said Ellen Steele energetically, 'dozens of them and it wasn't me, Sheila. Honest. And I just can't work out what happened to it.'

'Are we talking about that vase that stood on her shelf?' Shelves were few and far between in the less-than-ample residents' rooms at the Berebury Nursing Home. 'The pretty red and green china one?'

Ellen nodded. 'That's right. Beautiful isn't...wasn't it? It was the only thing that old Josephine would have there. She was really fussy about it.'

'I must say it looked valuable,' said Sheila, wondering what they would have to say about the breakage to the family.

'But if you ask me it was the only thing of hers that was, 'cepting those rings that she always wore. Lovely, they were.'

'Biggest diamond I've ever seen,' agreed Sheila, momentarily diverted. 'The other one was a sapphire...a Sri Lankan sapphire, I think she once told me it was.'

'Matched her blue eyes lovely, it did,' said Ellen. 'Like ice, they were.'

'But as to the vase being valuable, I couldn't say for sure,' said Sheila.

'Most of them stand their photographs along that shelf,' continued Ellen, 'but Josephine wouldn't never have nothing there but that vase. Ever.'

'I've an idea that she'd lost people in an accident and couldn't bear to look at their photographs,' said the deputy matron absently. Strictly speaking care in the home only related to the here and now, but in every care home the past always cast its long shadows towards the present.

'Kept all of them tucked away in a drawer, she did,' said Ellen, from whom no secrets of Josephine Short's room could very well have been hidden in the circumstances. 'Loose in a brown envelope. Didn't look at 'em much, though, I can tell you. Couldn't get to the drawer herself, not lately anyway.'

'Josephine wasn't ever one for talking about the past, either,' said Sheila, who took her share of the caring when someone else on the staff didn't come in.

'Unlike some,' groaned Ellen feelingly. 'I tell you, Sheila, if I have to hear about that Kathleen in number 11's safari trip one more time I shall scream. I've begun to wish those lions she saw had eaten her. Or, come to that, Lady Alice's tale about crossing the Bay of Biscay in the war with U-boats about when she was in the Wrens...'

'I hope, though, that that vase wasn't as valuable as it looked,' said the deputy matron, sticking to the point. She sighed. 'I don't know what Linda will say when she gets back from the church, I'm sure. I don't know when the family'll be coming back here either but we'll have to tell them then about its being broken.'

'But that's not it...' insisted Ellen with vigour.

'No?' said Sheila, puzzled.

'What you don't understand, Sheila, is that that room has been kep' locked ever since Josephine died.'

'Someone must have knocked it over,' pointed out Sheila mildly, careful not to cast aspersions. 'It can't have fallen on its own. Not short of an earthquake.'

'So they must,' agreed Ellen, 'but if it wasn't me – and I tell you it wasn't – then who was it? That's what I want to know.'

'And what were they doing in there, anyway?' asked the deputy matron, catching on. 'Nobody had any business to be in that room after the old lady died, never mind that it was kept locked and the key hung on the board on the wall in Linda's office here.'

'Exactly. That niece of hers – if that's what she is – Jan somebody...'

'Wakefield,' supplied the deputy matron. 'Wife of Josephine's next of kin. It should have been him taking care of things, only he's away somewhere on business.'

'Her, then. Linda was with her all the time she was here when she came up to get the old lady's papers for the registrar and that vase will have been all right then or we'd have heard all about it and no mistake.'

'We would,' sighed Sheila, on whose shoulders much of the minutiae of running the place fell. Mrs Luxton, the matron, dealt with the paperwork and the ever-burgeoning requirements of the regulatory authorities.

'So,' said Ellen ineluctably, 'short of that earthquake you mentioned, how come that vase fell off the shelf and broke if the room has been kept locked ever since? Or, at least, until I went in this morning to give the room a bit of a tidy before the family come?'

Sheila frowned. 'Think carefully. Is there anything actually missing from the room that you can see?'

Ellen Steele shook her head. 'Not that I noticed. Mind you, there wasn't a lot left in it to start with – not since them lovely rings went with the body to the undertaker's, like Morton's said Josephine had asked.' She sniffed. 'Not, I must say, that that stopped that young woman who come having a good hunt for anything valuable. Never been near the place before, either.'

'She did say that neither she nor her husband knew anything about his great-aunt being in here or they would have visited.'

Ellen sniffed again, not mollified by this. 'Didn't stop the old lady naming him as her next of kin, did it? Funny that, if you was to ask me. Mind you, Sheila, that wife of his got here pretty quickly after she'd died. People always do.'

The deputy matron did not attempt to dispute this. Instead she stood up and said she'd go and look at the room herself, and then perhaps Ellen would go ahead and sweep up the pieces before Linda and the other staff came back from the church at Damory Regis, and certainly before the relatives got to the Home. She halted suddenly on her way out and said, 'On second thoughts, perhaps not, Ellen. Just leave the broken pieces on the floor where they are. It might be better.'

She had hardly got to the door before the cook appeared, her sleeves rolled up to the elbows. ''Scuse me interrupting, Sheila, but you'd better come and take a look at the pantry. Someone's taken the window out.'

While Janet Wakefield struggled to sing the words of the hymn, her mind now in a complete whirl, her neighbour beside her in the front pew appeared quite at home with them, joining in the singing with ease.

'I nearly didn't make it,' he bent down and hissed into Janet's ear as they settled down and prepared to listen to the reading. 'I got lost on the way down.'

'Where from?' was all Janet could manage in the way of speech before the vicar welcomed the congregation and announced that the sentences of scripture would be from Ecclesiastes: '"To everything there is a season, and a time to every purpose under the heaven..."'

The Reverend Derek Tompkinson had reached '"A time to be born, and a time to die"...' before she got an answer.

'The airport. I hired a car there,' he said, sotto voce, under cover of the vicar's walking back from the lectern. 'I stayed there last night on my way here. My plane was too late in, yesterday evening, to come on here.'

'Where from?' she asked again.

'Lasserta,' he whispered. 'The sheikhdom thereof.'

Janet Wakefield settled herself back in the pew, trying to place Lasserta in her school atlas. Somewhere out East was all that came to her mind, it being the mysterious East in more senses than one as far as she was concerned since she couldn't think exactly where Lasserta was. With an enormous effort of will she turned her mind back to the matter in hand – the funeral service.

The vicar was talking about the late Josephine Eleanor Short. 'There will be those of you present here today who will have known she whose death we are gathered together to mark. I am not numbered among you but I join with you in bidding farewell to an old lady who chose to spend her last years here in our county of Calleshire and who had especially asked to be laid to rest among the villagers of this ancient settlement. She had asked, too, that you all be invited back to the Almstone Towers Hotel after this service for suitable refreshment.'

The Reverend Derek Tompkinson then gave his gentle smile and went on with practised fluency, 'In medieval times a candle would be lit in the church porch when a parishioner died to guide them to church. It was called a "fetch-candle" and while we do not know what it is that fetched Josephine Eleanor Short to our church and churchyard we assure those who mourn of our welcome here and of our love.'

Janet let her glance slide towards the man at her side, and wondered if he knew what there was about Damory Regis that had drawn Josephine Short – his grandmother, that is – here in death. She would ask him as soon as she could but not before she found out how it came to be that the deceased, apparently always known as Miss Short, had had a grandchild whom nobody – well not her Bill, anyway – had known anything about.

Janet's own husband was certain he had never heard of his great-aunt having had any children, that was for sure or he would have said so. As far as Bill Wakefield had been concerned, his Great-Aunt Josephine had always been called Short, which had been his own mother's maiden name, too.

'What's your name?' she hissed suddenly in the direction of the man sitting at her side.

'Joe Short, short for Joseph.' He bent his head down towards her again and said out of the corner of his mouth, 'What's yours?'

'Jan Wakefield,' she answered.

'Bill's wife?' he said, surprising her.

Before she could do more than nod, the vicar had started to speak again. 'I am going to read to you a piece by Bishop Brent called "What is Dying?".' The Reverend Derek Tompkinson cleared his throat and began:

'*A ship sails and I stand watching till she fades on the horizon and someone at my side says, "She is gone." Gone where? Gone from my sight, that is all; she is just as large as when I saw her. The diminished size and the total loss of sight is in me, not in her, and just at the moment when someone at my side says, "She is gone", there are others who are watching her coming, and other voices take up a glad shout, "There she comes!" and that is dying.*'

Quite unexpectedly and much to her own surprise Janet became aware of the trickle of a tear down her face. She told herself that this was utterly ridiculous – she hadn't ever set eyes on Josephine Short and she wasn't even a relation of the woman, let alone a close one. She was very conscious, though, that in some indefinable way the vicar had skilfully introduced into the ceremony an atmosphere of real devotion.

She gave a covert glance along the pew in the direction of her neighbour but his head was bowed and his face hidden from view. It was only when the final hymn began and Joe Short unfolded himself and stood up beside her that she could see his face again. His expression was suitably composed as he once again turned his attention to the singing.

As the last hymn drew to a close, Janet was aware of a rustle of movement at the back of the church as the undertaker's men prepared themselves to come forward. That was when the vicar and congregation began to sing the 'Nunc Dimittis'. This was something that Janet did know and she hastened to join in the familiar words: 'Lord, now lettest thou thy servant depart in peace...' while the undertaker's men lifted the coffin, swung it round with practised ease under the watchful eye of Tod Morton, and set off down the aisle.

Janet stepped out of the front pew behind the bearers and, with Joe Short now by her side, followed the cortège down the aisle and out through the open west door of the church. 'I didn't know Great-Aunt Josephine had had any children,' she said as soon as they were outside in the open air, speech then seeming somehow less constrained.

'One,' said Joe Short. 'My father.'

'Ah,' said Janet alertly. 'She had been married, then.'

'No,' said Joe Short. 'At least, not that I ever knew about.'

'Ah,' said Janet again. She searched about in her mind for something to say that sounded suitably broad-minded. 'Never mind...it was a long time ago.'

'She did mind,' said Joe Short flatly.

'Perhaps in those days—

'Especially in those days,' he said bitterly. 'She was thrown out of the parental home and told never to darken the door again. Talk about Victorian melodrama...'

'We forget how much times have changed...' Janet began but fell silent as the undertaker's men reached the open grave with the coffin and the rest of the congregation gathered round as the vicar began to pronounce the committal.

It was after that when Janet nearly lost her composure altogether. It was as Joe Short stooped and cast some earth down on the coffin. Shakily she followed suit – it was something she had never done before – and then the vicar brought the proceedings to an end.

As soon as Janet had raised her head and straightened up again she turned to Joe Short and said, 'Your parents aren't here, though, are they?'

A spasm of pain crossed his face. 'Didn't you know? Mum and Dad were killed in that air crash coming back to England from Lasserta nearly three years ago now. That's why Granny had to go into that nursing home in Berebury. She couldn't cope alone – not without Mum and Dad, anyway.'

'I'm sorry,' she stumbled contritely. 'I didn't know.'

'No, I suppose you won't have done.' His expression was set now in a controlled way that made him look suddenly older. 'They'd come out to visit me, you see, and were on their way back home afterwards.'

'I can see how that would make it worse,' she said sympathetically.

'Nothing could have made it any worse, believe you me,' he said grimly, 'especially for poor Granny. Losing my father and mother, and with my working so far away, she was very alone. All I could do was telephone…'

'That must have been a help,' she said, at a loss for the right thing to say since redeeming features in the situation seemed very few and far between.

'Oh, it was all right until Granny began to get so deaf that she couldn't hear me properly.'

'Oh, dear,' said Janet helplessly.

But Joe Short's attention had been diverted. 'Do you know who all these people are?' he asked, looking round as the congregation started to leave the graveside.

Janet pointed out the solicitor and the matron and two care assistants from the nursing home. 'Who the others are, I'm sorry, I just don't know myself.'

He thanked her and dutifully peeled off to shake hands with the vicar.

Very slowly the group round the open grave broke up as first one and then another of those present began to move away towards the church gate and the waiting cars, some making themselves known to Janet or Joe. Then Janet looked round to see her erstwhile companion punctiliously taking leave of the matron before moving over to talk to Simon Puckle, while just at the right moment Tod Morton appeared at her elbow again and steered her to the funeral car.

'What about…?' she began and then relaxed when she saw a hire car – presumably Joe Short's – parked behind several others alongside the church wall.

Tod Morton handed her into his firm's large black limousine, waved a gloved hand at the driver and sent her off to the Almstone Towers in solitary splendour. There she was welcomed by the black-coated manager who escorted her in his stately way to a reception room.

'If madam would like to receive the mourners here,' suggested the manager, 'they can then go straight on into the dining room...'

Obediently Janet took up a stance just where he had indicated. As she explained at length to her friend Dawn afterwards, she wasn't usually so biddable but he wasn't the sort of man to argue with. The manager clicked his fingers just once and a waiter appeared with a tray of glasses of sherry and took up his stance slightly to one side and a little behind her, advancing with his tray as other members of the congregation arrived one by one.

The thought that she would have to receive people had not occurred to Janet. She began involuntarily, 'But her grandson'll be getting here in a minute...'

'Very well, madam. I'll see that as soon as he arrives he is told where you are,' murmured the manager, melting away.

But it was quite a while before Joe Short turned up at the hotel and when he did arrive he was with Simon Puckle. The solicitor was suggesting to Joe Short that he came to his office at eleven o'clock tomorrow morning for the reading of the will, adding, 'I take it that this will be all right with you?'

'Sure,' said Joe Short politely.

Janet, joining them, said, 'Will you be staying here?'

The young man looked round at the Edwardian amplitude of the Almstone Towers. 'What? Not on my salary. I'm only a lowly mining engineer, you know.' He grinned. 'Actually I've booked myself in at the Bellingham in Market Street. Granny said she'd heard it was all right.'

Janet nodded, relieved that he'd found himself somewhere to stay, and thus that she had been saved the worry of whether she should have offered him hospitality. 'You should be very comfortable there.'

She turned as Mrs Linda Luxton, the matron of the nursing home, approached her and when she looked back Joe Short had gone.

CHAPTER THREE

'Ah, there you are, Sloan. I wanted to see you. Come in and sit down.' Police Superintendent Leeyes waved at a chair in his office. 'Something very funny's cropped up at the Berebury Nursing Home. That upper-crust one down the road in St Clement's Row.'

'I know the place,' said Sloan cautiously. 'The Earl of Ornum's eccentric aunt's in there. Lady Alice. I met her when they had an outbreak of food poisoning there once.' It hadn't been food poisoning but murder, though this didn't seem the moment to remind his superior officer of this.

'Said to be top of the shop as such places go,' said Leeyes. 'Expensive.'

'I'm sure, sir.' Detective Inspector Sloan − known as Christopher Dennis to his family and 'Seedy' to his friends and colleagues at Berebury Police Station − was head of the tiny Criminal Investigation Department of 'F' Division of the Calleshire County Constabulary and thus ultimately responsible for looking into most matters illegal in the eastern half of the county. Such crime as cropped up in the superintendent's manor was therefore usually handed over to the inspector to solve as speedily as possible. 'Has Lady Alice been up to something, then?' he asked warily. He devoutly hoped not. Tangling with her ladyship, as he knew from hard experience, could be very time-consuming.

'No, no, nothing like that, and nothing really to get your teeth into either as yet,' said the superintendent, 'but you never know.'

Sloan thought about saying something about great oaks from little acorns growing but decided against it. Instead he waited in silence.

'We've just had a report of a breaking and entering there,' said Leeyes.

Inspector Sloan did not find this very cheering. The superintendent only used the royal 'we' when he wanted to share the responsibility for something difficult with someone else.

'Just that?' he asked, since simple housebreaking didn't usually attract his superior's professional attention – not in the first instance, anyway. Or, come to that, usually his own attention either. He wondered if the presence of the earl's aunt explained the superintendent's interest.

'Not quite, Sloan. Constable Simpson, who attended in the first instance, reported that he wasn't happy about it being just a simple burglary, especially as, as far as the staff there can see, nothing has been taken.' The superintendent flipped over a flimsy message sheet on his desk in front of him and added sententiously, 'But you never can tell.'

'No, sir.' This was very true. Mental inventories always let people down and it was sometimes months after a burglary before the owner realised something really valuable was missing.

'There are, however, grounds for believing that an intruder might have been in at least one resident's room there.'

'I see, sir.' That was puzzling. Nursing homes were seldom the subject of acquisitive crime, although the old did tend to take their most valued possessions with them there, hanging on.to them until the very last.

'But no immediate signs of anything being taken,' repeated the superintendent.

That was puzzling too. 'I take it, then, that the matron has good reasons for wondering why this should have happened?' said Sloan, opening his notebook at a new page.

'Yes and no,' said Leeyes unhelpfully. Ever since the superintendent had attended an evening class on philosophy he had been inclined to equivocation. It had been the tricky proposition that a Japanese Noh play in a knot garden was not a special variety of the double negative that had made the greatest mark on the senior policeman.

'Ah,' said Sloan, still waiting for elucidation.

'Mrs Linda Luxton – she's the matron there – got back from attending an elderly resident's funeral to be told about a broken pantry window and signs that a search might have taken place.' He grunted. 'Actually she thinks the intrusion was during the night and has reason to believe it was in the room of the same resident that had died but she says she hasn't the remotest idea why.'

'Signs?'

'A broken vase...that sort of thing.'

'Someone looking for something in the dark,' concluded

Sloan. 'And in a hurry,' he added, since professional searchers seldom left signs of their incursion.

'Exactly. But the matron hasn't a clue about what it could have been.'

'Therefore she doesn't know whether or not they found whatever it was they were looking for,' murmured Sloan, half to himself.

Leeyes said, 'No. At least, not yet.'

'I'll go round there, sir, and see what I can do,' promised Sloan.

'And as far as I'm concerned, Sloan, you can take that detective constable of yours with you when you go.' He sniffed. 'That man'd cause trouble in an empty room.'

Sloan sighed. It was true that Detective Constable Crosby was by no means the brightest star in the constabulary's firmament but he didn't see why it was that he, Sloan, should always have to be the one to do the puppy-walking of the constable.

'Keep me in the picture, Sloan,' went on Leeyes, waving a hand dismissively. 'Can't have this sort of thing going on in a toffee-nosed place like that. Unsettling for the inmates.'

Detective Constable Crosby's reaction to a visit to the nursing home was different but instant. 'That's what they call God's Waiting Room, isn't it?'

Janet Wakefield could hardly wait to get home from the Almstone Towers Hotel and telephone her friend, Dawn. Avid for detail, Dawn listened spellbound to Janet's account of the start of the funeral.

'And then,' said Janet dramatically, 'you'll never guess in a thousand years what happened next...'

'So why don't you tell me now and save time?' said Dawn.

'This man came and sat beside me in the front pew and said he was Josephine's grandson!' exclaimed Janet.

'I thought you said she wasn't married,' objected Dawn.

'That's the thing,' said Janet eagerly. 'She hadn't been...'

'But she'd had children, though?' deduced Dawn.

'One. A son.'

'Without telling anyone?'

Janet paused and considered this. 'I don't really know about that. My Bill didn't know, I'm certain about that, but of course my in-laws – his parents – might have done. I don't know and it's too late to ask them now since they died before Bill and I were married.'

'Cool,' said Dawn. 'For those days, I mean,' she added hastily, mindful of several of their mutual friends who were single mothers without being in the least bit cool – quite the contrary, in fact.

'Very,' said Janet, determinedly broad-minded.

'So what is he like, this grandson?'

'Quite nice,' said Janet, frowning. 'His clothes were a bit... well, un-English – and they didn't fit very well. You see, he's been working out in Lasserta for ages.'

'That's somewhere in the East, isn't it?'

'I think so,' said Janet uncertainly, privately again resolving to get the atlas out as soon as she could. 'He's an engineer or something and both his parents were killed in an air crash out there two or three years ago, which is why his grandmother Josephine had to go into the nursing home.'

'That figures,' said Dawn, adding sympathetically, 'but it must have been a bit hard, all the same.'

'She was old, of course,' said Janet a trifle defensively. 'I mean, if she'd wanted us to visit her there she'd only have had to say and I'm sure we'd have gone. After all, she gave the Berebury Nursing Home our address, so she knew where we were, even if we didn't know where she was.'

'That's very odd,' mused Dawn. 'I mean, if she hadn't any other family around you'd have thought she'd have been glad to have had any visitors at all, whoever they were.' Realising that this didn't sound exactly flattering, she added quickly, 'But they say that the very old do get a bit funny, don't they?'

'All that the grandson – he's called Joe Short by the way—'

'Just like her,' observed Dawn.

'What?'

'Didn't you say she was called Josephine?'

'Oh, yes, I see what you mean now. Josephine and Joseph. All her grandson said to me was that she had got very deaf which had made telephoning a bit difficult as time went by.'

'He could have written.'

'I expect he did,' said Janet. 'No, wait a minute. I think they said at the nursing home that her eyesight had gone, too.'

'*Sans* everything...' said Dawn.

'What?'

'Shakespeare,' said her friend dreamily. '*As You Like It.* We did it in year twelve, remember? I loved Rosalind. That was the play with "*Sans* teeth, *sans* eyes, *sans* taste, *sans* everything..." in it. So sad.'

Janet shuddered. 'Don't. It must be awful to get like that.'

'You must be able to eat still, though,' countered Dawn, who was noticeably fond of her food. 'Or you'd die.'

Janet wasn't listening. She couldn't get back to telling Dawn about the funeral quickly enough. 'And afterwards, we went back to the Almstone Towers and then...' Her voice trailed away.

'And then...' prompted Dawn.

'He sort of melted away and I didn't see the going of him.' She hesitated. 'Now what I can't decide, Dawn, is whether to ask him over here. What do you think? He seems to be quite alone.'

'And so are you,' said Dawn perceptively.

'Exactly,' said Janet, 'and I don't quite like to...not without Bill being here, if you know what I mean.'

'Yes,' said Dawn. 'I know what you mean.'

'After all, I don't know him at all. I didn't even know about him, did I?' Janet brightened. 'I expect he'll be in touch, though, all the same.'

She hadn't realised how soon that would be. She had barely put the telephone down before it rang again and a rather husky voice said that it was Joe Short.

'Hullo, there,' she said uncertainly.

'I'm sorry I didn't see you again before you left the hotel,' he apologised. 'I got nabbed by an old friend of Granny's from the Rowlettian Society. I've no idea who he was but he said he had known her very well in the past—'

'Hang on,' Janet interrupted him, suddenly remembering something. 'I may have the answer to that.'

'You do? How come? I just couldn't get away from him but now I can't even remember his name.'

'Tod Morton – that's the undertaker, you know – handed me a little pile of those cards that people fill in at the funeral to say that they were there. I've got them here. I've been wondering what to do with them and—'

'What I have been wondering,' he interrupted her

unceremoniously, 'was whether you would consider having supper with me tonight here at the Bellingham. That's if you haven't got children or anything.'

Janet's acceptance bordered on the eager. She didn't say anything about not having children, this being an unspoken sadness that was never far from the front of her mind.

'Good. Then I'll be waiting for you in the foyer at half past seven,' he said. 'I say,' he added, 'you couldn't bring those cards with you, could you? I'd like to know who the old boy was.' He gave a little laugh. 'For all I know the man might even be my grandfather. He did keep on saying how well he knew Granny in the past. "Very well indeed," were his exact words.'

Mrs Linda Luxton, the matron of the Berebury Nursing Home, was ready and waiting for the two policemen when they arrived. Her funeral-going clothes had been rapidly exchanged for her blue uniform and she was once again on duty and very much in charge of her own domain.

Detective Inspector Sloan glanced down at his notebook. 'We understand, madam, that an unauthorised entry to the premises would appear to have been effected through a pantry window.' Choosing broadly neutral words with care was important at the outset of any investigation; they could always be refined and redefined later when more was known.

'At the back,' she said at once. 'It's just to one side of the kitchen door and it looks as if the window itself has been prised out,' she added, leading them to the pantry doorway and pointing to a space where the window would once have been. 'This must be where he got in...'

'Or she,' put in Detective Constable Crosby, who had

just attended an equal opportunities course.

The matron gave him an odd look but only said, 'We haven't gone any further into the pantry than this.'

'Very wise, madam,' said Sloan, a believer not only in giving praise where praise was due but more importantly in keeping women in uniform onside. In his experience of the female of the species, it was members of this subspecies who were the most frightening.

'And the cook didn't come in here and notice the missing window until just before we rang you.' She pursed her lips. 'I may say she's not very happy that she can't get at what she wants now.'

'I can see that she mightn't be,' said Sloan. Actually, he could see for himself that she wasn't because the cook was standing in the kitchen behind them, arms akimbo, visibly idle and anxious about the next meal. 'We'll be as quick as we can,' he promised. 'Now, has anyone noticed anything having been taken from their rooms?'

'We've asked all the residents,' said the matron, 'and they say not, but you will understand that not all of them are up to knowing one way or the other.' She shrugged. 'We are always reminding them about valuables not being kept in their rooms but some of them like to have them around or on their person. At their stage in life it often becomes important for the old ladies to keep their mementos where they can see them. Sometimes it helps them keep a hold on reality.'

Sloan nodded.

'Then there's the broken vase,' said Mrs Luxton. 'In room 18, that is. No one on the staff admits to having knocked it over, and there certainly wasn't any reason for anyone to enter that room until Ellen went in this morning to give it a tidy before the family came back again, the resident there having died last week. When we realised that there had been a break-in, though, we left it as it was.'

Sloan stood in the doorway of room 18 and considered the pieces of the smashed vase on the floor. 'Quite right. There may be footprints on the carpet...' Crosby, he decided, could summon up the Scene of Crime people to examine the room after they looked at the back of the building and the missing window.

'She – that's the late Josephine Short, the resident whose room this was until she died – always had that vase on the edge of her shelf,' said the matron.

Sloan nodded. An intruder working in the dark – or at least, in very little light – could have easily knocked it over when feeling along the shelf. It would have been where most residents would have kept their ornamental bits and pieces. He stepped across to a little chest of drawers and opened each in turn.

'As far as we know, Inspector,' said the matron, 'the resident here had no real valuables save the rings that she always wore. They were very nice, though, I must say.'

He nodded and carried on with his examination. The top drawers were full of toiletries and suchlike but the bottom one yielded a tattered brown envelope. He lifted this out and spilt the contents onto the bedside table. They were mostly old black and white photographs. He riffled through them, noting only one newish one. It was of a tall, cheerful, young man, presumably the grown-up version of several ones of a child, including a faded one of a little boy steadying himself beside a table labelled 'Joe aged two and a half'. There were several of a young couple standing under the canopy of a variety of tree he didn't recognise and more of the same couple a little older with a small boy standing between them but with a totally different background.

'Did anyone hear anything?' he asked.

'The night staff made a note that Lady Alice in the room above complained of a bump in the night, but,' she sighed, 'Lady Alice complains about everything and I'm afraid they didn't take too much notice of her at the time.'

'I'd better talk to all the residents presently,' said the detective inspector conscientiously.

Mrs Luxton hesitated, searching for the right words. 'Don't ask the one called Mavis how she is, though, will you, Inspector?' she said anxiously. 'You'll never get her to stop if you do.'

'Gives you a full organ recital, does she?' asked Detective Constable Crosby chattily.

'What about the key to this room?' Sloan asked, ignoring this.

'On a hook on a board in the office,' she said.

'A numbered hook?'

'Oh, yes, naturally.' She gave him a rueful look. 'We'd never keep track of anything here otherwise.'

'And where would the night staff have been during the night?'

'They would have been doing the ironing, preparing the breakfast trays, answering any bells,' said the matron piously, although she personally suspected that that wasn't always the case. 'That sort of thing. There would have been two of them on and, of course, they have a break.'

'A woman's work is never done,' muttered Crosby under his breath.

'So the intruder might have knocked over the vase and got out before he could take anything,' reasoned Sloan aloud.

'I'm sure I hope so,' said Mrs Luxton warmly, 'but if he was in room 18 then he – or she – remembered to lock the door again on his – or her – way out and put the key back on its hook before he left.'

'Funny that,' observed Detective Constable Crosby.

'But nothing has been taken, which is so odd,' said the matron.

'Alternatively the intruder might have been disturbed anyway,' pointed out Sloan. 'He could have heard the staff moving about and so forth.'

'He—' began Mrs Luxton.

'Or she,' put in Detective Constable Crosby once again, the lesson on sexual discrimination having been well learnt.

She looked at him and said deliberately, 'Come this way, gentlemen. To my office. He or she,' she invested the words with ironic significance, 'had enough time to go through my bureau over there.'

The policemen regarded the matron's burr walnut desk with interest. 'How do you know?' asked Sloan.

'The papers have been put back in the wrong pigeonholes,' she said. 'I always keep current bills in the left-hand slot. Always. That way I know when they're due, and when they've been paid I put them somewhere else.'

'Just so,' murmured the detective inspector. In the Sloan household unpaid bills hung around like a miasma until the end of the month. 'Crosby, whistle up that SOCO, pronto, will you?' He turned to Mrs Luxton. 'I think I'd better just have a word with the woman who first went into the room. Ellen, did you say her name was?'

'Ellen Steele,' said Mrs Luxton, putting her finger on a bell.

The name rang a different sort of bell with Detective Inspector Sloan who had spent all his working life in and about the market town of Berebury and thus knew all the malefactors. The entire Steele clan were known to the police in every sense of the phrase. 'Matthew's mother,' he said immediately when she entered the room, recognising her at once from numerous court appearances involving her son.

'That's right, Mr Sloan,' she said anxiously. 'He hasn't been and done anything, has he?'

'Not that I know about,' said Sloan dryly. Matthew Steele came into the category of persistent offender, in and out of trouble all his life, lacking in both brains and morality.

'He hasn't been in trouble for quite a bit now,' she advanced tentatively.

'I'm very glad to hear it,' said Sloan. 'Now, tell me all about this broken vase.'

CHAPTER FOUR

Janet Wakefield had put the telephone down after talking to Joe Short with something bordering on relief that he hadn't offered to come and collect her. Having her own car gave a girl a certain independence.

Deliberately making herself just a little late, she duly made her way to the Bellingham Hotel as evening fell. An old coaching inn, it sat in the middle of the market town of Berebury, the stable yard now its car park. It was a little bit on the shabby side these days and distinctly old-fashioned, but unpretentious and comfortable. Joe Short was waiting for her in the entrance hall and led her to the lounge. He was still in the same rather crumpled darkish suit, but very welcoming.

'Now, what will you have to drink?' he asked.

Janet settled herself into a chair while he busied himself at the bar. Looking over at him while he did so, Janet decided he must be about thirty years old, perhaps a little less. He was tall and well built, with short brown hair surmounting a considerable suntan, and broad workmanlike hands.

'There we are,' he said, soon returning with a glass in each hand. He set them down and waved a hand round the hotel's lounge. 'I'm sorry it's not the Almstone Towers but Granny did recommend the Bellingham Hotel for good value. And until the insurance people settle up for Mum and Dad's accident, the Bellingham it will have to be. There's nothing wrong with it anyway. It's a lot more comfortable than Mathabo – that's where I live in Lasserta.'

'I expect that sort of thing takes time,' said Janet vaguely. 'Insurance claims, I mean.'

'It's going to take a lot more than time,' he said bitterly. 'They were on a Lasserta Airlines plane...'

'So surely the insurance—'

'But unfortunately the accident happened on a Lassertan runway...'

'And each is blaming the other?' divined Janet without difficulty.

'Too right, they are. It'll take years before they finish arguing. And Lassertans love arguing. They're famous for it. And insurance companies never hurry themselves either.'

'What I want to know,' said Janet, never a time-waster and conscious of a need to change the subject, 'is how you heard about the funeral.'

'Easy,' he relaxed. 'We may live on a benighted island but we can go online and therefore read the papers even out in the wilds of Lasserta.'

'But why weren't you told properly?' she asked. 'By the nursing home or the undertaker's, I mean?'

'Granny said I wasn't to come,' he said simply.

'What?' exclaimed Janet. 'Oh, I'm sorry, I didn't mean to sound rude.'

'Don't worry. I know it sounds odd but it isn't really. First of all, Granny was the most unsentimental person I've ever known. She said she'd had all that knocked out of her when her family kicked her out of the house because she was pregnant.'

'That must have been quite awful,' said Janet.

'And anyway I'd had to come home and sort things out when…after the plane accident.' He raised his glass to her and went on, 'Then, you see, I'd changed jobs after that and so I hadn't really clocked up enough leave to come back again in the ordinary way.'

'But you came all the same,' she said, taking a sip of her drink.

'Cartwright's – that's Cartwright's Consolidated Carbons who I work for these days – were really decent about it and said I ought to go.'

'I should hope so, too,' said Janet, whose knowledge of overseas employment practices began and ended with those of her husband's firm.

'Actually,' Joe looked down and seemed a bit confused, saying in a muffled voice, 'I'd lost a mate – he went off trekking in the jungle and couldn't be found – just as I went to work for them and I think they were a bit sorry for me.'

'Bad luck,' Jan said gently. She stayed quiet for a moment and then, 'There's something else. Something I'd really like to know,' she said.

'Fire away,' said Joe Short, his poise recovered, 'and then, when you're ready, we'll go in to supper.'

'What made your grandmother choose to be buried in the churchyard over at Damory Regis? Nobody in the village there had ever heard of her.'

He shook his head. 'I have absolutely no idea and she'd never said anything to me. I didn't even know that was what she'd arranged.'

'And what on earth is the Rowlettian Society?'

He laughed. 'That one's not so difficult. It's the Old Boys' Association of the school where Granny used to work. Rowletts.'

'The prep school? I've heard of that, of course. It's over Calleford way, isn't it? I should have put two and two together and realised the Rowlettian Society was to do with it, shouldn't I? Silly of me.' She gave a shy little laugh. 'It's where Bill says any children we ever have should go. It's out in the country between Calleford and Kinnisport, isn't it?'

'That's right. In the real Calleshire hinterland,' he said, his lips tightening again. 'The Calleshire hinterland isn't as dangerous as the Lassertan one, though. That's where Brian got lost – he was my best mate.' He pushed his chair back and stood up abruptly before she could say anything and said, 'Let's go and eat and I'll tell you all about Lasserta.' He waited until she'd finished her drink and then led the way into the hotel's dining room. 'Now, what are you going to have?' he asked, picking up the menu as soon as they were settled at the table. 'It all looks good to me – where I live you don't get as much choice as this.'

Janet chose the roast beef. 'It's not something a grass widow ever cooks for herself.'

'The beef'll do me, too,' he said. 'It doesn't often come my way in Lasserta. No cattle there to speak of.' He didn't resume the subject of the Rowlettian Society until their first course arrived.

Then he said, 'When Granny's family showed her the door she had literally nowhere to go—'

'And was having a baby,' put in Janet. Pregnancy was a subject never far from her own mind.

'Exactly. So she had to find somewhere to live for starters and then get a job to keep herself and the baby when it came.'

'Tough,' said Janet.

'I'll say. It doesn't really bear thinking about. Well, to begin with, I was always told that she farmed the baby out.'

'I think you mean fostered,' said Janet dryly.

'Do I?' He grinned. 'It can't have been much fun, all the same, whichever it was.'

'No,' agreed Janet soberly.

'So, being Granny, she soon found a job where she could be resident. She was quite clever really, because always having had a proper nanny herself—'

'I guessed she was from that sort of a family because of things Bill had heard about her parents from his mother,' nodded Janet. 'Toffee-nosed and in the money.'

'From that sort of a family,' agreed Joe Short. 'Very well off and well up the totem pole. So because of knowing the nanny business from the receiving end she thought she could look after small children herself. She'd had the benefit of having seen it done the right way and on the strength of that she got a position as junior matron at a preparatory school – Rowletts.'

Janet's face cleared. 'Ah, I understand now.'

'Anyway, I'm told she proceeded to make herself quite indispensable there and first of all she was allowed to stay at the school in the holidays and then in the fullness of time to have Dad – her baby, that is – there as well. Later on they let him be educated there, too, and at very reduced rates.'

'Good for her, and them, of course,' Janet added hastily.

'I'll say. She was soon babysitting for everyone and was promoted to senior matron before very long and became a bit of a personal assistant to the headmaster into the bargain, when necessary.'

'It was a bargain,' said Janet thoughtfully. 'I don't know what I would have done if I had been her...' Because babies were yet to arrive in the Wakefield household Janet spent quite a lot of time wondering how she would cope when – if – they did.

'As far as Dad was concerned Granny was always a bit of a legend and it sort of rubbed off on me.' He looked into the distance. 'She was great.'

'I'm sure,' said Janet warmly. 'I'm beginning to wish I'd known her myself.'

'That reminds me. You did bring those names and addresses that the undertaker gave you, didn't you? I might find some people who did. Especially that old gentleman who was so keen to have a chat with me. He was a bit tottery – and quite as old as Granny, I would have said.'

Janet handed over the little pile of cards that Tod Morton had given her and Joe Short gave them a quick flick through. He stopped at one and looked it over carefully. 'There's a Sebastian Worthington here with an address over Calleford way. I wonder if it was he who spoke to me – it could well have been. The handwriting's a bit spidery – it looks like an old man's.'

Janet said mischievously 'Did he look like you?'

'I never thought of that.' He frowned and then said seriously, 'I should have looked at him more carefully.'

'Only joking,' said Janet swiftly. She wasn't sure, though, that Joe Short had been joking.

He went on flicking through the undertaker's cards. 'None of these other names mean anything to me.'

'You don't have any cousins or anything?'

'No first cousins,' he said seriously. 'Mum's only brother was killed by a mine when he was yomping towards Port Stanley in the Falklands, but I've probably got loads of remoter ones from Granny's side of the family who I don't know about because of her being ostracised by them in the past.'

'Such as my late mother-in-law,' said Janet.

'Wasn't she called Eleanor, too? That was Granny's middle name, you know,' he said.

'Yes, she was Eleanor Wakefield after she married, so her parents must have stayed friendly with your grandmother or they wouldn't have called their daughter after her, would they?' Janet gave a little laugh. 'I'm not a blood relation, of course, because I wasn't descended from the Shorts. I'm only married to the son of one of them.' She frowned. 'I'm not even a cousin german.'

'What's that?'

'First cousin. I'm only related by marriage. Affine, I think it's called, but my late mother-in-law – she would have been a blood relative, all right, because Josephine was her aunt. Her father would have been Josephine's brother. I know he was called William because my husband Bill was called after him.'

'So your mother-in-law would have been a first cousin to my father, wouldn't she?' he said, frowning.

'That's right and that means my Bill is a connection of yours, too,' said Janet.

'First cousin, once removed or something,' said Joe, adding, 'him and an unknown number of others.'

'Kissing cousins,' said Janet lightly, 'that's what they all are.'

'I haven't kissed any of them,' he protested, laughing for the first time and going a little pink.

'I wonder if any of them came to the funeral,' said Janet, pointing to the little cards, still on the table.

Joe Short scooped them up and put them into his pocket. 'I'll go through them in the morning. I haven't got to have an early start. I don't have to be at the solicitor's until eleven. Now, what are you going to have after the beef?'

Someone who did have an early start the next day was Superintendent Leeyes. He was never at his best first thing in the morning and wise subordinates usually took good care to see to it that they were engaged elsewhere until their superior officer had mulled over his in-tray and had the first of many mugs of tea brought to him at his desk.

Detective Inspector Sloan had no such option to hand when summoned to his presence. The request that he appear at once in his superior's office had been rather more than peremptory.

'Come in, Sloan, come in and don't waste time. I don't know what you were planning to do this morning but—'

'Look into that rather odd break-in reported at the Berebury Nursing Home yesterday, sir. There's something there that doesn't quite add up.'

'Well, it'll have to wait, that's all. This is more important.'

Detective Inspector Sloan tugged his notebook out of his pocket and opened it at a fresh page.

'Never mind the paperwork now, Sloan,' snapped Leeyes. 'I want you to get over to Billing Bridge pretty pronto.

There's a dead girl there. On the north bank.'

'Right, sir,' promised Sloan, snapping his notebook shut, getting to his feet and starting to edge towards the door.

'She was pulled out of the water first thing this morning,' said Leeyes, consulting a message sheet. 'Two men out fishing saw the body and grabbed it.'

Detective Inspector Sloan noted that between sentences, so to speak, the dead body of the girl – whoever she was – had gone from being referred to as 'she' to the more depersonalised 'it'. It wasn't a good sign.

'Any name known?' he asked. The girl would have been a person still to somebody.

'There's been nobody reported missing so far today,' said the superintendent elliptically, starting to scrabble about amongst the papers on his desk again, 'but it's early days yet.'

Rightly taking this to mean that decomposition had not yet set in, Sloan said he would go straight to the riverside. And he would take Crosby, he added to himself, even though it would be puppy-walking again; the dead were beyond harm.

CHAPTER FIVE

'Mr Short? Good morning to you.' Simon Puckle rose to his feet as his visitor was shown into the solicitor's office. He welcomed him with a handshake and waved him into the client's chair. 'I have here,' he began without further preliminary, 'the last will and testament of Josephine Eleanor Short of the Berebury Nursing Home, St Clement's Row, Berebury…'

'My grandmother,' said the young man opposite him.

'Precisely,' said Simon Puckle. 'It is dated – let me see now – just under three years ago.'

'That would have been when she first went into the nursing home,' supplied Joe Short, nodding, 'which was soon after my parents were killed. She sold her house then and almost everything in it.'

'Just so,' said Simon Puckle, specialist in the winding-up of homes as well as estates. 'If I may say so, that is quite clear from the provisions of the will.'

Joe Short visibly relaxed. 'That's quite a relief, Mr Puckle.

Sorting out my parents' estate is being quite a problem, my being out in Lasserta and the airline people and the airport owners there still being at loggerheads after the accident. I just can't get anywhere with them yet...'

'And you are described here as an employee of United Mellemetics plc in Lasserta...'

'I was with them,' replied Joe Short immediately. 'I moved to Cartwright's Consolidated Carbons not long after I lost my parents. A good friend of mine had gone missing about the same time and I thought a change of scene might help...'

The solicitor, a man still working in offices in a fine early Georgian house bought by his great-great-grandfather and by both nature and profession therefore constitutionally opposed to change, nevertheless nodded sympathetically.

'But it didn't,' admitted the younger man, 'at least, not much.'

Simon Puckle, mindful of a famous legal comment made when people were straying from the point, soon got back to his muttons. 'The will appoints myself and failing me, members of this firm, as sole executors of the will...'

Joe Short nodded again. 'That figures. Granny knew I couldn't get back to England very easily or often and she didn't want me to have to. And anyway she always said her family's obligation was to the living not the dead and that was what mattered.'

Simon Puckle, who dealt with the estates of the dead as much as with those of the living, and did feel an obligation to them, made no comment on this and said instead, 'In my capacity as sole executor I can therefore advise you of its contents.' Something of a specialist in reading body language, he waited for any increase in tension in the man opposite, but there was none that he could observe. Joe Short seemed very relaxed and so the solicitor deduced that what was to come was probably not news to him.

'As her only grandchild, you are her residuary legatee,' said Simon Puckle formally, 'and subject to the obtaining of probate and paying the necessary inheritance tax and, of course, making the small bequests she listed, to the Rowlettian Society and so forth, and seeing to a gravestone for her in Damory Regis churchyard – she wanted your parents' names on it, too, by the way, as well as the old-fashioned plumb line—'

'Plumb line?' said Joe Short, a bewildered look on his face.

'A medieval symbol meant to represent the expression "Death levels all".'

His face cleared. 'I see.'

'...the remainder of the estate will be coming to you. In due course.' He added the caveat carefully.

Joe Short nodded. 'Poor Granny.'

It wasn't what the solicitor had expected him to say. At this stage most legatees only wanted to know how much money would be coming to them.

'Subject, naturally,' continued Simon Puckle fluently, 'to your also providing satisfactory evidence of identity.'

Joe Short jerked his head. 'Of course. I quite understand that.' He fumbled in his jacket pocket. 'I've got my passport here if you want to see that,' he said, putting it on the desk.

'Thank you.' The solicitor picked it up, glanced at the man and the photograph, made a written note of its number, and then rang for a clerk and asked her to make a photocopy of it. She was back in minutes and he handed it back to Joe Short, who stowed it away in his inside jacket pocket.

'Let me see now,' said Simon Puckle, delicately casting a fly with all the finesse of an experienced freshwater fisherman, 'I am not sure if the source of your late grandmother's money is known to you.'

Joe Short frowned. 'And I'm not sure that I know all the details myself. I can only tell you what my father told me.'

'Which was?'

'That round about the time when Dad had just left school Granny's own mother died...'

'Ah, I see, an inheritance...'

'No, no. Well, not exactly. Only in a way. Her mother didn't leave Granny any money at all. In fact, believe it or not, the family actually tried to cut her off with a shilling...'

As it happened Simon Puckle had no difficulty in believing this: that the making of testamentary dispositions didn't always bring out the best in people was a lesson learnt early in the legal profession.

Joe Short was still looking at him across the desk. 'That bit about a shilling's an old saying, isn't it? At least someone once told me it was.'

'Indeed, it is, and one with some legal significance.'

Joe Short looked up. 'Tell me.'

The solicitor rested his elbows on his desk and steepled his fingers before he said, 'To be cut off with a shilling is to be disinherited. To be left a shilling in a will indicated that the testator had not forgotten or overlooked the person concerned but had intentionally disinherited him or her by bequeathing them a trifling sum.'

'There was plenty of room on Granny's side for hurt feelings,' Joe Short sniffed, 'so in my opinion it should have been the other way round: Granny cutting them off.'

'Ah,' said the solicitor alertly.

'It must have been like rubbing salt into an old wound as far as Granny was concerned,' said Joe Short heatedly, 'her own mother trying to do her out of what was rightfully hers.'

'Indeed, but do go on. You were telling me about your grandmother's family and this inheritance.'

'I was told that the family tried to cut Granny out of her share of her own grandmother's estate but they found they couldn't. By the provisions of some old trust – I don't know anything more about it than that – when Granny's own mother died all that was held in it had to be divided up between her descendants *per*...' He stopped and looked uncertainly at the solicitor.

'*Per stirpes?*' suggested Simon Puckle. He coughed and explained that the distribution would therefore be equally shared between the immediate heirs and not according to the number of children they had if they had predeceased the testator.

'That's it. I didn't know what it meant, but anyway I know Granny was entitled to her fair share all right, just like the rest of her grandmother's descendants – all her own sisters and brothers.'

The solicitor nodded and added pedantically, 'And cousins, if any.'

'They – well, all but one of them, her brother, William – tried to stop her having it but you didn't know Granny.' Joe Short's face broke into a smile for the first time that day. 'She was a fighter. She took them to court and won her share. Her family found out the hard way that they couldn't do her out of the money in that trust however hard they tried.'

The solicitor glanced down at the will and said wryly, 'She seems to have put it to very good use.'

Joe Short was still smiling. 'There were no flies on Granny, Mr Puckle. I can tell you that. No flies at all. That money bought her house and put my father through university and then some.'

'Your father...' said Simon Puckle. 'Let me see now, his name was...'

'George Peter Arden Short,' supplied Joe Short. 'Inevitably known as "Lofty" at school.' He grimaced. 'When I was at school they used to say "Short by name and tall by nature".'

'Ah, I was going to ask you about your schooling, too.' Simon Puckle's pen was poised over the notepad on his desk.

'Here, there and everywhere,' said Joe Short cheerfully. 'Dad was working all over the world – he was an engineer, like me – and Mum didn't want me sent back to some boarding school thousands of miles away so I got sent to school wherever they happened to be at the time.'

Simon Puckle made a note and then went on, 'Presumably this money that your grandmother inherited was the basis for her...er...shall we say – future prosperity?'

Joe Short said, 'That's what I've always been led to believe. My father told me that she went into property a bit earlier than most people.'

'A lot earlier, I should say,' said the solicitor approvingly, 'judging by the size of her estate. She would appear to have been very far-sighted.'

Again the man in the client's chair did not say what Simon Puckle had expected. Instead he shook his head sadly and said, 'After my parents died Granny said money didn't matter. All the money in the world wouldn't bring them back.'

'It's the hardest lesson of all,' murmured Simon Puckle, a man trained to be the interface between money and life.

Joe Short started to get to his feet. 'There was one thing, though, that I'd rather like to know...'

'Yes?'

'Suppose I'd died before Granny – what would have happened then? You know, another plane accident – not, I can assure you, that I'll ever travel by Lasserta Airlines again. Ever. But working with querremitte can sometimes be dangerous, too.'

The solicitor scanned the pages in front of him. 'Let me see, now...ah, yes, here we are. Any wife and children of yours would take first, then someone called William Wakefield of The Old Post Office, Staple St James, would inherit.' He looked interrogatively at Joe Short. 'Presumably he is the husband of the Mrs Janet Wakefield who made the funeral arrangements and was the person the deceased gave as her next of kin?'

'That's right. And it makes sense. As I said, his grandfather, a William, too, was a brother of Granny's and the only one of the family who kept in touch with her after...after...'

'Shall we say the "disruption"?' The solicitor was more used to dysfunctional families than most and had found over the years that this word – carefully selected from the history of the Scottish Church in the nineteenth century – had come in very useful.

Joe Short grinned. 'I couldn't have put it better myself.'

'So this William Wakefield, or failing him, any heir male of his body, would have become the residuary legatee,' resumed Simon Puckle punctiliously.

'That figures, doesn't it?' said Joe Short, suddenly rising and putting out his hand. 'Thank you.'

'I take it you'll be staying at the Bellingham for a little while?' said Simon Puckle.

'Just a very few days. I have to get back to Lasserta as soon as I can, the firm having been so good,' said Joe Short from the doorway. 'But first I'm going over to Kinnisport to look up an old boy called Sebastian Worthington who came to the funeral. I want to talk to someone who really knew Granny well and he seemed to fit the bill.'

And then he was gone.

The bridge across the River Alm at Billing was situated at the lowest point downriver at which it had been possible to build a bridge with the tools, materials and know-how around in rural Calleshire in 1485. Its pointed stone piers had deflected the waters of the Alm between the arches ever since.

What the piers of the bridge hadn't done today was to deflect the body of a fully clothed girl through them and into the mainstream. Instead, some vagary of the current had caused her body to fetch up in a little patch of still water near the northern bank.

'Bream,' spluttered one of the fishermen, when Detective Inspector Sloan arrived. 'We were fishing for bream.'

Sloan nodded. People said the oddest things when under stress. This man was clearly stressed. His friend was a bit more composed. 'I got a hook into her clothes, Inspector,' the other fisherman said, 'though it seemed a bit disrespectful.'

Sloan was reassuring. 'You did the right thing. Looking for her lower down the river would have been more difficult.'

'And then we hauled her out,' said the first man, adding anxiously, 'hope that was all right, too?'

'In case the river took her away again,' explained his friend.

'It could have done. Easily. The Alm can come up quite quickly when it has a mind to.'

'After heavy rain upriver,' supplemented his companion. 'And you don't always realise here downstream when that's been happening. Takes time to get here does heavy water, but when it comes, it comes down sudden.'

'I know you're not supposed to touch a body...' The first fisherman still needed reassurance.

'It's better than letting her go out to sea,' said Sloan firmly. 'Now, both of you keep well back and let me have a proper look...'

Not only the two fishermen but Detective Constable Crosby, too, kept their distance as the detective inspector advanced carefully towards the body of the girl. He judged that she was aged about twenty-four or -five and certainly hadn't been in the water long. She was wearing a very light coat over a blouse and brightly coloured summer skirt, strands of auburn-coloured hair falling wetly round her face. As far as he could see at first glance there was no sign of injury on the body but that was something that would have to await the arrival of Dr Hector Smithson Dabbe, the forensic pathologist. Post-mortem evidence was what would be wanted, not the unskilled observations of anyone else.

'Tape off the site, Crosby,' he ordered, 'watch out where you walk and establish a single route to the scene.' He turned to the fishermen. 'You two stand over there until we've had a chance to take down your names and addresses.'

'But I told my wife I'd be home for breakfast,' began one of them.

His protest fell upon deaf ears. Sloan thought he himself would be lucky to get home for his supper. Making a mental note to ring Margaret, his wife, and tell her so, he pointed authoritatively to the spot where he wanted the men to stand and then got back to business – police business.

Meanwhile Detective Constable Crosby was obediently pegging out the ground. Then suddenly he raised his head, dog-like, for all the world like a pointer scenting game. 'I can hear a car coming.'

'Then get back up to the road, Crosby, and if it's the doctor let him know exactly where we are.' Injuries examined *in situ* after death were in the first instance a matter for Dr Dabbe, not a policeman. Police interest, if any, usually only arose after that. Natural causes let everybody off the hook – except perhaps the doctors. 'The photographers should be on their way, too,' he reminded Crosby.

'And the river bailiff,' said one of the fishermen. 'He's always about.'

'You can count on it,' added the other fisherman bitterly.

Sloan made another mental note. The river bailiff, then, might well be the man to ask about the rate of flow of the River Alm. And if the pathologist could tell him how long the body had been in the water, then working out where the girl had gone in the river shouldn't be too difficult. And if neither of them could help, the River Board should be able to provide the answer.

'Ah, there you are, Sloan.' The pathologist advanced across the grass and stepped carefully down the slope towards them. He was followed by his perennially silent assistant, Burns, who was carrying the doctor's black bag. The doctor waved his hand airily. 'Your photographer chaps are on their way, Inspector. They'll be here soon. I overtook them about four miles back.'

This came as no surprise to Sloan. The pathologist was one of the fastest drivers in Calleshire and that was without even having the excuse that his patients were urgent cases. 'I expect they were obeying all the rules of the road, Doctor,' he said without inflexion. 'It wouldn't do for them to be caught speeding, would it, now?'

'Point taken, Sloan,' said the pathologist jovially. 'Now then, what have you here for me?'

The detective inspector indicated the body of the girl outstretched on the riverbank.

'She was floating in the rushes, Doctor.' One of the fishermen hurried into speech. 'On her back.'

'Just like Ophelia,' murmured the pathologist. 'At least, just like Sir John Millais' portrait of Ophelia.'

'Beg pardon, Doctor?'

'A girl in a famous painting, Inspector, who had drowned herself for love. Amazing what some girls will do for love, isn't it?'

'So I'm told,' said Sloan austerely, not diverted from the matter in hand. What he himself had done for love was not something he cared to reveal to anyone. His wife, Margaret, knew and that was all that mattered. All he was ever prepared to say on the matter was that faint heart had never won fair lady.

'Ophelia but without the flowers,' said the pathologist, taking in the surroundings with a practised eye. 'Burns, we'd better have the ambient temperature.'

'What flowers?' asked a bewildered Crosby, looking round and seeing nothing but grass and water in the countryside.

'In that painting,' explained the pathologist. 'The artist, Millais, sent out for plants that grew at the water's edge while he was working on it. He had some trailing willow branches brought round, too. Mind you, I don't blame her...'

'Who?' asked Crosby, totally lost now.

'Ophelia. Her lover was a very funny chap with big problems.' Dr Dabbe's manner changed as he peered at the body. 'Millais's model caught pneumonia but I think this girl might have drowned. Too soon to say, of course. Much too soon. But how and why is a different matter. Or to put it another way it's the difference between "I shall drown and no one will save me", which is a cry of despair, and "I will drown and no one shall save me", which is suicidal.'

'Yes, Doctor,' Sloan said stolidly.

The pathologist was looking round now as two men, heavily burdened with equipment, started to struggle across the field. 'Ah, here come your happy snappers. When they're done, Sloan, perhaps I could get a bit nearer and tell you whether she did an Ophelia or her Hamlet pushed her.'

CHAPTER SIX

At her home, The Old Post Office, in the village of Staple St James, Janet Wakefield was pushing a mug of coffee across the kitchen table to the woman sitting opposite her.

'Now, Jan, tell me about last night. Everything, mind you,' said her friend, Dawn. 'I'm all ears. What's this Joe Short really like?'

Janet screwed up her face. 'Difficult to say.'

'Oh, come on. You can't have spent an evening with any man without getting to know something about him. That wouldn't be natural, not knowing you.'

'He didn't give much away, really,' Janet protested.

'Tall or short? Fat or thin?' Fatness was forever at the forefront of Dawn's mind. She always asked if the milk for her coffee was semi-skimmed.

'Oh, quite tall. What you might call well built rather than fat – oh, and sunburnt,' replied Janet. 'Very pleasant, though, I must say. That's all, Dawn, honestly.'

It wasn't anything like enough for Dawn, who carried on

with her interrogation. 'Married? If not, why not?'

'I don't know whether he is or not. He didn't mention a wife or say anything at all about having any attachments...oh, except that conditions in the wilds of upcountry Lasserta were no place for anyone's wife and family but he hoped not to be staying there for ever.'

'What's his job?' Dawn's husband was something unspecified in insurance.

'He's an engineer with Cartwright's Consolidated Carbons. They do something important with querremitte ore – whatever that might be – after it's been mined.'

'Bully for them.'

'Sounds to me more like profits for them,' said Janet on whom some at least of the essentials of her own husband's work had rubbed off.

'How old?'

'About our age,' said Janet. 'Well, under thirty, anyway,' she added delicately, since she knew Dawn was approaching that highly time-sensitive watershed. 'About twenty-eight, I should say, now that I've seen him properly. What I can't understand is that while Joe seemed to know all about us – Bill's family, that is – we didn't know anything about him. I've certainly never been told anything much at all about the history of the Shorts.'

'Not even that this particular one existed,' remarked Dawn pertinently.

'No.' She shook her head. 'Bill's never talked about that side of the family at all. I'm not even sure that he knew a lot about it himself, although now I come to think about it I remember there were some hints about there being a black sheep in the past.'

'One is always at the mercy of the older generation for that sort of information,' said Dawn largely. 'I mean, they only tell you what they want you to know, don't they? Parents are the same all over.' She took a sip of her coffee. 'Me, I got an aunt to spill the beans about my grandfather. Drink,' she said lugubriously.

Janet, who heard about Dawn's grandfather's overfondness for alcohol every time her friend was offered a glass of wine, reverted to her husband's family. 'That was why I was so surprised, remember, when we got that call out of the blue from the nursing home.'

'Perhaps the Wakefields didn't want to tell you about someone in the family being born on the wrong side of the blanket,' suggested Dawn. 'Don't they call it the bar sinister or something?'

Janet Wakefield hesitated before she spoke. 'I know there was some big trouble a long time ago about something called the Kemberland Trust... But what exactly it was all about I just don't know. Money, anyway.'

'Trusts always mean money,' declared the worldly-wise Dawn. 'And money means trouble.'

'It did,' said Janet slowly, taking a long sip of her coffee before she spoke again. 'Not that I know any of the details except that I was told that there was a great row about it... lawyers and that sort of thing.'

'Families,' exclaimed Dawn. 'They're always the same. So is money,' she added more thoughtfully.

'But on the other hand I was told that Bill's parents' share of the money from that trust made a big difference to Bill's mother, Eleanor, that is. Put Bill through school and that sort of thing. Gave him a good start in life, all right.'

'And therefore made a difference to you and Bill, too,' concluded Dawn ineluctably, looking round the nicely appointed kitchen at The Old Post Office.

'Well, yes, in a way,' admitted Janet honestly. Her home was her pride and joy, the furniture carefully chosen and much polished, the soft furnishings colour-coordinated in a way advocated by the best magazines. 'I must say it gave Bill a good start in life, his having had a good education. It put him through university and that sort of thing.'

The lacuna in the conversation which followed was due to the desire of both women to not mention that quite a lot of Bill and Janet's present income was presently being spent by the couple on infertility treatment. That the trust money would give any child of Bill and Jan's marriage a good start, too, should one come along, was not mentioned by either of them. So far, though, no baby had appeared and the fact, appreciated but unspoken, hung between both of them like a cloud.

'Joe Short was going to look up some old boy near Kinnisport who'd been at the funeral and told him he'd known his grandmother really well a long time ago,' volunteered Janet, breaking the silence and adding lightly, 'just in case he was his grandfather.'

'That would be a real turn-up for the books,' said Dawn, who had never placed a bet in her life.

'Wishful thinking, if you ask me,' said Janet robustly. 'I think the poor fellow – Joe, I mean – is a bit short of relations these days and wouldn't mind a few more seeing as he's lost both his parents, too.'

'Well, he's got you two now, hasn't he?'

'I hadn't thought of that,' said Janet slowly. 'Perhaps I ought to ask him round. I'll have to think about it. More coffee?'

'Please.' Dawn pushed her mug forward and then cocked her head to one side, listening hard. 'Isn't that your phone I can hear ringing somewhere?'

Janet slid off her chair and went into another room. When she came back she was a different woman, exuding excitement and pleasure, her eyes glowing. 'Dawn, you'll never guess what's happened! That was Bill,' she announced excitedly, 'ringing from London.'

'London? But I thought he was in Brazil...'

'Head Office,' she said impressively. 'He was called back there yesterday all in a hurry. His flight landed during the late morning our time...'

'When you were over at the funeral, of course.'

'Exactly. That's what I told him. He said he'd tried to ring me later as well but it was too late to come home after he'd seen the boss man at work and he was too tired after the flight to be safe to drive anyway.'

'Something wrong?' enquired Dawn curiously. In her own husband's world the words 'Head Office' usually spelt trouble.

'On the contrary,' said Janet, smiling broadly. 'He said it was good news but he wasn't going to tell me what it was until he got down here. I explained that I was out last night too.'

'At the Bellingham with Joe Short,' supplied Dawn. 'So what did you tell him?'

Her lips curled mischievously. 'That I was at a hotel with another man. All evening.'

'You'll be lucky if he doesn't come straight down with a horsewhip.'

'But,' went on Janet serenely, 'I assured him he hadn't anything to worry about.'

'Good,' said Dawn seriously. 'Now what about that second cup of coffee?'

Janet moved towards the stove and then turned. 'Of course, if Bill is back at home we can ask Joe Short round, can't we? After all, he is a sort of relative.'

The two police photographers, Williams and Dyson, had reached Billing Bridge now and were busy setting up their equipment on the riverbank. While the pathologist was taking in as much as he could about the body from what could be determined at a suitable distance, Detective Inspector Sloan raised his head and looked at his surroundings properly for the first time.

This was an area of the Calleshire countryside that the watercolourists greatly favoured – something about the rows of willows by the water always attracted painters – and it was one that the nature conservationists were wont to wax lyrical about. If the noises nearby were anything to go by, it suited the bird life, too. The thought stirred Sloan into action.

'Crosby, take statements from those two fishermen, and then get onto the local twitchers and find out if any of them saw anything like a body coming downstream at any stage before it got here. I understand some of them get up quite early.'

'Don't they call it the "dawn chorus" or something?' said the constable naively. Getting up in the morning was something he had always found difficult.

'Very probably. And find out who was on duty last night in the bridge area of Berebury. They might have seen something.' Personally, he doubted it. A constable on the beat on foot saw a lot, two policemen in a car patrolling a wide sweep of the town after dark usually saw very little. 'You might check up on any houses by the riverside, too.'

'Yes, sir,' said Crosby, glad to get away from the body lying on the riverbank.

'And when Williams and Dyson have taken as many pictures as they need – get them to take as pretty a one as you can for identification purposes – you can let Dr Dabbe get started on his examination while I—' He was interrupted by a ring on his earphone. It was Superintendent Leeyes at his desk in Berebury Police Station.

'That you, Sloan? We've just had a missing person reported. Might be a help.'

'Missing how long?' asked Sloan cautiously. The body on the riverbank hadn't been in the water more than a few hours – even he could see that.

'Sounds like just since last night.'

'That figures, sir.' He reached for his notebook.

'Girl of twenty-four, a nurse at Berebury Hospital, didn't turn up for work this morning when she was meant to be on duty.' Leeyes grunted. 'Apparently someone from the hospital went round to her house and tried to knock her up. She didn't answer the door but the lights are still on and the curtains are drawn. Name of Lucy Lansdown. No description available yet.'

Detective Inspector Sloan dutifully conveyed this information to Dr Dabbe.

'Any note?' asked the pathologist.

'None that's been found so far, Doctor.'

'Tell them to have a good look when you do get into the house,' said Dr Dabbe. 'A suicide note can help. And if she's been reading Goethe, it might explain her going in the river.'

'Who's he?' asked Crosby, not yet out of earshot.

'A German poet who said "Know myself? If I knew myself I'd run away." Girls get funny ideas sometimes, you know.' The pathologist waved a hand. 'Not that I'm jumping to any foregone conclusions, Sloan. You know me too well for that.'

'I do, Doctor.' Getting a really firm opinion out of the pathologist until after the post-mortem was always difficult.

'No handbag round her shoulder, I see,' said Dr Dabbe. 'Handbags are as important to women of this age, you know, as they were to Lady Bracknell.'

'I know that and we'll be examining the house of the missing woman as soon as we can, Doctor, for that or a note. And we'll be looking at the bridge area in Berebury and any other spots where she might have gone into the river, too.'

'Sometimes they take their handbags with them when they jump...' The pathologist peered at the body's fingertips and changed his tone suddenly. 'That is, if they do jump, Sloan. It rather looks as if this woman tried to grab something as she went into the water. These hands have been scratched by something. I'll need a closer look later.'

Detective Inspector Sloan cast an eye in the direction of the hands of the body on the riverbank. Giving the deceased a name somehow made the death more poignant. A pretty girl, he thought. 'She might have been called Lucy Lansdown. That's the name of the only girl notified as missing in our manor last night.'

The pathologist was not interested in names. 'Superficial grazes on the right forearm, too,' Dr Dabbe was already dictating to Burns, his taciturn assistant. 'I'll get you some samples of the grit in the abrasions as soon as I can.'

Sloan made a mental note to get some samples of the grit from the bridge in Berebury, too.

Dr Dabbe peered at the supine figure. 'I can't see from here if there are any bruises round the neck or anywhere else, but I'll be examining the subject more carefully later.' Then he raised his head and called across to the fishermen. 'There's a weir upstream from here, isn't there?'

'At Lower Malcombe,' answered one of them.

The pathologist nodded. 'She might have got bumped about going over that – that's if she went in higher up. I can't tell you any more yet, Sloan. Not until I've had a better look all round back at the mortuary.'

CHAPTER SEVEN

Simon Puckle depressed a switch on his office desk and asked if Miss Fennel would come in, please. It was a measure of the length of time that Florence Fennel had been with the firm of Puckle, Puckle & Nunnery that Simon Puckle, now a partner, still always addressed her as Miss Fennel. Although he wasn't frightened of her any more – as he had been when he was a small boy playing under his grandfather's big partner's desk – he hadn't yet ventured to call her Flo as everyone else in the firm did, even though that same big desk was the one he was sitting at himself now.

'Yes, Mr Puckle?' She came in promptly, notebook at the ready. Florence Fennel had managed the matter of addressing her employer rather better, moving seamlessly between calling him 'Simon', 'Master Simon', 'Mister Simon' and – now that he was a full partner – to 'Mr Puckle'.

'In the matter of the executry of Josephine Eleanor Short,' Simon began, 'we shall first need to establish that there are no other claims on the estate...'

She nodded. 'I'll draft the usual advertisement for *The Berebury Gazette* asking for anyone who thinks they have one to let us know by the end of...say...next month.'

'That will do nicely. And then could you please look into confirming that the residuary legatee...let me see, now,' he consulted his notes, 'this young man Joseph Arden Short, is who he says he is.'

'Establish his credentials...' she said, nodding.

'Exactly. I've seen his passport but we'll need the marriage certificate of his parents. I've got a note of the names of his former employers and his present employers out in Lasserta. Perhaps you would check with them, too?'

'Certainly, Mr Puckle.'

'But there is also the matter of the deaths of his parents. This will need proper confirmation, as well.' Simon Puckle went back to his notes. 'Ah, yes, I've got their names here – George Peter Arden Short and Helena Mary Short. They died in an aeroplane accident in Lasserta two or three years or so ago.'

'The British consul should have a casualty list,' said Flo Fennel. 'I'll email him.'

The solicitor frowned. 'I rather think it's an embassy there, not just a consulate. There's a lot of valuable querremitte mines out in Lasserta and our supply line needs an eye kept on it.' He smiled and said neatly, 'A case of the flag following trade, you might say.'

'I don't know what querremitte is but I'm glad to hear somebody is looking after our interests,' said Miss Fennel, who did not have a high opinion of government administrators of any sort.

'A hard metal of great industrial value, I think,' murmured

Simon, privately resolving to look it up to make sure and then speedily returning to the matter in hand. 'I can give you the approximate date of the air crash anyway because the testator made a new will immediately afterwards.'

'Very commendable,' Miss Fennel nodded approvingly. 'Great presence of mind in difficult circumstances. So many people leave it too long.'

'Oh, yes.' He nodded. 'There can be no doubt about Miss Short's mental capacity at the time, which is a help. There would certainly be no question of a successful challenge on those grounds.'

'Is there any likelihood of a challenge on any grounds at all?' enquired Miss Fennel with detached professional interest, her pencil hovering over her notebook.

Simon Puckle paused before he spoke. 'I hope not but I understand that some years ago there was...er...considerable family dissension over an inheritance – a very considerable inheritance – from a long-standing family trust.' He squinted down at his notes again. 'The Kemberland Trust, I understand it was called. I think it might be as well for us to be briefed about that as the legatee may have a legitimate interest in it now.'

'Just in case,' agreed Miss Fennel composedly. 'I'd better send for a copy of his birth certificate, too, since I take it he didn't bring it with him.'

'No, he didn't, so please follow that up, too.' Simon handed over his copy of Joe Short's passport. 'The date of birth is here. And you might let the Berebury Nursing Home know that I've given him permission to collect his grandmother's things from her room there.'

Miss Fennel nodded. 'They'll be wanting the room cleared as soon as possible.'

'And redecorated, I expect,' said Simon Puckle, a veteran of many nursing home visits. 'I gathered from Mrs Janet Wakefield – she's a connection of the family on the distaff side – that there wasn't a great deal there...' He paused and raised his eyebrows. 'I quite forgot that there isn't another side.'

'No. I've made a note that the father of Miss Short's child is unknown,' said the secretary.

'Undisclosed,' Simon Puckle corrected her mildly.

'Of course, Mr Puckle.' She paused, her pencil hovering over her notebook. 'Failing this Joe Short or his heirs-at-law, who takes? The Crown?'

'A distant cousin, William Wakefield of Staple St James.'

'Who is presumably therefore also a member of the family which had some connection with the trouble over the Kemberland Trust?' said Flo Fennel intelligently. 'Since, as you say, there isn't another side.'

'Another known side,' qualified Simon Puckle again, 'but as you say, this William Wakefield's family would probably have been involved in the trust, too.'

'I'll look into it,' she promised, closing her notebook and rising to leave. 'Was there anything else, Mr Puckle?'

He smiled. 'I think you'll find that'll be quite enough to be getting along with, Miss Fennel.'

Sebastian Worthington was very welcoming when Joe Short arrived at Curfew Cottage in the hinterland of the fishing village of Kinnisport beyond Calleford. 'Let me see, now...oh, yes, of course. Joe Short.' He peered at him. 'I saw you at the funeral, didn't I?'

'That's right, sir. I'm Josephine's grandson.'

'Of course. Come along in and sit down.' The old gentleman turned to address the wire-haired terrier barking at his feet. 'Quiet, Sparky! Down, boy! You don't mind dogs, do you?'

'No,' said Joe Short, attempting to pat the little dog that was making a determined effort to bite his ankles.

'If you sit down quickly,' advised Mr Worthington, 'he's less likely to take against you.'

'That's good,' said Joe, heading swiftly for the nearest chair, adding lightly, 'Where I come from dogs have rabies.'

'No, not that chair, my boy. That's Sparky's favourite. It's beside the fire, you see, and he likes that.'

Joe Short moved hurriedly away from a chair covered in dog hairs and instead made for one deeper into the room.

'That's better,' wheezed Sebastian Worthington. 'He won't bother you any more. Not now you've sat down. Look, there now, he's gone to his own chair and settled down already. There's a good boy. So what is it you wanted to talk to me about?'

'My grandmother,' said Joe Short, taking a look round the crowded room. The walls of the cottage were covered in framed school photographs. Pictures of rows and rows of the indeterminate faces and figures of little boys in school uniform hung there, all against the background of the same school building.

'A great girl in her day,' Sebastian Worthington sighed. 'And such good fun, always. She was forever quoting Martial's epigram: "Tomorrow's life is too late. Live today". And she did.'

'You see, sir, you came over to Damory Regis for her funeral and I wondered...you knew her well, I take it?'

'Ah, yes,' the old man sighed, a faraway look coming into his rheumy eyes. 'I knew her from the old days when I taught at Rowletts – that's the prep school, you know – that's how and when. I taught there for the best part of thirty years.' He sighed as if looking into the past from afar. 'They were the best years, too. The very best.'

Joe Short nodded sympathetically. 'I was...well...just wondering exactly how well you knew her.'

'As well as she would let anyone know her,' replied the old man gruffly, peering at Joe Short over the top of his glasses. 'I can tell you that that meant that you had to keep your distance. Oh, dear me, yes. There was no question of anyone taking liberties with your grandmother.'

'That figures.' Joe nodded. 'She seems always to have been a very private person...'

'If,' responded the old schoolmaster energetically, 'I didn't so disapprove of the modern idiom, I should have said that you could say that again.'

'Very private,' said Joe Short ruefully. 'There's a lot even I don't know.'

The glasses had slipped even further down Sebastian Worthington's nose. 'There was a child – a son – but of course you know that since she was your grandmother and that's your name, too.'

'Yes,' agreed Joe Short solemnly. 'That son was my father.'

The old schoolmaster pushed his glasses back up his nose and gave Joe a quizzical look. 'Unless, that is, she married in secret after I knew her, but as she wouldn't marry then, I don't suppose she married later.'

'No,' said Joe Short. 'At least not that anyone knew about.'

'Her boy was at Rowletts.' Sebastian Worthington

waved a hand towards the wall. 'George.'

'My father,' said Joe Short again.

Sebastian Worthington wasn't listening. 'He'll be on one of those photographs. If you could lift that one over there down, you'll find him on there. The third from the left in the second row.'

'My father,' said Joe Short, even more firmly, getting to his feet to the accompaniment of a low growl from the fireside chair.

'Quiet, Sparky,' said the dog's master. He turned back to Joe and said, 'I taught him, you know. Nice boy. Quiet and hard-working, quite good at games but not good enough to ruin his work, which always helps. Sorry to hear about the accident,' he added awkwardly. 'Quite awful. Your poor mother, too. We put it in the Old Boys' magazine. Mr Thompson – he taught geography in your father's day – wrote the obituary.' He scrabbled about through a pile of papers by his chair. 'I've got a copy here somewhere.'

'I've seen it,' said Joe Short with constraint.

'Yes, naturally you would have done. Well, Josephine cut herself off from everyone after that. Went into a nursing home and wouldn't see anyone at all. Quite understand that, of course. Would have done the same myself. Not much fun, though, all the same, to end up like the poet said of the old oak tree "dry, bald, sere".'

Joe said sadly, 'She didn't even want me to come back home to see her.'

Sebastian Worthington pushed the glasses back up his nose again and said pointedly, 'But you didn't come to Rowletts.'

'No,' said Joe, answering the accusation implicit in the statement. 'You see, Dad was working out in Africa then and they thought I was too young to come home alone.'

The schoolmaster sniffed, unappeased. 'A lot of boys did, though.'

'My mother didn't want me to come back to England anyway – besides, Granny had retired from the school by then and Dad thought Rowletts mightn't have been the same there without her.'

'It wasn't,' said Sebastian Worthington with great feeling. 'At least, not for me.'

'I think she had come into some family money by then, too,' explained Joe. 'I expect that had something to do with it.'

'Very possibly,' said the old gentleman. 'But there was no chance of her marrying anyone, anyway. Not then.' A wistful note came into his voice. 'She told me once she was still in love with your grandfather's memory.'

Joe Short looked up sharply. 'That meant he was already dead by then, doesn't it? You see, we...that is, I...never knew who he was.'

'Neither did I,' responded the old gentleman crisply. 'As I say, your grandmother always played her cards very close to her chest.'

Joe Short said, 'And why burial at Damory Regis, sir? That's something else I don't know about.'

'Neither do I,' responded Sebastian Worthington, 'but knowing your dear grandmother as I did for many years I am sure she will have had her reasons. Good ones, I should say. Hers always were good reasons.'

Joe Short shook his head. 'I can't imagine what they were. The vicar said she didn't seem to have gone to church there or have any connection with the place that anyone knew about.'

'Life's full of mysteries,' sighed the old schoolmaster. 'And the longer you live, the more you realise it, and I don't only mean the *Mary Celeste*. Now, what about something to drink?'

CHAPTER EIGHT

Janet Wakefield paused in her rapid tidying up of the house as the telephone rang. Pushing the vacuum cleaner to one side she picked up the receiver and said, 'Hullo?'

'Is that you, Jan? It's Joe Short here. I'm really sorry bothering you again but I just wondered if you'd be free to come over to the nursing home at Berebury with me? Simon Puckle says it's all right for me to go ahead and take away Granny's things now.'

'Oh, Joe,' Janet sounded quite breathless, 'I'm so sorry but I just can't. Something's happened…'

'Nice or nasty?' he asked quickly.

'Oh, nice. Very nice. It's Bill – that's my husband, you know. He was called back to his head office yesterday all of a sudden from Brazil – no warning at all. He only flew into the UK in the evening and tried to ring me but of course I was with you at the Bellingham, wasn't I?'

'You were,' said Joe.

'And he said that anyway it was much too late to come on down here last night by the time Head Office had finished with him – they're like that, you know – these big firms.'

'You don't have to tell me,' said Joe Short feelingly. 'Remember, I know all about big firms and their merry little ways.'

'No warning at all,' she repeated. 'Well, he's just rung me again now. I asked him where he was and he said he's going to be catching a train from London as soon as he could get away from his head office. I promised I'd meet him at Berebury station – that was going to be after I'd done some shopping and got some food on the go for us.'

'Couldn't we just slip over to the nursing home now, then?' asked Joe Short persuasively. 'It shouldn't take too long and you could do your shopping and then go straight to the station from the nursing home. I'm sure there'd still be time.'

'Well...' she hesitated.

He sounded diffident. 'You see, it's that I don't really like to go through Granny's things on my own...'

'Of course, I quite understand that,' said Janet readily. 'There isn't a lot of stuff there, of course. I do know that.' She hesitated and then said slowly, 'I suppose I could take in going there with you since I've got to be in Berebury afterwards anyway to meet Bill off the train.'

'Bless you,' said Joe swiftly. 'I'll meet you at the place in twenty minutes.'

He was as good as his word, standing waiting on the forecourt of the Berebury Nursing Home as Janet's car drew up.

The matron, Mrs Linda Luxton, came to the door herself, explaining over her shoulder as they walked down the corridor about the break-in and the broken vase. 'We don't know what the burglars were after,' she said, giving a light laugh. 'Anyway, we're pretty sure they didn't find anything.'

'About this broken vase,' said Janet, suspecting diversionary tactics.

'We found it in pieces on the floor,' said Mrs Luxton. 'We don't know how that came about but I'm very sorry about it.' She unlocked the door to the room and stood back for them to enter. 'The police have had the room examined and say we can go in again now.'

'Poor Granny,' said Joe, looking round the bleak little bedroom. There was a bed, a wardrobe, a chest of drawers and precious little else in the room.

'We let residents bring their own furniture when they come here,' said Mrs Luxton defensively, 'and you must remember that by the time they come to us they've probably only been living in one or two rooms in their own homes anyway. Besides, most of our residents are usually quite glad not to have to bother looking after their own houses and possessions any longer.'

Joe Short said, 'My grandmother – tell me, had she sort of given up on life?'

The matron's expression softened a fraction. 'It was difficult to say,' she hedged. 'Josephine was one of those who never talked about the past at all. We knew there had been some sort of a tragedy—'

'I'll say,' interjected Joe with vigour.

'But, Mr Short, she didn't tell us any of the details. She was always...well...very self-contained. She didn't complain at all.'

'What about?' demanded Janet immediately. 'What was there to complain about here?'

Mrs Luxton shot her an unfriendly look. 'Nothing here, Mrs Wakefield, I can assure you,' she said stiffly. 'I was talking about her physical ailments, that is the normal loss of powers and faculties that usually accompany old age. Sight and hearing normally decline with time, and naturally illness inevitably overtakes all our residents in the end.'

'Death and taxes being the only certainties in this world,' chimed in Janet as Joe Short drifted towards the chest of drawers at the far side of the room.

He pulled a long face and said solemnly, 'As Robert Louis Stevenson wrote, "Old and young, we are all on our last cruise", but it can't have been much fun for Granny, all the same.' He stooped and pulled each of the drawers of the chest open and shut in turn, pausing at the bottom one.

'That was where Josephine kept her papers,' announced Mrs Luxton, adding half apologetically, 'which I only know because towards the end she couldn't bend down to open it herself.'

Joe put his hand in and withdrew a tattered brown envelope out of which spilt a handful of old photographs. He picked them up and looked at them one by one. Janet moved to his side and said, 'Do tell me who they are.'

'That's me, for a start,' he said, offering her a head and shoulders photograph of himself.

Janet regarded it critically. 'That's a good likeness.'

He smiled a little and reached for another one. 'And there's me in rompers. Mum must have given her that.' He turned a rather faded snapshot over. 'There – it says on the back that it was taken when I was two and half. Can't say I remember that one being taken.'

Janet took the snap in her hand, too. A little boy was

steadying himself against a chair by a dining room table set for a meal, his head only just level with the top of the table. Joe dipped his hand back into the pile of photographs and handed her another one. 'That's an old one of Mum and Dad taken when we were in rural Africa. Very rural, it was, too. From the look of it I think Dad must have developed it himself.'

The matron stirred. 'It would be a great help, Mr Short, if you would be kind enough to check that there isn't anything missing from the room. We have no reason, of course, to believe that the intruder was actually in here...'

'Except for the broken vase,' chipped in Janet quickly.

'Indeed, Mrs Wakefield,' said the matron smoothly. 'Furthermore, as far as we knew Josephine had nothing of... well...intrinsic value in here anyway, except, of course, for the rings she always wore.'

'I'm sure she hadn't.' Joe Short shook his head and said with deep feeling, 'She'd already lost everything that mattered to her.'

The matron inclined her head. 'So I understand...but in any case for obvious reasons we don't encourage residents having really valuable things in their rooms—'

'Those rings,' interrupted Janet suddenly. 'What happened to them? I certainly wasn't given them when I came here after she'd died.'

'They went with her to the undertaker's just as she had requested,' said the matron. 'Perhaps you should check with Morton's...'

'Could the vase have been really valuable?' began Janet tentatively. 'You never can tell with old china.'

'Naturally we haven't thrown the pieces away,' said Linda Luxton stiffly.

'I expect someone could tell from those if it had been a real antique,' said Janet.

Joe shook his head. 'I don't know for certain but I wouldn't have thought it was. I'm sure I would have heard about it if it had been Ming or something. She would have said.'

'It might have had a sentimental value,' suggested Janet.

Joe Short shook his head. 'I very much doubt it. Believe you me, Granny was the least sentimental person I've ever met.'

Suddenly Janet glanced at her watch and gave a little start. 'Oh, my goodness, look at the time. Joe, I really must go now or I shan't meet the train.'

'Right,' he said. 'I think I've been here quite long enough, too.' Joe Short stuffed all the photographs back into their old envelope and bent down to put them back in the bottom drawer. When he straightened up he looked the matron in the eye and said, 'Tell me, I haven't asked anyone yet. What exactly did my grandmother die from?'

'Heart failure,' said Mrs Luxton immediately.

'That's something we all die from,' countered Joe Short.

'Perhaps so, Mr Short,' she responded stiffly, 'but that is what is on her death certificate. That and nothing more.'

Janet Wakefield stood on tiptoe as the London train drew into Berebury Station. She was still a little out of breath following her last-minute dash onto the platform. Parking the car at the station had been a problem as usual and she had only just found a space and got into the station before the London train rounded the last bend and drew to a standstill.

She stood as conspicuously as she could near the 'Way Out' sign, scanning the passengers as they descended from the train.

'Here, Bill,' she called out, waving madly as she caught a glimpse of her husband. 'I'm over here.'

William Wakefield, tanned and open-shirted, stepped off the train and looked round. He caught sight of her and waved, letting the other travellers go on ahead of him.

'Darling,' he said, his words tumbling out as he kissed her. 'Isn't this a lovely surprise? You could have knocked me down with a feather when Carruthers called me back to the office from the site. He'd had this email from Head Office, you see...'

At this point the train driver sounded his horn preparatory to departure, the noise echoing round the station, drowning whatever else William Wakefield might have said.

'What email?' asked his wife when she could be heard.

'The one ordering me to report to Head Office in London without delay, of course.' He grinned. 'As Carruthers pointed out it was marked "Private and Confidential" and he said he didn't know anything about it so he couldn't tell me anyway, darling, and I couldn't tell you – not until I'd been back to Head Office. Then they said it was all right if I let you know now.'

'Let me know what?' she asked anxiously. 'You haven't been sacked or anything, have you?'

He chucked her cheek. 'No, I have not. What on earth put an idea like that into your head?'

'Your being called back to Head Office like that,' she retorted promptly. 'Have you just dropped a clanger or something, then?'

'No, my dearest, I have not. On the contrary, you might say.' He started to fumble for his ticket.

'And what does that mean?' she asked, still anxious.

'It means, Mrs William Wakefield,' he said impressively, 'that I've had some promotion.'

'Darling!' Impulsively she kissed him on the cheek and then stepped back. 'Bill, where on earth did you get that bruise on your face?'

'The hotel bedroom door. I didn't realise the spring was as strong as it was and hit the door as it closed behind me. I thought you'd be pleased about the promotion,' he said modestly.

'But why all the secrecy?' she said as they stepped out of the station. 'Oh, dear, I do hope I haven't got a parking ticket.'

'I daresay we'll be able to afford it now,' he said comfortably.

'I still don't see why it's all been so hush-hush,' she protested.

'I didn't either to start with,' he said, slipping automatically into the car's driving seat and adjusting it to accommodate his legs as opposed to his wife's, 'but I do now.'

'Tell me.'

He steered the car carefully out into the stream of traffic, deftly joining the inner lane. He stretched luxuriously in the driving seat. 'If you could see the roads I have to drive on out there.'

'Hang the roads, Bill, and tell me what's happened.'

'You are now talking to a regional manager, South America!'

'Bill, how lovely. Isn't that good?' A shadow crossed her face. 'But won't that mean you're going to be away from home more than ever?'

'It might,' he admitted.

'The specialist isn't going to like that,' said Jan.

'No.' He twisted his head round to look at her. 'But I couldn't turn it down, could I?'

'No, no, of course not, darling. It's only…'

'I know.' He reached over and patted her knee. 'I know.'

'So why all the secrecy?'

'Oh, I can understand that now,' he said confidently. 'You see, old Carruthers really wanted the job for himself and they couldn't very well let him find out from an email to me that I'd got it and he hadn't. Now, could they?'

'No, I suppose not.'

'Definitely not,' he said firmly. 'Now, young lady, suppose you tell me what man it was you were out to dinner with last night. I'm quite jealous.'

Mrs Connie Marshall was hovering expectantly outside number 2 Stortford Villas, in Stone Street, Berebury, and welcomed Detective Inspector Sloan and Detective Constable Crosby with evident relief. A house key was prominent in her hand.

'I can't imagine what's happened to Lucy, officer,' she said, scarcely bothering to glance at Sloan's warrant card. 'She's not answering the door but the lights are still on and her curtains haven't been drawn back. What can possibly have happened to her?'

'When did you last see her?' asked Sloan. He'd noticed that his own doctor always responded to a question he didn't want to answer with a question of his own. Sloan did that now.

Mrs Marshall paused for thought, her brow wrinkled. 'Not for a few days, come to think of it. Last Friday, I would have said it was. We had a chat when we met in the street – she'd just come off duty at the hospital and I was on my way home with the shopping.'

'And you have Miss Lansdown's spare key,' Sloan prompted her gently.

'That's right,' she said, handing over the key with alacrity. 'I usually keep an eye on her house for her when she's away – she's got a married brother in the North – and I always take any parcels in for her if she's out when the delivery people come. That sort of thing.'

'So she lived alone,' concluded Sloan. Whether the girl was in a relationship or not was something that could await what were euphemistically known as 'further enquiries'.

Mrs Marshall nodded. 'That's right. She did. At least I've never seen anyone else around. Otherwise I didn't see a lot of her. Mind you, she does the same for me on the looking-out side for deliveries and she feeds my cat when I go over to my daughter's in Calleford.'

'Very neighbourly,' said Sloan absently. 'It must have been a great help.'

'It's not like Lucy to go away without saying anything,' she persisted.

'No,' said Sloan. 'Nurses are usually very responsible people.'

'That's what the hospital said – and that it was not like her not to come in to work when she was on duty. Mind you, she had some time off yesterday but they said they knew all about that at the hospital.'

'What was that for?' asked Sloan casually. 'Did she mention it?'

Mrs Marshall shook her head. 'No, but I just happened to notice her coming home yesterday afternoon, that's all.' The woman was clearly working out how much noticing was a neighbour taking a kindly interest and how much was an old woman spying on someone else.

'Dressed for work?' asked Sloan, determinedly low-key.

'Oh, no,' said Mrs Marshall instantly. 'She wasn't in uniform then. Very neat and tidy, she was. Best grey coat and all that.'

'And so she came home later or earlier than usual?'

'Oh, earlier. I just happened to look out of my window as she came up the road. About half past four that would have been.'

'That's very helpful,' said Sloan gravely, turning towards the door of the house.

Mrs Marshall did not leave her position on the pavement.

'I'll just have to get my constable to check the lock to make sure that there hasn't been any forced entry,' said Sloan, jerking his head in Crosby's direction.

That worthy suddenly became alert and approached the door. He examined it closely for scratches. 'Seems OK, sir,' he said presently.

'That's good, it looks as if she went out voluntarily, if she did,' said Sloan, addressing the neighbour. 'Thank you for your help, madam, we'll be in touch again if necessary.'

He entered the house first, as always feeling an intruder himself. A police visit even to an empty house was never a welcome incursion. The light in the front hall was indeed still on but the rest of the house was in darkness, all the curtains drawn against the daylight. He switched on the light in the sitting room with a gloved hand and looked first towards the mantelshelf, taking in the fact that there was no note propped against the clock on there nor, indeed, lying prominently on the table.

The deaths of suicides who didn't leave notes behind – preferably addressed to the coroner, who could decide for himself whether to read them aloud at an inquest – could remain inconclusive and everyone unhappy. Sometimes hurting the living was only what the dead had in mind.

There was no sign of disturbance in the sitting room, he noted methodically, or in any of the other rooms on the ground floor. The spare, simple furnishings and their surroundings had the unpolished look of belonging to someone who had their real being somewhere else. Although there was a pot plant on the table there was a shower of pollen under it that had not been dusted off.

Still wearing the rubber gloves that were mandatory these days, Sloan picked up the telephone and dialled the code designed to record the number of the last incoming call. Someone unknown had telephoned Lucy Lansdown just before ten-fifteen the night before, leaving no number.

'Crosby,' he said, 'you go and check upstairs. See if the bed has been slept in for starters...'

Sloan made his way into the kitchen. It was neat and clean, with what looked like yesterday's supper dishes washed and stacked in a drying rack beside the sink. He pulled open the odd cupboard and saw nothing out of the way. Standing on the work surface was a tin of cocoa, a mug ready beside it. He went back to the sitting room as a clattering on the stairs heralded the return of Crosby.

'Bed not slept in, sir,' he reported. 'Everything seems OK up there otherwise.'

'It looks as if she went out of her own volition, at a guess sometime after a telephone call a little after ten o'clock last night,' murmured Sloan, 'but whether that was in response to that particular call or not remains to be seen.' He looked round the room again. 'Can you see a handbag anywhere?'

Crosby took a good look round and then shook his head. 'No, sir.'

Sloan said, 'Then I don't think there's anything more here for us just now... Wait a minute, though, Crosby, wait a minute...'

'Sir?'

There was a little stool beside a fireside chair with a pile of magazines on it, topped by a copy of the local paper. Sloan had stooped and looked at it more closely.

The Berebury Gazette was opened at the page carrying the notices of deaths and the announcements of funerals. The time of that of Josephine Eleanor Short at the church at Damory Regis the day before was ringed in black ink.

CHAPTER NINE

'Come in, sit down and say that again, Sloan,' barked Superintendent Leeyes. He was sitting in his office behind his desk on which lay only a flimsy message sheet. His pencil hovered over this but he wasn't actually writing anything on it. Two telephones sat at his elbow, both silent for a wonder.

'After your message, sir,' repeated Detective Inspector Sloan, 'we visited the house in Berebury of the missing person whose name you gave us, that is a young woman called Lucy Lansdown.' Sloan took a chair and got out his notebook. 'Formal identification has not yet been carried out but the visible characteristics of the deceased match the description we have been given of this Lucy Lansdown.' Checking the DNA and tracing dental records was all very well, thought Sloan, but they took time. Those could and would come later. After Dr Dabbe had done his work.

Leeyes grunted. 'Go on.'

'We're keeping the probable identity under wraps, sir, for

the time being and at least until we've traced any relatives.'

Leeyes grunted again. 'House keys?'

'There were none with the body and no handbag has been found yet. It was a neighbour, who did have a spare key, who let us into the house.' Mrs Marshall, the neighbour, had called it a 'crisis key', which in the circumstances perhaps it was, although Sloan hadn't said this to her.

'And?' grunted Leeyes.

Sloan plodded on. 'There was no note immediately visible in the house...'

'Nothing propped up in front of the clock, then,' said Leeyes.

Sloan shook his head and took a deep breath before saying, 'No, sir, but we did find something else...'

The superintendent tapped his desk with a pencil. 'Go on, man.'

'A copy of last week's local newspaper—'

'That's no surprise, surely...'

'With a notice about a death and funeral highlighted in ink.'

'Ah...' Leeyes sat up.

'It announced the date and time of the funeral yesterday, at Damory Regis, of an old lady called Josephine Eleanor Short.'

Leeyes bristled. 'Sloan, are you trying to tell me that this girl chucked herself in the river from grief?'

'No, sir,' said Sloan stolidly, resisting the temptation to say that he had been trying to tell his superior officer something quite different; after all, he had his pension to think of.

Leeyes drummed his fingers on his desk. 'Then what are you trying to say, Sloan?'

'That it was also the same Josephine Eleanor Short's – the late Josephine Eleanor Short's – room that would appear to have been broken into at the Berebury Nursing Home.'

'What!'

Since there could have been no doubt that Superintendent Leeyes had heard perfectly clearly what he had had to say, Sloan said nothing in response to this.

'Why?' demanded the superintendent.

'I couldn't say, I'm sure, sir. Not at this stage.'

'Stop talking like a civil service spokesman, Sloan, and give me a proper opinion.'

'Quite difficult, sir. There would appear to have been nothing missing from the room at the nursing home when we examined it.'

'Forget the words "would appear", too, Sloan,' snapped Leeyes, 'and tell me whether there was or there wasn't.'

'Impossible to say, sir, not without further investigation.' Standing one's ground with the superintendent was easier said than done. 'It seemed pretty bare there when we made our examination and the only known damage was to a Chinese vase, which would appear to...that is to say...which had been knocked over and broken. I've telephoned the home and requested that the room in question be locked and kept locked until we get there. I'm going straight over there again now.'

'I should hope so, too,' snapped Leeyes.

Sloan paused and then said, 'I'm afraid I was informed by the nursing home staff that the relatives of the deceased were actually there in the room when I rang.'

'Pity, that,' said the superintendent at once. 'They'll want watching.'

'Yes, sir.' This sentiment he understood. The superintendent was a firm believer in the fact that a death brought out the worst in everyone but in relatives in particular.

'What did the old lady die from?'

'I don't know that yet,' said Sloan, making a note. 'I have been told that Dr Angus Browne was in attendance and signed the death certificate, and he's usually reliable.' Christopher Dennis Sloan might have been a policeman but he was also a husband and father, and as such did not subscribe to the myth that all qualified doctors were as good as each other.

The superintendent grunted in agreement. 'Pigs might be equal, but doctors aren't.'

'No, sir.' It was the evening class lecturer who had decided that the superintendent and he were never going to see eye to eye on the works of George Orwell.

'This girl in the river, Sloan, you will remember is said to have been a nurse at the Berebury District General Hospital...'

'So I understand, sir.' That nothing should ever be taken on trust was a lesson learnt early on in every police career, but since Lucy Lansdown worked at the hospital, this seemed to be taking the precept to extremes, especially since it was the hospital that had declared her missing. But, as always, he would check.

Leeyes tapped his pencil on his desk again. 'The girl could have gone in for mercy killing and then been overcome by remorse, couldn't she?'

'Yes, indeed, sir. Theoretically, that is. We don't know yet whether the deceased had been a patient in the hospital at all during her last illness. I'll look into it. There is one thing, though...'

The superintendent sighed heavily. 'There always is, isn't there? Go on, tell me.'

'Dr Dabbe says he found some grazes on her hands as if she had clutched at some stonework as she fell.'

'The Amy Robsart question,' mused Leeyes.

'Sir?'

'Did she fall or was she pushed?' It wasn't for a disagreement over literary fiction that the superintendent had been asked to leave his evening class on Tudor history. It had been for letting his heavy endorsement of capital punishment get in the way of proper historical assessment. 'Is that what you're trying to say, Sloan?'

'It's whether she jumped or not that we have to worry about, sir.'

'Well, you'll have to find that out, won't you? And soon. It won't be long before we have the coroner on our backs.'

Mr Locombe-Stapleford, Her Majesty's Coroner for East Calleshire, was an old sparring partner of the superintendent's and not given to allowing the police as much leeway as Leeyes would have liked.

'The body is on the way to Dr Dabbe at the mortuary now,' promised Sloan, 'and I'm on my way to the Berebury Nursing Home.'

'Take Crosby, will you?' said Leeyes. 'Anything to get him out from under my feet would be a good thing as far as I'm concerned. He's nothing but a nuisance here.'

'Yes, sir,' said Sloan stiffly. No one could call the detective constable an asset to any investigative team. He gritted his teeth and said, ingrained discipline overcoming any other response, 'Certainly, sir.'

'But,' added Leeyes, a specialist in the unanswerable Parthian shot, 'don't let him hold you up.'

* * *

'Walk?' echoed Crosby in tones of disbelief. Walking had never appealed to the detective constable. It was driving fast cars very fast indeed which was his greatest delight.

'You heard,' said Sloan briskly. 'Walk. It's what bipeds do. They put one foot in front of the other. And we're going to do it, too. Now. The Berebury Nursing Home is only in St Clement's Row. Not at the North Pole. Come along.'

The detective constable looked dubious. 'We went by car last time.'

'Well, we're walking this time.'

'Yes, sir.' He sounded mulish.

'All we have to do is cross over Division Street and we're there,' said Sloan.

'Never 'eard of it,' muttered Crosby under his breath.

This was not surprising since there was no road called this in the market town of Berebury. The name had come from an evening class on sociology attended by Superintendent Leeyes; attended, that is, until he had parted brass rags with the lecturer over the little matter of the causes of youth crime. To say that the two men had not seen eye to eye on this was a considerable understatement.

'Division Road,' explained Sloan patiently, 'is where the better houses are on one side and the less good on the other, divided by the road running between them.'

'I get you, sir. And one's the wrong side of the tracks.' Crosby nodded his understanding. 'And we're heading for Nobs Row now. That's it, isn't it?'

'I couldn't have put it better myself,' murmured Sloan as they turned into St Clement's Row. The houses there had once been the biggest and best in the town. The Berebury Nursing Home building, formerly a large family house, was no exception. Its elegant brickwork exuded Edwardian skill and confidence.

The two detectives crunched up the gravel drive, Sloan automatically taking a look at the cars parked outside. Since none of them was a high-powered sports car Crosby's interest was more cursory. The matron herself met them at the door.

'The family were here earlier, Inspector,' she said. 'I take it you will wish to talk to them, too?'

'Presently,' said Sloan easily. He could recognise an attempt to shift the police emphasis from the nursing home to the relatives of the deceased as well as the next man. 'But first we should like to re-examine the room in question.'

'As I said before, as far as we are aware there is nothing missing,' said Mrs Luxton tautly.

'Good,' said Sloan.

'So why—?' she began.

'There has been an unexpected development.'

That silenced Mrs Luxton. She led the two policemen to Josephine Short's room without further demur, drew the key from her pocket and opened the door. As far as Sloan could see at first glance everything was just as it had been before. All that was different was that the pieces of china from the broken vase had gone.

'Tell me, madam, had the late Josephine Short been in hospital lately?'

Mrs Luxton shook her head. 'Not for some years. We would have liked her to have gone there when she got so ill last month but she declined.' Her lips twisted. 'Very vigorously.'

'Dangerous places, hospitals,' remarked Crosby. 'You can catch things there.'

Mrs Luxton turned her basilisk gaze on him. 'Although

we know the Berebury Hospital is a good one, Josephine very much wanted to die here and not there. She made that abundantly clear on several occasions.'

'She knew she was dying, then, did she?' hazarded Sloan.

'Oh, yes, Inspector. Moreover, she wanted to die. She had also made that quite clear to us all. Many times.' She gave him a meaningful look. 'And to Dr Browne. I'm sure he would confirm that. And, of course, he would also confirm the fact that Josephine declined to go to hospital. I may say she did so with more animation than either the doctor or I had thought possible in her state of health at the time.' She waved a hand. 'It will all be in our records as well as his.'

'I'm sure,' murmured Sloan. 'So, in that case, did you have any outside nursing help for her while she was so ill?'

Mrs Linda Luxton drew herself up to her full height and said impressively, 'Here at the Berebury Nursing Home, Inspector, we pride ourselves in being able to look after all our residents ourselves until the end.'

'What about visitors?' asked Sloan, ignoring this shameless promotion of the nursing home. 'Do you have a record of who came to see her?'

'We have a record that she had no visitors,' responded the matron promptly. 'In fact, she instructed us that were any to come here they were to be told that she didn't wish to receive anyone.'

'And did anyone come?' enquired Crosby, showing interest for the first time.

'Only once. When she was first here. An old gentleman. I must say he seemed not to be at all surprised when we told him what Josephine had said and he went away again. In fact,' the matron unbent a little and said, 'it was when we happened to have a girl working here – a student, who wanted a bit of pin money...'

Detective Inspector Sloan forbore to say that the only students he knew wanted money for items quite different – needles rather than pins, often enough.

Mrs Linda Luxton went on, 'This girl said that it reminded her of a poem where a traveller knocked in vain on a moonlit door.'

'Really?' said Sloan, his mind elsewhere.

'She quoted it to us. She was reading English, you see. "Tell them I came, and no one answered, that I kept my word",' said Mrs Luxton, who had always been privately intrigued by the late Josephine Short and was even more so now. 'Walter de la Mare, she said wrote it.'

'Really?' said Sloan politely. 'And now can you tell me the names of the people who have been – who are known to have been, that is – in her room since she died?'

Mrs Luxton frowned. 'Apart from the staff here, the doctor, of course, he came first and then Morton's, the undertaker's. Then Mrs Wakefield – she's the wife of William Wakefield, who is the next of kin whom Josephine had named for us in our records. I understand that he – that is her husband – was in South America at the time of Josephine's death so she came instead.'

Detective Inspector Sloan was conscious of somehow being made aware that Mrs Janet Wakefield was not Mrs Linda Luxton's favourite person. He said, 'I'd like her address, please.'

'She insisted,' the matron informed him in the same flat tone, 'that neither she nor her husband had been aware of the existence, let alone the proximity of his great-aunt.'

'Funny, that,' interjected Crosby.

'Indeed.' Mrs Luxton clearly thought so too. 'The funeral was yesterday as you already know and then today...'

'Yes?' said Sloan.

'Today Josephine's grandson – that's a young man called Joe Short – came here with Mrs Wakefield to take some of Josephine's things away. He'd arrived from overseas for the funeral. He said the executor had told him that he could, although in the event he didn't take anything away. That's Mr Simon Puckle from the solicitors down by the bridge – he got his secretary to ring us to confirm that.'

'Go on.' No policeman needed to be told where to find the solicitors in their manor.

'Then you came,' finished Mrs Luxton astringently. 'First yesterday and then again now.'

'Someone broke the vase,' put in Crosby, 'didn't they?'

'That's apart from the staff, of course,' said Mrs Luxton quickly. 'They came in, naturally, to clean the room and so forth.'

'I'll bet the breaker and enterer came in here, too,' said Crosby rather too informally. 'The breaker, anyway,' he added under his breath.

Detective Inspector Sloan, ignoring this clear breach of police protocol when interviewing, said instead, 'So Josephine Short died here in this room?'

Subconsciously all eyes became centred on the empty bed, now stripped to the bare mattress.

Mrs Luxton inclined her head and said, 'That is so. We telephoned the doctor at once, of course, and he came and left the death certificate here. That was when we got in touch with Mr Wakefield's home.'

'Not before?' said Sloan with raised eyebrows.

'We had been given instructions by Josephine – very specific instructions, I may say – not to do this until after her death.'

'Got it all arranged, hadn't she?' came in Crosby chattily.

'Josephine knew her own mind,' said Mrs Luxton repressively. Then her tone lightened a little and she sighed and said, 'Not all of our residents do, of course, which can be even more difficult.'

'Quite so,' said Sloan. The totally irrational were a problem to the forces of law and order, too. A fool was even more trouble than a criminal and the fact that notably unpredictable behaviour was the most difficult of all to police, whether criminal or not, Sloan had learnt early on the beat. 'What happened to the room immediately after she died?'

'Nothing, Inspector. Apart from the bed, of course, which you can see has been stripped.' She indicated the empty bed, which was still the cynosure of all eyes.

'And when Mrs Wakefield came?'

'She went through the drawers of that little chest there looking for the papers the registrar wanted. Sheila – she's my deputy – was with her while she was here and says she didn't think Mrs Wakefield took anything away except some official papers. Not that there was anything to take...'

'I'm coming to that,' promised Sloan.

'The young woman was in an awkward position, of course,' conceded Mrs Luxton, 'what with not having known anything at all about Josephine herself and her husband being away.'

'Then?'

'Then Sheila locked the room again.'

'But we do know someone else has been in here,' murmured Sloan. He prompted her. 'The broken vase...'

Mrs Luxton flushed. 'My staff are adamant that none of them broke it.'

'But then they would say that, wouldn't they?' remarked Detective Constable Crosby to no one in particular.

Mrs Luxton stiffened. 'Our staff policy does not encourage victimisation.'

For a fleeting moment Sloan wondered if the woman would be available to do some missionary work along these lines with Superintendent Leeyes. This happy thought passed immediately and he said instead, 'Nevertheless you will appreciate that in the circumstances we shall have to interview them all individually again.'

Mrs Linda Luxton inclined her head in what appeared to be a gesture of gracious acquiescence.

'All breakages to be paid for,' said Crosby cheerfully. 'Like it says in china shops.'

'Tell me, Mrs Luxton,' intervened Sloan quickly, 'does the name Lucy Lansdown mean anything to you?'

There was no hesitation in the matron's response. 'No, Inspector. Occasionally we have to employ agency staff here and I could check our records but I don't know the name myself.'

'These agency staff,' said Sloan, struck by another thought, 'are they sometimes moonlighting from other jobs?'

'Quite often, I'm afraid,' sighed Mrs Luxton. 'And that means that they're usually tired out before they get here, let alone after a night's work. It's usually nights they do.'

'Then if you would be good enough to check...'

'Certainly, Inspector,' said Mrs Luxton, making a move towards the door. Sloan stayed her with his next question.

'What did the late Josephine Short die from?'

'Heart failure,' said Mrs Luxton once more.

Before Sloan could say anything in response to this, his telephone earpiece sprang to life with a message that the pathologist was ready to begin the post-mortem on the body of the unknown female recovered from the river at Billing Bridge, and would Detective Inspector Sloan make his way to the mortuary as soon as possible as there were two people there from Berebury Hospital prepared to identify the deceased.

CHAPTER TEN

Detective Constable Crosby fetched up at the offices of the Calleshire River Board in Calleford without enthusiasm.

'Police,' he announced at the desk with considerable import, usually gratified by the response that this simple statement elicited. He was destined to be disappointed today.

'I never,' responded a young man with spiky hair and earrings, throwing up his hands in mock surrender. 'Don't hit me. I'll go quietly.'

'Not you, mate,' said Crosby.

'It must be the boss you're looking for, then. Bald, fat and never lifts a finger.' He smirked at Crosby. 'On second thoughts it can't be him. Too lazy to commit a crime. If he was a sloth he'd fall off out of his tree.'

'I've come about the river,' said Crosby.

'What's it gone and done, then?'

'Carried a body downstream, that's what.'

The youth changed his manner immediately. 'Where from?'

'That's what I've come about. We don't know yet.'

'Where to, then?'

'Billing Bridge.'

'Ah,' said the youth, suddenly wise, 'that's where the tide turns. If it's travelling downstream and the tide's coming in when it gets there, then it tends to stop just there wherever upriver it's come from.'

'It did,' said Crosby tersely.

'When?'

'Last night or early this morning. What I...we...want to know is when the tide turned.'

The youth turned to a computer, punched a few buttons, frowned prodigiously, drummed his fingers on the desk and then leant down, opened a plan chest instead and produced a tide table. 'The tide at Billing Bridge would have turned at half five this morning. The incoming tide would have slowed anything going further down until after that. Pushed it into a backwater, more like.'

'So when would anybody...' Crosby stopped and changed the emphasis, 'I mean any body have gone in the river at... say...Berebury for it to get there, then?'

The youth pursed his lips. 'Is this for the law?'

'It sure isn't for fun, laddie,' Crosby said portentously.

'Then I'll have to ask my boss to be certain sure...that'll get him out of his chair, all right. He won't be pleased, I can tell you.'

'Doesn't like putting anything in writing?' deduced the constable. 'Is that it?'

'That's him...but if you was to ask me... '

'I am asking you,' said Crosby flatly.

The young man reached for a calculator and put some

figures in. He looked up. 'The river runs at about five knots per hour this side of the weir at Lower Malcombe – that's if there isn't too much rain about...'

'There wasn't,' said Crosby.

'Even so, naturally the weir slows it up a bit...'

'Naturally.'

'So if you was to be talking about...say...the bridge at Berebury...'

'Just for instance,' said Crosby cautiously.

'Well, there aren't any other bridges between Berebury and Billing.'

'We'd got as far as that,' said Crosby with exaggerated weariness. 'And we do also know that there are other ways of getting into the river than from a bridge. Like a boat and the riverbank.'

The youth scribbled some more. 'Then I'd say you're looking for sometime between half ten and elevenish. Maybe a bit earlier if there was rain upriver.'

'And,' said the constable, 'just supposing – only supposing, mind you – we were to want to drag the river below the bridge.'

'Depends on the size of what you were looking for,' said the youth.

'Something small.'

'Then frogmen would be your best bet. Grabs don't pick up little things downstream of the piers of the bridge – they get in the way and push up the rate of flow – but if whatever it is you're looking for is there, you might find it in the dead water below the piers.'

'Thanks, mate,' said Crosby, starting to take his leave. He got to the door before he turned and said, 'Are you the biker here?'

'What if I am?' The clerk bristled.

'There's a Bandit 600 Suzuki in the car park.'

'Well, I can tell you for starters it's not the boss's,' responded the youth vigorously. 'He couldn't get his leg over it. Not being the weight he is.'

'Then your road fund licence expired last month,' said Detective Constable Crosby, sweeping out, adding as he did so, 'and we know where you live.'

In the view of Detective Inspector Sloan there was very little to be said in favour of the surroundings in which post-mortems were conducted. One thing, though, as far as he was concerned, was the complete absence of any attempts to ameliorate the starkness of the Berebury police mortuary. In his view, any such attempts would, if possible, have made the ambience even less attractive. Crematoria might enjoy polished walnut fittings and flowers galore, and green-lawned cemeteries might lie beyond stately wrought-iron gates, but Dr Hector Smithson Dabbe's place of work boasted none of these.

The little door at the back of an anonymous, nondescript brick building, which could only be reached down a blind alley, boasted neither number nor nameplate. It wasn't, either, somewhere where even the most mischievous child could play 'Knock-down Ginger' with a doorknocker and run away. Entry was by a door without a handle on the outside – and ingress could only be gained after a verbal exchange through a microphone set discreetly to one side of it.

Crosby had conducted this with an unseen guardian of official privacy and soon the two policemen had been admitted to the pathologist's sanctum.

'Ah, there you are, Sloan,' said Dr Dabbe. 'You got

through the postern gate, all right, then?'

'Yes, thank you, Doctor, whatever that might be,' said Sloan, mystified.

'Meant to be wide enough for men but not horses, postern gates. Now, come along in. The parish bearers are ready and waiting to produce the subject.' He gave a wolfish grin. 'That's what they used to call 'em in the olden days, anyone who was supposed to give a hand taking the body to the coroner. Now it's something much more highfaluting.'

'Always is,' said the detective inspector.

'Didn't have superintendents in those days either, did they?' said Dabbe solemnly, tongue in cheek.

'Nor pathologists,' said Sloan agreeably.

'What, no slicers and dicers?' said Crosby in an undertone.

'All they did have, gentlemen, were those old women called the searchers who sat by the dying and then said what it was that they had died from,' said the pathologist, adding piously, 'I hope I can do better.'

'So do I,' said Sloan, policeman on duty, first and last. 'I understand that someone from the hospital where the deceased worked is here and prepared to confirm any provisional identification.'

'She's in the waiting room now with her friend, the thoroughly modern Milly.'

Sloan looked blank.

The pathologist waved them away without explanation. 'My man Burns will take you along there.'

The two policemen followed the pathologist's taciturn assistant through a door and into a waiting room. At the far end of this was a narrow, funnel-like passageway that ended not in a door but in a window. As they entered the room two women in mufti rose and turned towards them. They introduced themselves as having come from Berebury Hospital. 'Helen Meadows, director of nursing,' said the taller woman.

'Colleen Bryant, modern matron,' said the other.

'Ah...' As far as Sloan was concerned the slight woman in front of him bore no connection to the legendary matrons cast in the Florence Nightingale mode on whose memory his mother had brought him up. He promptly resolved that this appellation be kept from Superintendent Leeyes: matron, perhaps; modern, no – the two words together a red rag to a bull. Neither woman carried the weight of uniform, either. A plain-clothes man himself, he often missed its unspoken authority.

The director of nursing was saying, 'Lucy Lansdown was due on duty at the hospital at half past seven this morning, Inspector, but when I was told she hadn't reported to the ward by nine o'clock we naturally instituted enquiries.'

Sloan nodded, wondering briefly why it was that the higher up a professional ladder everyone climbed the more circumspect their speech became. Perhaps there was a moral there somewhere...

The woman was still speaking. 'Since it was highly unusual for her not to come to work we sent a porter round but there was no answer to her knocking...'

'The bird had flown,' muttered Detective Constable Crosby impatiently under his breath.

'She was not there,' finished the director of nursing, hardened to irreverence.

'You didn't telephone?' said Sloan.

The tiniest frown crossed the woman's face. 'I'm afraid that there are some of our staff who decline to give us their home telephone numbers. It means that we can't call them in when they are off duty.'

'That's a good idea—' began Crosby.

'If you would both come this way, then, please, ladies,' interrupted Sloan, making for the viewing end of the room and anxious not to put words into their mouths.

He stood back while the two women advanced to the window and looked through the glass at the body beyond. It was placed on a trolley, clearly in sight but out of touch, only the head being visible.

Helen Meadows took a deep breath, and visibly wincing, said, 'Yes, Inspector, that is Staff Nurse Lucy Lansdown.'

'And I was talking to her only yesterday,' murmured Colleen Bryant, equally distressed. 'Poor Lansdown.'

Detective Inspector Sloan, officer of the Crown, had forgotten that there were other institutions, too, where surnames held sway.

'The wonder of death is nearly as mysterious as the wonder of life,' sighed Helen Meadows, the director of nursing. It was something she had said many times before having found it went down well with newly bereaved families.

Detective Inspector Sloan, police officer, was thinking of something else. 'Yesterday? When yesterday?' he said swiftly.

Colleen Bryant frowned. 'In the morning. That was when she first came on duty and she reminded me then that she had arranged to have some time off later that day to attend a funeral.'

'Did she happen to say whose funeral?' asked Sloan, leading the way back to the waiting room end of the viewing room.

The modern matron shook her head. 'No, and I didn't ask, but she was going home to change first.' She hesitated. 'She didn't seem inordinately upset or anything like that if that's what you wanted to know.'

'It helps,' said Sloan. He took out his notebook. 'So would anything else you can tell me about her.'

'She wasn't planning to come back on duty afterwards – I think the service was somewhere out in the country – so I can't tell you anything about the funeral or what she did afterwards,' said Colleen Bryant.

'How long had she been working at the hospital here, for instance?'

The more senior nurse answered him, producing a record card as she did so. 'Nearly three years now. She did her training over at Calleford – there's a big teaching hospital there – and then did a stint at the cottage hospital at Kinnisport. Then she came to us.'

'On promotion?'

The director of nursing nodded. 'Yes. To staff nurse.'

'What about next of kin?'

The woman consulted the record card. 'A brother in the North of England.'

Detective Inspector Sloan copied the name and address into his notebook.

'We haven't been in touch with him yet,' began the nursing officer tentatively.

'You can leave that to us,' Sloan said authoritatively. An experienced professional from the local force could not only impart the bad news but would be more able to assess the response to it. And glean what he or she could from the relatives. 'In fact, we would very much appreciate it if you didn't mention her name to anyone at this stage. Not until we've contacted her relatives.'

The women, no strangers to the importance of confidentiality, seemed relieved. Helen Meadows nodded. 'We quite understand.'

'Tell me,' he said, 'had she seemed depressed at all?'

'Not that we were aware of,' answered the senior nurse with circumspection.

'I'm sure we would have noticed,' put in the modern matron. 'It's not an easy thing to hide, anyway. She would have said, too, I'm sure, if there had been anything wrong.'

'No run of unexpected deaths on her ward or anything like that?' asked Sloan.

'No, and I can assure you, Inspector, that that is something that is always looked into if they do happen,' said Colleen Bryant firmly.

'I'm glad to hear it,' said Sloan, forbearing to mention several spectacular cases in recent times when they hadn't been. 'And there is no suggestion that she had been distressed over the death of any particular patient?'

The nursing officer stirred. 'Nurses are taught to leave the worries of the ward behind when they remove their uniforms. Life would be intolerable otherwise.'

Detective Inspector Sloan said warmly that he was glad to hear it, wishing all the while that this was something he had been taught when a raw constable. It would have saved him a good few sleepless nights in the course of his career. 'Now, if you would just sign a few forms for us... We'll keep in touch, of course.' He put them in front of the two women and said casually, 'By the way, do you know anything about her private life? Had she been lucky in love?'

'I couldn't say, Inspector,' said the senior nurse in tones that conveyed the unspoken message that she wouldn't say if she could.

'She hadn't been lucky in love,' said the younger woman firmly. 'She'd had a break-up with someone a couple of years ago and I don't think there's been anyone since.' She frowned. 'I rather think that's why she came over here from Calleford.'

'Any idea who?'

Both women shook their heads, the older one quite forgetting that she had denied all knowledge of any love affair minutes before.

By the time the paperwork had been accomplished the body was back in the mortuary and Dr Dabbe was waiting for the two policemen, gowned and masked, and quite serious now. The pathologist pulled the microphone dangling above his head down to the right level and started dictating. 'Body of a well-nourished female, said to be aged about twenty-four, recovered from the riverside three hours ago by Billing Bridge...identification confirmed...'

Crosby started unobtrusively to inch his way back from the post-mortem table and towards the edge of the room. He didn't like watching autopsies.

'On macroscopic examination,' continued the pathologist, utterly absorbed in his work now, 'there are grazes on the palmar aspect of both hands – no sign of any rings having been on either hand – but several broken fingernails.' He turned in the direction of the policeman. 'I daresay you'll be wanting samples of the grit in the grazes, won't you, Sloan?'

'Please, Doctor,' he said, for all the world as if they were something being handed to him over a shop counter.

Dr Dabbe continued to stare down at the hands. 'From the

direction of the minor lacerations in the skin I think she might have been trying to clutch at something as she fell…and there are some bruises on the hands, too.'

Detective Inspector Sloan, experienced police officer that he was, didn't like what he was hearing. The pathologist's words conjured up a picture of a young woman desperately struggling in the dark for a handhold as she fell into the river.

'Hullo, hullo…' said Dr Dabbe, 'what have we here?'

'What, Doctor?' Sloan leant forward.

'More bruises round her throat.' The pathologist adjusted an overhead lamp, the better to see what he was doing. 'Someone or something has grasped her round the neck. There are bruises on both sides of her throat.'

Sloan made another note, thankful that the doctor didn't call them ecchymoses, something that always annoyed Superintendent Leeyes.

'I'll be examining the hyoid bone in a minute, Sloan,' said Dr Dabbe, 'but I'm beginning to think that we may be looking at the mark of Cain here.'

CHAPTER ELEVEN

There was an unexpected little knock on the door to Simon Puckle's room. The solicitor looked up from studying a complicated lease to one of the Earl of Ornum's outlying farms. He was doing this with a view to making absolutely sure that as usual all reversionary rights fell back into the estate at its termination. Since his grandfather had done much the same for the earl's grandfather he knew what to look for. The trouble was that the earl's current land agent liked to think of himself as a new broom, sweeping clean. New brooms, though, did not go down well with either Simon or the earl...or, now he came to think of it, the earl's equally long-standing tenants.

'Come in,' he said.

The office junior entered and said nervously, 'I'm ever so sorry bothering you, Mr Puckle, but Miss Fennel hasn't come back after the lunch hour and we're a bit worried. It's over an hour now and it's just not like her...'

'No,' agreed Simon at once. 'It's not.'

'And we wondered if you happened to know why,' she went on timorously.

'No.' He frowned. 'She might have just gone into the library, of course.'

'So she might. I'm sorry, Mr Puckle, we never thought of that.'

Since both of them knew what he suggested to be untrue – Miss Fennel invariably let the office know if she wasn't coming straight back – there was nothing more to be said and the girl withdrew.

Simon pushed the lease away and was just toying with the idea of telephoning her home – Florence Fennel lived at the other side of the town – when the door opened and she came in and in something of a fluster.

'I'm very sorry, Mr Puckle, to be late back but I couldn't get back over the river. The police have closed the bridge off at both ends and—'

'There isn't any other way round, of course,' he said before she could. Berebury only had the one bridge.

'And the place was swarming with people in those white suits.'

'Scene of Crime officers,' he said. No solicitor was unfamiliar with photographs of them.

'And I particularly wanted to be back on time to get to work on the Josephine Short executry.'

Since this was a fiction, too – Miss Fennel was never late back whatever she wanted to do – Simon nodded sagely.

She hurried on. 'I've already had an email back from the embassy in Lasserta giving me the date of the plane crash out there – it was just under three years ago – and confirming that the names of George Peter Arden Short and Helena Mary Short were on the casualty list and that there were no survivors.'

Simon winced. Dry as dust the law might be but its practitioners weren't entirely without human sympathy.

Miss Fennell carried on. 'I have also been in touch with the United Mellemetics office in Lasserta – that is the firm that the client's grandson was working for at the time of the accident. They confirm that their employee Joseph Arden Short left them soon after that to go to work for Cartwright's Consolidated Carbons at the other side of the island.'

'Whatever Consolidated Carbons might be,' said Simon Puckle, an unworthy vision of charcoal biscuits rising in his mind.

'That I could not say, Mr Puckle. It wasn't long after the plane crash, anyway. United Mellemetics say they did their best to get him to stay but they understood his need for a change at the time and sent him off with their blessing. A good worker, they said, and they had been happy to give him a reference stating that he had left the firm entirely at his own wish for personal reasons.'

Simon made a note.

'The firm of Cartwrights say much the same thing and confirm that he is presently employed by them as an engineer on their mining side and that they are looking forward to his return.'

'Good. Winding up his grandmother's estate will take some time, being quite substantial.'

'And,' she went on, knowing, good secretary that she was, that all estates took their time to be wound up, 'I haven't got anywhere yet with the Kemberland Trust but I'm working on it. Since I understand that it came to court there will naturally be some record. If we knew where the appellants lived that would help.'

'Josephine Short worked at Rowletts Prep School over Kinnisport way, that I do know,' he said, 'but as to where the rest of the family were at the time of the dispute over the trust funds I can't tell you. I'm not sure that her grandson knows either. He doesn't seem to know too much about it.'

'I might try the newspapers if we can work out an approximate date.'

'Good thinking. With that amount of money involved I should imagine the case will have hit the headlines,' said Simon, 'to say nothing of its having an unmarried mother as the plaintiff.'

'I'm sorry to say,' said Miss Fennell, pursing her lips, 'but that sort of case invariably attracts the less attractive elements of the press.'

'I'm afraid that some newspapers nearly always consider family disputes to be cases of human interest,' said Simon Puckle as Miss Fennell left his office, 'which, of course, they are,' he added when she had gone. 'It's what sells.'

He picked up the Ornum lease again when she had withdrawn but his concentration had gone.

'Now,' said Bill Wakefield, pulling up his chair to the kitchen table in his own home and cradling a mug of coffee, 'sit down and tell me about this Joe Short. I'd never heard of him myself.'

'Well, I can tell you he knows all about you – us, I mean,' said his wife. 'That's what's so funny.'

'Not half as funny as his being here at all,' declared Bill. 'That's what I can't understand. I never knew Great-Aunt

Josephine had had any children. Or even been married.'

'She hadn't.'

He grinned. 'That explains why I hadn't heard of her, then. Where did you say he'd come from?'

'Lasserta – wherever in the world that might be. I meant to look it up.'

'Querremitte,' said Bill Wakefield, sitting up suddenly and looking every bit the alert businessman. 'They mine it there. Hardest element known to mankind and pretty valuable, I can tell you.' He paused. 'Are you sure, Jan, that he's not pulling a fast one on us all? I mean to say, why should this fellow have only just come out of the woodwork and at this particular point?'

'Because of his grandmother dying, I suppose.' Janet Wakefield wrinkled her nose, a characteristic, had she known it, that had always enchanted her spouse. 'He seems all right,' she said slowly, 'and he certainly knows his family onions, although I agree it's all a bit odd.'

'Anyone could mug those up,' pointed out Bill Wakefield.

'That's true, but he's pretty clued up all the same.'

'That doesn't mean he's pukka.' In the course of his business career Bill Wakefield had had a spell in India.

'No, but,' she brightened, 'his photograph's still in his granny's drawer at the nursing home. I've seen it there myself.'

Bill Wakefield laughed and relaxed. 'That clinches it, I suppose. Well, in that case, we'd better invite him to supper tonight, hadn't we?'

'I'll ring him at the Bellingham if he's still there...' She turned, cocking an ear. 'Isn't that the front doorbell?'

'I'll go,' he said, pushing his chair away from the table. 'It may be this Short fellow.'

It wasn't Joe Short on the Wakefield doorstep but Detective Inspector Sloan and Detective Constable Crosby. Sloan introduced himself and asked if they might come in.

'Certainly,' said Bill Wakefield immediately. In some of the far-flung places in the world where he had worked the police didn't ask if they could come in – they came in. 'Come through this way and tell us what brings you.'

'The death of your great-aunt,' said Sloan truthfully.

'What about it?' he asked. 'From what the nursing home told my wife I thought it was all pretty straightforward.' He looked across at Jan. 'That's so, darling, isn't it?'

She nodded. 'Heart failure was what they told me, Inspector, and that was what was on the death certificate that Dr Browne gave us.'

'We'll be talking to him presently,' said Sloan.

'When he gets back to his surgery,' added Detective Constable Crosby by way of adding a touch of verisimilitude.

'I don't know that I can give you any help at all, whatever it is you want to know,' said Bill Wakefield, frowning. 'As my wife will tell you, I was rather out of touch when the old lady died – in one of the remoter areas of the hinterland of Brazil.'

'So I understand, sir,' said Sloan. He reached into his case and produced a photograph of the face of the girl who had been found in the river, suitably touched up by Dyson, one of the police photographers. He handed it to Bill Wakefield. 'Now, what we want to know, sir, is whether you have ever seen this woman before at any time?'

Bill Wakefield took the photograph in both hands and regarded it for a full moment before handing it back to the detective inspector with a shake of his head. 'No, never.'

Sloan handed it to Janet Wakefield. 'What about you,

Mrs Wakefield? Have you ever seen her before?'

Janet scanned the photograph and said readily, 'Oh, yes, I have, Inspector. It's the girl with the auburn hair. She was at Bill's great-aunt's funeral yesterday over at Damory Regis. That's where I saw her.'

'Did you speak to her?'

'No, I didn't. I didn't know her, you see.' Janet caught her breath. 'Actually I didn't know anyone there at all, Inspector, except the people from the nursing home and Mr Puckle. Truly. But I do remember the girl's hair. It was quite striking.'

'Was she there with anyone else? Can you remember that?'

'Not that I noticed.' Janet frowned. 'I'm almost sure she was alone.'

'Did you see her talk to anyone else?'

Janet shook her head. 'Not that I remember but then almost everyone else there were strangers anyway. Should I have known her? Who is she?'

'That,' said Detective Inspector Sloan, responding to Janet's first question but not her second one, 'is one of the things we are trying to establish.'

Janet gave a sudden start and said, 'Inspector, I've just had a thought. After the funeral, Morton's, the undertaker's, gave me a pile of those little attendance cards that people sometimes are asked to fill in at funerals. I passed them on to Joe Short, that's Josephine's grandson who came over for the funeral. Perhaps you could find out from those who she was. He's staying at the Bellingham.'

Sloan took the photograph back and stowed it carefully away in his case. 'Thank you.' He turned back to Bill Wakefield. 'Right. Now, sir, if we might just have a note of your firm's address in London.'

'Inspector, what is all this about?' Bill demanded, patently puzzled. 'What's gone wrong?'

Janet protested, 'We hadn't even known about Josephine Short's existence here before her death anyway, had we, Bill?'

'Not even that she was still alive,' insisted Bill, 'let alone the fact that she was holed up in a nursing home in Berebury so near us.'

'I'm sure that we'd have gone to see her if we'd known about her,' said Janet.

'In any case,' went on Bill Wakefield firmly, 'I only got back to this country yesterday.'

'When yesterday?' asked Sloan.

'If you must know I flew in and got to Head Office just before six o'clock in the evening. They wanted to see me straightaway, you see.'

'If I might have the name of the person there whom you saw,' said Sloan, pen poised.

'If that's what you want,' said Bill Wakefield in a voice that was now distinctly surly.

'And after that, sir? What did you do after you left the office?'

An angry flush rose steadily up Bill Wakefield's cheeks. 'Look here, officer, what is this all about?'

'The police ask the questions,' put in Detective Constable Crosby.

Bill Wakefield gave him a baleful look. 'If you must know...'

'Yes,' said Crosby sotto voce.

'It would be very helpful, sir,' said Sloan smoothly, reminding himself to tell Crosby sometime that you don't get a second chance to make a first impression.

'As soon as I got away from Head Office,' said Bill Wakefield, 'I naturally tried to ring my wife but there was no answer.'

'I was having supper at the Bellingham with Josephine Short's grandson then,' put in Janet Wakefield quickly. 'I'd met him at the funeral, you see, and it seems he's part of the family.'

'So,' went on Bill with considerable determination, 'I thought if there was no one at home here in Berebury for whatever reason there wasn't much point in my coming down that night. I don't take my house keys out to Brazil with me, you know.'

'No spare under a flowerpot, then?' said Crosby chattily.

'No,' said Bill Wakefield coldly. 'And I must remind you that the last train from London leaves pretty early.'

'Yes, sir, I do know that,' said Sloan patiently. 'So what did you do next?'

'I booked myself in at the Erroll Garden Hotel. At the firm's expense, of course,' he added, catching sight of his wife's expression.

'And then, sir?' persisted Sloan.

'Had a good meal and went to bed early. I was pretty short of sleep by then, I can tell you. Brazil's a long way away.'

One of Detective Inspector Sloan's early mentors had been the sergeant with whom he had first walked the beat. That wise old policeman had a theory that a person being questioned turned their head to the left when spontaneously speaking the truth and to the right when thinking up a good lie. He had held that it had to do with the functioning of the left and right parts of the brain, the right side being used for memory and the left for the creative thinking necessary for telling a good lie – not forgetting that the two pathways crossed over in the brain.

As a very young police constable Sloan had thought instead that it was just policeman's instinct and experience on his sergeant's part. Whatever it was – instinct or simple observation – there was no doubt in his own mind now that Bill Wakefield was lying. A slight trembling in that young man's left hand confirmed this view.

CHAPTER TWELVE

'Where are we now, Sloan?' asked the superintendent. The question was purely rhetorical in that Detective Inspector Sloan was standing in front of him in his superior officer's room.

'Dr Dabbe is of the opinion that the body pulled out of the river, now identified as far as we are concerned as a young woman called Lucy Lansdown, was the victim of an attack.'

The superintendent grunted. 'Sit down and go on.'

'This is on the basis of some bruises to her neck, perhaps designed to stop her crying out for help.'

'It has been known,' said Leeyes heavily.

'There were also grazes on both her hands...'

'From clutching at the quoins of the bridge on the way down?' he asked.

'We're checking on that,' said Sloan.

'But she wasn't dead when she hit the water?'

'Dr Dabbe thinks not. He is of the opinion that she probably died from drowning. She had inhaled some river water and there were diatoms in the lungs. He also found a bruise on her head so it is possible that she could have been stunned before she went into the river.'

The superintendent stirred uneasily. 'There's doesn't sound to me anything at all accidental about all this, Sloan.'

'No, sir, I'm afraid not.' He coughed. 'Dr Dabbe is working on his report now but he states quite categorically that the deceased was not pregnant.'

Leeyes grunted again. 'Or drunk?'

'No, sir. Her blood alcoholic levels showed that she had drunk nothing last evening.'

'And no note, you said?'

'No note that has been found so far,' stated Sloan precisely. 'All we discovered in the house in the first instance was the piece in the local paper announcing the funeral of Josephine Eleanor Short over at Damory Regis marked in black ink.'

The superintendent gave a prodigious frown. 'And what, pray, is the connection between the – I mean, both – deceased?'

'That, sir, is what we are seeking to establish now.'

'You aren't issuing a carefully prepared statement to the press now, Sloan. You're talking to me in my office.'

'Yes, sir.'

'And so what's holding you up, then?'

'We have examined the late Josephine Short's room at the Berebury Nursing Home,' Sloan replied obliquely. 'The contents appear to have been undisturbed save for a vase whose breakage cannot be accounted for and an unconfirmed feeling the matron has that someone has riffled through her office records. Nothing missing there, though, that she can think of.'

'Now you're talking like an accountant, Sloan.'

'There is no doubt, though,' Sloan ploughed on steadily, 'that there had been an intruder on the premises the night before the funeral, although there is no evidence so far that he was in Josephine Short's room, save only for the fact that it was in her room that the vase was broken and none of the staff admit to knocking it off the shelf.'

Leeyes grunted. 'So what's new?'

'Matthew Steele's mother works there, by the way, as a care assistant.'

'Heaven help the inmates, then.'

Sloan coughed and said delicately, mindful of both political correctness and the matron, 'I understand, sir, it is more usual to refer to them as residents.'

Leeyes drummed his fingers on his desk. 'Mark my words, Sloan, that's what they'll be calling prisoners any minute now, too.'

'Very possibly, sir. And Ellen Steele is, as I said, the mother of the troublesome Matthew.'

'Nobody in that tribe would ever have broken anything that they could sell for ready money. Ever,' pronounced Leeyes. 'Any of them. Certainly not her Matthew.'

'No, sir.' Sloan carried on, 'The Scene of Crime people have now taken all the information they can from the nursing home and we have confirmed that the girl in question—'

'The girl in the river,' said the Superintendent.

'Her,' agreed Sloan, since there was never a lot of point in disagreeing with his superior officer anyway. 'She was seen at the funeral by Mrs Janet Wakefield who has since been shown the photograph. Although she states she doesn't know her name, she did identify the woman in the photograph as being among those attending the ceremony.'

'Mourners, Sloan, that's what they're called.'

'Yes, sir, but what we don't know as yet is why she should have been mourning the old lady.' He paused and then went on, 'Or what the connection between the two could be. There must have been one or she wouldn't have been at the funeral.' He wondered briefly if he should mention that sometimes people represented other people at funerals but decided against it. Instead he said, 'We propose checking next with the deceased's grandson if he knew her.'

'Who benefits from her death?' asked Leeyes simply.

'The girl's? We don't know yet, sir. We've been told that there's a brother living in the North of England and that's all I can tell you so far. In the meantime we're keeping the victim's name under wraps.'

'Never does any harm,' opined Leeyes, constitutionally opposed to giving information of any sort away. 'And the old lady's heir?'

'This grandson I mentioned. He's called Joe Short.' Simon Puckle, the solicitor, had been guarded in his talk with the police but helpful. He hadn't known the girl with the auburn hair either, although he, too, had seen her at the funeral.

'Where there's a will, there's a relative,' observed Leeyes largely.

'Just so, sir,' said Sloan. 'We are also carrying out a routine check on this William Wakefield – it was his wife, Janet, who organised the funeral. He says he only arrived in England yesterday evening.'

'Good thinking. The checking I mean.'

'And it would seem, sir, that he – this William Wakefield – inherits should...er...anything happen to the deceased's grandson, Joe Short.'

'I take it, Sloan,' said the superintendent loftily, 'that you will see that nothing does happen to him.'

'I'll try,' said Sloan warily. He coughed. 'I have also instituted enquiries in the town about whether anyone saw anything untoward on the bridge last night, although I'm afraid it's rather unlikely if it was after dark.'

'There's not a lot of traffic at that hour of the night,' agreed Leeyes, adding mournfully, 'and it's about the only time when there isn't.'

Detective Inspector Sloan snapped his notebook shut and got to his feet. In 'F' Division of the County of Calleshire Constabulary, cars, unless used in the deliberate killing of someone, were not his problem. Anyway, he had a feeling that he'd got quite enough on his plate already. 'There's one other thing, sir...'

'Which is?'

'Lucy Lansdown's handbag.'

'What about it?'

'We can't find it.'

'So?'

'So I'm having the river just below the bridge dragged. Just in case.'

Detective Inspector Sloan was not unknown at the Bellingham Hotel. Old-fashioned and comfortable, he had rarely been called there in the line of duty but he had from time to time looked in when not working. Once upon a time, though, he had frequented dances in their ballroom hoping that a certain young girl would be there in an electric-blue dress...a girl called Margaret. He had it in mind to take her back there on their next wedding anniversary.

Pulling himself together he asked at the desk if a Mr Short was in his room. The receptionist pointed across the hall. 'I think you'll find him in the lounge, Inspector. He's just asked for a pot of tea.'

'Make it for two. No,' Sloan corrected himself, now conscious of a figure at his side stirring. 'For three, please.'

'A cake would be nice,' said Crosby plaintively, 'seeing as how we didn't get any lunch.'

'With cakes,' sighed Sloan.

'We do toasted teacakes,' said the receptionist, obviously a born saleswoman.

Crosby brightened. 'Lovely.'

'This way, Crosby,' said Sloan, making his way across the Bellingham's hall. The lounge was comfortable, furnished with sensible leather-covered chairs into which a guest could sink. He picked out Joe Short without difficulty since he was the only solitary male in a room otherwise mainly full of women, who judging by their parcels, were resting after heroic shopping. True, two other men were huddled over a table in the far corner of the room. They were mulling over papers, their briefcases spilling out over the floor, but they were older and patently busy.

Sloan advanced towards the young man. 'Mr Short, I'm Detective Inspector Sloan.'

Joe Short got to his feet. 'My goodness, Inspector, that was quick...where I come from you practically have to bribe the police to take an interest in a murder let alone a stolen passport.'

'Sir?'

'I've only just been into your police station to report that my passport has been stolen.'

'Really, sir?' Sloan sat down across the table from the young man. 'Tell me.'

'It was my own fault,' he admitted. 'At least, I think it was.'

'Go on,' said Sloan. If Crosby said anything at this moment about a dead girl he'd have his guts for garters.

'I've been staying here in Calleshire for my grandmother's funeral,' explained Joe Short, 'and I went over to see an old boy – a friend of hers, who'd been at the funeral, called Sebastian Worthington. I got his name and address from some cards Mrs Wakefield brought round after the funeral...'

'Ah, yes,' said Sloan with apparent indifference. 'Perhaps we could take a look at those sometime.'

'Sure. Well, this guy lives out in the country, inland from Kinnisport, and by the time I left him I was a bit hungry and so I cast about a bit for a good pub...'

'And found one?'

'The Shipwright's Arms. I guess that figures since they're near enough to the sea there.'

'Ah, food,' said Constable Crosby to the waitress as she approached their table. 'Put it here, please.'

'You know the pub?' said Joe Short to Sloan.

'I know of it, sir,' said Sloan. And he did. A big old country pub with a large clientele, some of them sailors ashore.

'It was pretty crowded at lunchtime, I can tell you. I suppose that should have made me more careful...'

'Yes,' said Detective Constable Crosby indistinctly, wiping some butter that had dripped from the toasted teacake off his fingers.

'Yes, well I will be in future I promise you,' grimaced Joe Short.

'Did you lose anything else besides your passport?' asked Sloan. 'Your wallet, for instance...'

'No,' Joe Short patted his trouser pocket. 'That's safe enough.'

'Not now you've shown everyone in the room where it is, it isn't,' remarked Crosby insouciantly.

'Where was your passport, then, sir?' asked Sloan.

'Ah, that was in my jacket pocket and like a fool I took that off after I'd had a beer and began to feel warmer.'

'And you hung it on the back of your chair, I suppose,' said Crosby censoriously. He reached for another teacake, then withdrew his hand. 'Do you want the last one, sir?'

'I think, Crosby,' said Sloan acidly, 'that your need is greater than mine.'

'As Sir Philip Sidney said at the Battle of Zutphen,' remarked Joe Short. He grinned apologetically. 'Schoolteachers were hot on the history of England if they were abroad.'

'I can see that they might be, sir,' said Sloan. Distance might well have lent enchantment to some of the more inexcusable incidents in British history. 'Now, this passport that you have reported missing...'

'I shall have to apply for a replacement one pretty pronto or I shan't be able to get back to Lasserta.'

'Lasserta?'

Joe Short sketched a circle in the air. 'Large island, sandy desert in the north and tropical jungle in the south – with the odd hill in both.'

'Ours?' enquired Crosby. He'd once been given an old atlas, its maps mostly in pink.

'Sort of,' replied Joe. 'That is, it was once. A British protectorate or something like that. It isn't now but I think we have some kind of presence there.'

'Why?' asked Crosby, never a child of Empire.

The young man relaxed in his chair. 'That's easy. They mine querremitte ore there. Hardest metal known to man.'

'Very valuable, I'm sure,' said Sloan.

'It sure is.' Joe Short picked up his cup. 'And I won't be able to get back there without a new passport. I've just booked a slot on your library computer here in the town so that I can get cracking today. Before I lost the thing I was all ready to start booking a return flight home now that the funeral's over.'

Sloan nodded. 'Now, sir,' he went on, opening his notebook, 'as it happens we came to see you about something quite different.'

Joe Short started. 'Not about Granny surely? The matron at the nursing home said that everything was hunky-dory... sorry, I mean that there was nothing to worry about with her death. Expected and all that. Oh,' he subsided, 'I suppose you mean about that break-in there that I was told about. Very odd.'

'Yes and no,' said Detective Inspector Sloan, reaching into the folder he had brought with him.

'I don't get it, Inspector,' said Joe. 'What exactly do you mean?'

Sloan opened the folder and pulled out the photograph of the face of the girl pulled from the river. 'Have you ever seen this girl?'

Joe took it in both hands and studied it carefully. 'No, I don't think so...ah...wait a minute, wait a minute. Yes, I have. The girl with the auburn hair.' He handed the photograph back to Sloan. 'I remember her now. She was at Granny's funeral. Why do you ask?'

'Did you speak to her?'

'Not really. She dropped her handbag in the churchyard and I picked it up and handed it back to her.' He screwed up his face in an effort of recollection. 'I think she must have thanked me but that's all.'

'I see, sir. Did you notice anything else about her?'

'Apart from her hair,' put in Crosby unnecessarily. He had cleared the plate of toasted teacakes and was eyeing a chocolate bun.

'I'm sorry,' said Joe Short simply. 'I was a bit preoccupied at the time – they were getting ready to lower the coffin in the grave just then and I had to go on.'

'And afterwards?' prompted Sloan.

'I didn't see her afterwards. She certainly wasn't at the bunfight at the Almstone Towers Hotel. I'm sure that I would have noticed her if she had been there. She was very pretty.'

At the mention of the word 'bun' Detective Constable Crosby's hand descended on the plate.

CHAPTER THIRTEEN

Joe Short arrived at The Old Post Office at Staple St James that evening armed with a bunch of flowers and a bottle of sherry. William Wakefield met him at the door and welcomed him with a hearty handshake.

'Come along in, Joe,' he said, steering his guest towards the sitting room. He'd changed into comfortable slacks and an open-necked shirt and looked quite relaxed.

'Thank you.' Joe Short indicated his rather stiff suit. 'Sorry to be a bit overdressed but I came to Berebury for a funeral and wasn't expecting to stay.' He waved his hands and explained about the theft at The Shipwright's Arms. 'And now I've got to go to London tomorrow to try to get a new passport or permit to travel, or something issued instead.' He grimaced. 'And I can't go back to Lasserta until I do.'

'Bad luck, that,' said Bill Wakefield. 'You're obviously not used to our friendly little English ways with other people's passports.'

'True.' He pulled the corners of his mouth down. 'Out in Lasserta I assure you that they don't bother stealing passports. It's money they're after as a rule. And with some of the native tribes really deep in the jungle it's their enemies' scalps they go for.'

'That sounds gruesome,' exclaimed Janet Wakefield, coming through from the kitchen still in an apron. Her appearance had undergone something of a sea change since the return of her husband. Gone was the rather businesslike suit she'd worn that morning – now she had on a soft green dress. She was being altogether more domestic in her manner now, too.

Bill Wakefield laughed. 'We'll have to talk about that over supper. Jan's been slaving over a hot stove for hours.'

'Don't you believe it, Joe,' said Jan. 'You're only getting a simple casserole. Nothing elaborate.'

'Sounds lovely,' Joe said politely.

Her husband gave an expansive sigh. 'I can assure you that anything home-cooked is an improvement on what I've been living on in the Amazon hinterland. What about you, Joe?'

'Oh, the food's not too bad in Lasserta, but it gets a bit monotonous and Mathabo – that's the place on the island where I'm working – is really remote. Supplies take their time getting through to us, and unless they're tinned, often enough they're bad by the time they do. That's the trouble.'

'Give him a drink, Bill,' said Jan, 'and I'll be with you in a minute.'

William Wakefield stood back and regarded Joe Short with a long appraising look. 'So we're both from the same stable, are we, Joe?'

Joe Short shrugged himself out of his coat and said lightly, 'Well, if we were Arab stallions I think we could say we've come from the same bloodline, that's all.'

'But a bit way back,' said Wakefield.

'So I'm told,' said Joe Short, 'although with regard to appearance my mother always said I favoured her side of the family.'

'And she wasn't a Short, of course,' said William Wakefield.

'No, no, but she wasn't actually – what is it they call it these days? – wasn't vertically challenged, that is to say she was quite tall.' He smiled, displaying a row of white, even teeth. 'They do say all boys are taller than their mothers and I did manage that – just.'

'Anyway,' said Bill Wakefield, 'it was my mother and your father who were first cousins so it doesn't apply to the two of us so much.'

'True,' agreed Joe.

'But you haven't both got the same colour eyes,' said Janet, who had come back into the room without her apron. 'Bill's are blue and yours are brown. What colour were your grandmother's?'

'Search me,' said Joe. 'Boys don't notice that sort of thing.'

'Except in girls,' teased Janet. She put her arm round her husband's shoulder and said affectionately, 'Bill's my blue-eyed boy, anyway.' She straightened up. 'Now that we've got that sorted out, Bill,' she said, 'why don't you stop talking and give Joe that drink while I dish up the supper?'

William Wakefield moved obediently towards the sideboard. 'What can I offer you, Joe?'

Joe Short spread out his hands in a negative gesture. 'Nothing but a soft drink or water for me, thank you.'

William Wakefield raised a quizzical eyebrow and said, 'Water rusts ships, you know.'

Joe said, 'I'm driving and I'm well aware that I'm not in Lasserta now.'

'No speed cops and breathalysers there, then?'

'No cops at all to speak of,' he said. 'They've got some, of course, in the capital but where I'm working, if anything really awkward crops up, they call out their tribal chiefs. They're the real boss men out there.'

'What about the firm's boss men?'

'Like all boss men the world over, I guess. Oh, they're not bad really. Just like everyone else out there – working hard for their retirement somewhere else. Anywhere else where living's not so darned uncomfortable and you can have a wife and children with you.'

'Join the club,' said William Wakefield feelingly. 'And have you got a wife hidden away somewhere?'

'Not yet but I daresay it won't be long before I do. Not just now, though. And if she'll have me, of course.'

'Quite, quite,' said William Wakefield hastily. 'And is there what is delicately called "a British presence" in Lasserta?'

'Sort of.' Joe Short frowned. 'At least, there's an ambassador, a chap called Anthony Heber-Hibbs. I must say they were all very decent at the embassy after the plane crash – sent messages of sympathy and flowers, that sort of thing – although the man himself was on home leave by the time they had the big memorial service. Jan's told you about that, hasn't she? United Mellemetics, who I was working for at the time, were pretty good, too. They gave me instant leave for as long as I needed which was a great help.'

'You're in mining, I think Jan told me,' said Bill.

'In a way. I'm an engineer with Cartwright's Consolidated Carbons now and we're mainly prospecting for new seams of querremitte. It was more looking for new sources of oil at United Mellemetics, although I can't say we ever found that much. And you?'

William Wakefield waved a hand. 'My firm? We prospect for plants.'

'Plants?'

'Well, plants with prospects,' he admitted. 'Perhaps I should have said plants with potential.'

'For what?'

'Pharmaceutical use, mainly, but for any other developmental purpose that might come up...we use plant biologists and ethnobotanists and chemists...those sort of specialists.'

'For "development" you can read "exploitation",' said Janet tartly as she came back. 'Supper's ready, you two. It'll be getting cold soon.'

'Well, we're not exactly looking for querremitte for fun ourselves,' admitted Joe Short. 'It's a pretty valuable commodity these days.'

'That's enough business talk for tonight,' ordered Janet Wakefield. 'So, Joe, when did you last see your grandmother?'

He wrinkled his brow. 'It must have been nearly three years ago now. After the crash, anyway, when I had to come back to clear my parents' house. I'd come over on leave before, while Granny was still living in her house in Calleford, but she got ill while I was there and had to go into hospital. Actually I saw quite a lot of her in there. Mind you, my parents were around then, too, which helped.'

'Now, tell me,' said Bill Wakefield, ushering Joe Short into a chair, 'exactly how much do you know about the famous Kemberland Trust.'

'Not a lot, except that I understand that there was one hell of a row about it at the time it came to an end with great-great-grandmother's death.'

'Me, too,' said William Wakefield. 'I'd heard a bit about that but not everything, I'm sure.'

Joe leant back in his chair. 'I was told that when Granny's mother died it had to be wound up, and then at that point the rest of the family wouldn't give Granny her share of her grandmother's trust fund, and challenged her right to it.'

Bill nodded. 'And I was told that all her brothers and sisters or their heirs objected to Josephine having her share of it except my grandfather, who'd always been on her side.'

'Rotten, really, when you come to think about it,' said Janet Wakefield, passing a dish of vegetables in Joe's direction.

'It seems that there was quite a lot of money involved – at least I know that just her share put my grandmother on her feet financially for the rest of her life,' said Joe. 'Dad always said things were more comfortable for them all round after that.'

'I knew there was plenty of dosh about then, too,' said Bill Wakefield. 'I remember my parents telling me that my own grandparents were distinctly chuffed at the time.'

'I understand from what the solicitor told me that Granny went into property with her inheritance,' advanced Joe, 'which, when you think about it, at the time was pretty smart of her.'

'And don't say "for a woman", or you won't get any more supper,' said Janet sharply. 'Either of you.'

'Before the property surge anyway,' said Bill Wakefield.

'What about your grandparents?' Joe asked Bill. 'What did they do with it all?'

It was Janet who responded with a light laugh. 'Nothing so enterprising as property, Joe. No, they educated Bill at all the best schools and universities and then put the rest in a new trust they set up themselves. They put most of it beyond reach, you might say.'

'Entailed for the education of at least two generations of heirs of the body male in the first instance,' explained Bill.

Joe frowned. 'That's you, then, isn't it?'

'It's just me now and any children I may have,' said Bill Wakefield, carefully not looking at his wife.

'I see,' said Joe Short.

'They sort of kicked the capital into touch,' amplified Bill. 'Quite legally, of course.'

'And what about in the second instance?' asked Joe lightly.

'The reversion if there aren't any children, you mean?'

'Sorry, I didn't mean to seem inquisitive...' began Joe apologetically.

'It reverts to other descendants of my grandfather,' said Bill.

'More cauliflower?' interrupted Jan.

'Thank you,' said Joe even though his plate was already piled high. He tactfully changed the subject. 'Now, tell me what it's like up the Amazon.' A cloud passed over his face. 'We've got some tropical jungle in Lasserta, too.'

It was much later – while they were taking coffee in a sitting room that was just a little bit too tidy – when Joe told them about being asked if he had recognised a photograph of a girl that the police had brought round to the Bellingham Hotel.

'We were asked, too,' said Janet. 'I told them I'd only ever seen her at the funeral and that I didn't know why she was there anyway.'

'Me, too,' said Joe. 'She definitely didn't come on to the Almstone Towers or I would have noticed her there, I'm sure. She was very good-looking. I just wondered, though, if you knew why they were asking us at all.'

'No. Do you know?' asked Bill.

'No.' Joe shrugged his shoulders. 'Nor why she was at the funeral either.' He glanced at the clock. 'Talking of hotels, I think I'd better be going. The hall porter at the Bellingham goes off duty at twelve midnight. You have to knock him up if you're back later than that and I'm told he doesn't like it.'

'Quite right, too,' said Janet. She chanted the old proverb 'Early to bed, early to rise, makes a man healthy, wealthy and wise.'

'Then I must definitely be going, mustn't I?' he said, rising to take his leave. 'Otherwise I shall be bound to be ill, poor and daft and that wouldn't do at all, would it?'

Dr Angus Browne was sitting at his desk when the two policemen were shown into his consulting room the next morning. He pushed a blood pressure instrument out of the way and turned towards them, raising a bushy eyebrow quizzically in their direction.

'Well, now, gentlemen, and what can I be doing for you?' he said.

'You can be telling us about the late Josephine Eleanor Short who died last week in the Berebury Nursing Home in St Clement's Row,' responded Sloan in kind.

'I ken fine when and where she died,' said the doctor

irritably. 'I wrote her death certificate, remember?'

'Ventricular fibrillation, I think was what you put,' began Sloan.

'And ventricular fibrillation was what she died from,' said the doctor combatively. 'She'd had it ever since she came into my care when she arrived at the home. Is anyone saying anything different?'

'No, no,' said Sloan hastily. 'We just need it confirming, that's all. And that it was only that and nothing more.'

'Of course it wasn't only that, man,' snapped the doctor. 'By the time these old ladies get to their great age they pretty well all have some form or other of multiple pathology.'

'That sounds nasty,' said Crosby, diverting his attention from an eye test chart on the wall which he had been trying to read with one eye. 'Whatever it is.'

The doctor favoured him with a penetrating look. 'Multiple pathology, Constable, means that there are – or in her case, were – coexisting conditions.'

'Two for the price of one?' suggested Crosby.

'I'll have you know that there are quite often more than two,' countered the doctor briskly, 'and that the confusion of symptoms arising from several different conditions can sometimes make diagnosing them quite difficult.' He added after a pause, 'To say nothing about the problems of treating them and countering the side effects of the multiple medications at the same time.'

'Quite so,' said Sloan peaceably. He had never made the mistake of supposing that the police were the only ones with difficult and demanding jobs.

'She was having trouble with her chest, too. She'd had a continuous series of infections – none of them quite bad enough to carry her off.' Dr Browne gave Sloan a very straight look. 'They used to call pneumonia the old man's friend, you know, but as it happens she didn't die from that.'

'It wasn't the cough that carried her off,' chanted Crosby under his breath. 'It was the coffin they carried her off in.'

'Then, Doctor,' intervened Sloan speedily, resolving to overlook this only until he got Crosby on his own, 'presumably in your opinion there were no unusual circumstances arising around her death?'

The general practitioner sat back in his chair and considered the question. 'None that I am aware of, Inspector. She talked a lot about "all gone, the old familiar faces" as the poet puts it so well but she never mentioned suicide and I had no cause to suspect that. Besides in any case she knew she was dying and therefore didn't need to...'

'How come she knew she was dying?' asked Crosby inelegantly.

'Because she wasn't stupid,' retorted the doctor testily. 'She was an intelligent woman and she must have been aware that her heart was failing – these attacks were becoming more and more frequent and she lost a little more ground each time.'

'Two steps forward and one back,' suggested Crosby.

'More like one step forward and two back,' returned the doctor swiftly. 'And, of course, she actively wanted to die, which sometimes – but not always, naturally – accelerates the process.'

Detective Inspector Sloan, erstwhile schoolboy, knew about that 'not always' qualification. There had been that poor old man in Chaucer's 'Pardoner's Tale' forever seeking Death and not finding him. Or her, he added subconsciously.

'That I do know...' the doctor was saying.

'Do you mean she had said so?' interposed Sloan again before Crosby could say anything more.

'Many times. She often told me that she had had enough of life.' The doctor stroked his chin. 'A lot of patients say that, you know, but they don't usually mean it. Josephine Short did. After all, her sight was failing along with her heart and chest, she was very deaf and she had told me only a week or so ago that she was just waiting to die.'

'I can see that might be the case, Doctor, in her condition,' said Sloan, aware that he was still too young and committed to life to dispute the point. Besides, he wanted to see his son grow up. 'But...'

'But even so I can assure you that I did nothing to bring her death about before her time.' He regarded the policeman with a beady eye. 'Is anyone suggesting that I did?'

'No, no, Doctor,' said Sloan hastily. 'These are just routine enquiries as a result of something else coming up.'

'I myself was quite anxious that she went into the Berebury Hospital when she really started to go downhill,' went on the doctor, ignoring this, 'but every time I suggested it she got very worked up, not to say quite agitated. In fact, she made me promise that she could die in the nursing home where she was, as she felt she was being very well looked after in there and didn't want the disturbance of being moved.'

'Very understandable,' said Sloan and he meant it. Hospitals frightened him, too. 'Tell me, had she ever been in hospital here at Berebury?'

'Not that I know of,' said the doctor immediately, 'but she did tell me that she had had some treatment at the hospital at Calleford before she came into the nursing home and hadn't liked it. She only became my patient here when she came to Berebury but I can tell you that she was very anxious indeed not to go back into that hospital over there.'

CHAPTER FOURTEEN

'Where to now, sir?' asked Crosby.

'Anywhere where we can sit down and compile a list,' said Sloan, aware of a tiredness already seeping into his body. Sleep had come late and lightly to him the night before. 'Back to the station, I think.'

Crosby brightened. 'The canteen might be open now.'

It was.

Cradling his hands round a large mug of coffee, Sloan started to think aloud. 'We need to take a look at the hospital records at Calleford, Crosby, and see if one Josephine Eleanor Short was ever nursed by the dead girl when she was a patient there. That, if you can remember, was where Lucy Lansdown trained.'

'Yes, sir.' Crosby had opted for tea. He kept one hand on the handle of the mug and with the other pulled out his notebook. Swopping the mug into his other hand, he retrieved a pencil from a pocket and made a note. 'And whose say-so are they going to do that on, might I ask?' He sniffed. 'Not mine, I'll bet.'

'A court order, I expect, or a dispensation from God which comes to much the same thing. We might be able to suborn their director of nursing, Crosby, but I doubt it. We might try the chief executive man to man before we try her. Or we might not. And don't forget we want to know whether Josephine Short was being nursed at a time when Lucy Lansdown was around there. I'll remind them all that we could be talking murder here. That usually loosens tongues.'

'Righteo.'

Sloan sighed deeply and then stretched his arms up behind his head and locked his fingers together to make a headrest. 'And we'd better run a check on exactly when William Wakefield landed in the UK and what he did afterwards. You can talk to the airline he flew in on. Oh, and with the Met about the hotel where he spent the night. Sounds a very posh one to me. Theoretically I suppose he could have come down to Berebury, pushed the girl into the river and got back to London again in the time.'

'Easy-peasy-lemon-squeezy,' said the constable.

'Even by driving safely,' said Sloan with a perfectly straight face. Crosby's fast driving was a byword in the force. 'But why on earth he should have done so beats me.'

'Another mug, sir?'

Sloan handed over his empty mug and went on thinking aloud. 'And I suppose we'd better check up on this grandson of the old lady's, Joe Short, too, although he says he didn't know the girl from Adam.'

'Eve,' said Crosby.

'And get me something about this island he's supposed to have come from,' continued Sloan, rising above this.

'Yes, sir.'

'Another thing – get in touch with his firm over there to make sure he's all he says he is. Get them to send us an email photograph of him. His employers are bound to have one of him on file – that's if they're into keeping proper records out there, which if it's as benighted as some places they might not be.' He regarded the constable without enthusiasm and said, 'Oh, and make absolutely certain that Joe Short was safely tucked up at the Bellingham last night, too.'

Detective Constable Crosby made another note.

Sloan went on thinking aloud. 'There must be some connection between the girl in the river and the Wakefields because of her going to their great-aunt's funeral but as to what it is...'

'Or with the Short fellow...'

'True. Mustn't forget that.'

He was talking to the empty air.

'And,' resumed Sloan, three minutes later, when Crosby came back with two brimming mugs and a couple of Chelsea buns, 'get a trained search team to go through Lucy Lansdown's house. Tell them to come back to me with a report on anything and everything they find...and don't find – especially her handbag. We need a clear steer on the girl.' He took a sip of his fresh coffee. 'She's a bit shadowy at the moment.'

'Nothing known against,' contributed Crosby. 'I did the check.'

'Oh, and you can set up a press conference. Her picture in

the papers might just help to bring something up but don't give them her name. You never know...'

That you never knew with press conferences was very true. What came out of the woodwork after the press got hold of a story was an unknown factor. They could spin a tale better than any spider and they could dig deeper and less scrupulously than any police force in this country, too.

'Okey doke...' began Crosby, amending this when he caught Sloan's eye to, 'Yes, sir. I've got all that.'

'While I have a word with the coroner's officer,' finished Detective Inspector Sloan.

'A court order!' expostulated Superintendent Leeyes instantly the words were mentioned.

'For access to the medical records of the late Josephine Eleanor Short,' said Detective Inspector Sloan.

'You'll be lucky to get those out of anybody,' pronounced Leeyes.

'Because I don't suppose the hospital will give them to us without a court order,' finished Sloan.

'I don't suppose they will either,' snapped Leeyes. 'They'll go on and on about medical confidentiality and then they'll misplace a computer disc and lose all their data to the stolen identity specialists.'

'Records dating back at least three years,' persisted Sloan steadily.

'They can lose them quicker than that,' pointed out Leeyes. 'Whether they can find them again after so long is another matter altogether.' He shot Sloan a severe look. 'More than three years ago is a long time. What do you want them for, anyway? You said you were satisfied that the old woman died of natural causes and you've got a death certificate to prove it.' He hesitated and sniffed. 'Well, not prove it exactly.'

Detective Inspector Sloan agreed that a death certificate per se only proved the willingness of a registered medical practitioner to write one, not that it was correct. The police held what was known in diplomatic circles as 'a settled view' on this subject. Even if they did not publicise it.

'And yet the hospital's always creating about our not having someone in their Accident & Emergency Unit at the drop of a hat, Friday and Saturday nights, for the drunk and disorderly,' grumbled Leeyes resentfully. 'That sister there is a holy terror.'

'It isn't the old lady's death I'm worried about,' said Sloan, sticking to the point. 'It's the girl in the river we're really concentrating on.'

'Well it certainly doesn't sound like it to me,' rejoined the superintendent unsympathetically.

'What we need to know, sir,' persisted Sloan, 'is whether when Josephine Short was a patient in the hospital this girl taken out of the river—'

'Who you tell me has now been identified as Lucy Lansdown,' said Leeyes.

'Lucy Lansdown,' agreed Sloan, 'who you will remember was a nurse—'

'You've said that already, Sloan.'

'What we need to know,' repeated Sloan, clamping down hard on rising exasperation, 'is whether she treated Josephine Short or even visited her when she was a patient there.'

'Do I take it, Sloan, that you're hoping that there will

be records of which wards she worked on while she was there?'

'Yes, sir. They shouldn't be too difficult for the hospital to find because she was a student nurse in training at the time. I don't think that those sort of nursing records would be construed as confidential. Not in the circumstances.'

'Murder,' said the superintendent trenchantly.

'Those records might just help,' admitted Sloan. 'Although it may not take us any nearer knowing what the connection between the two women is.' He paused and added. 'If any.'

'And they're both dead now.'

'Exactly, sir.' A lesser man might have verbally patted the superintendent on the head for getting there at last. Instead, Sloan said, 'This court order to serve on the Calleford hospital, sir. Can I go ahead and apply for it?'

A beatific smile suddenly appeared on the superintendent's face. 'You did say Calleford Hospital, didn't you?'

'Yes, sir. Apparently Josephine Short lived over that way before she went into the Berebury Nursing Home and it's where Lucy Lansdown did her nursing training.'

'Why didn't you say so before, Sloan?' said Leeyes, sitting up alertly. 'That's quite different. If it's an enquiry called for over in "A" Division, then I think that Calleford can do the applying for us. After all,' he said virtuously, 'it wouldn't do for us to be seen trespassing in another manor, would it, now?'

Detective Inspector Sloan was unsurprised. No anthropologist was keener on the territorial imperative than Superintendent Leeyes.

The smile was still creasing across the superintendent's face. 'Give them over there something to do instead.'

The old-established – and rather old-fashioned – firm of Messrs Morton & Son Ltd, Funeral Directors, was well known in the market town of Berebury for the understanding and sympathetic service it rendered to the bereaved. As was proclaimed in letters of gold on the office door, these were available 'Night and Day'. The firm was also well known to the police force for its equally ready response when required by Her Majesty's Coroner to remove a body forthwith to the mortuary for further examination. That was a night-and-day service, too.

There was thus no delay in young Tod Morton's having speedy access to Detective Inspector Sloan when he called at the police station that morning, even though that officer was very busy indeed. The delay came later – while he got to the point.

'Sorry being a bother, Inspector,' began the young undertaker in the low-key manner that went with his calling.

Since all of Sloan's work involved a bother somewhere to someone – usually Sloan himself – all he said was, 'Go on.'

'I've just come from Damory Regis,' went on Tod. 'You know, over Almstone way.'

'I do know, Tod,' he said, reaching for his notebook. 'Tell me.'

'From the church – St Nicholas's – well, from the churchyard there, actually...'

Detective Inspector Sloan remained alert. Anything about Damory Regis was of interest to him now. 'And?'

'We did a burial there a couple of days ago,' said the young undertaker, in the same serious way.

'Go on,' said Sloan, suppressing an urge to shake him.

'Well, the vicar there, quite a decent fellow actually—'

'Do get on with it, Tod...'

'Well, he – Reverend Tompkinson, that is – rang and complained to Dad about the condition of a new grave there. Didn't like his churchyard looking untidy, he said.'

Sloan ground his teeth. 'Complain about what about the grave, Tod?'

'That's just it, Inspector. We didn't know ourselves at first.'

'I'm never going to know at this rate,' said Sloan, resisting a strong impulse to grab him by the lapels of his neat black coat and give him a good shake.

'So Dad said to pop along this morning just to check on what the vicar was on about. Didn't want to blame the sexton, you see. Can't be doing without the sexton's help, can we? I did say that Reverend Tompkinson's usually all right, didn't I?'

'Yes,' said Sloan shortly. 'You did.'

'Dad's always quite keen on checking anyway, gravediggers being what they are. "Alas, poor Yorick" and all that.' He looked anxiously at Sloan. '*Hamlet*, you know.'

'I know,' said Sloan, suppressing further comment with difficulty.

'And you never can tell with chalk.'

'Nor bees, Tod.'

'Doesn't settle well, chalk.'

Detective Inspector Sloan decided that silence might be a quicker way to the point.

'Well, it wasn't all right. The grave, I mean.'

'Not all right?'

'No.' Tod shook his head. 'Disturbed. We've never had that happen before. Not at Morton's. The grave not being all right afterwards, I mean. Never. I told Dad and he said to come straight round here and tell you.'

'In what way not all right?' asked Sloan carefully.

Tod still didn't relax. 'Well, if you were to ask me I should say that it had been disturbed overnight. A bit more than just disturbed, actually. And it must have been overnight. Stands to reason.'

'Foxes, little foxes?' suggested Sloan, well grounded in the *Song of Solomon* by a churchgoing mother, quoting with more than a touch of irony '"The little foxes that spoil the vine"?' A keen gardener himself, he knew only too well what damage foxes – little and large – could do. 'They like churchyards, Tod. Nice and quiet. Or badgers? Badgers can do a lot of damage overnight.'

'Neither foxes nor badgers,' said Tod Morton flatly, getting to the point at last. 'Not unless they brought a screwdriver with them. The coffin lid had been lifted.'

'What!' Sloan exploded.

'When I said the grave had been disturbed,' said Tod, professionally given to understatement, 'I meant it was the coffin that had been.'

'Opened, you mean?' said Sloan, abruptly bringing all equivocation to an end.

'That's right,' said Tod uneasily. 'The screws had been undone. We put six screw caps on coffins but only use four screws. It looks better, you know. Besides, nobody's going to know.'

'These small economies...' began Sloan. What he should have been saying was that exhumations were a matter for the Home Office and a lot of palaver.

'We always put on six handles, though,' responded the undertaker immediately. 'Most firms only use four.'

'The coffin, Tod…'

'But he – whoever got in there, that is – didn't know about the dummy screws and he must have tried to unscrew one of the screw caps that didn't lead anywhere and knocked it off trying.'

'That all, Tod?' He needed to get going on this as quickly as he could.

'Well, no, Inspector. Actually, it's even worse than that.'

'In what way worse?' asked Sloan, visions of black masses being celebrated in rural Calleshire churchyards with stakes driven through the heart and suchlike arcane practices rising before him. 'Surely the body…'

'Oh, the body was all right,' said Tod, a man accustomed to bodies. 'Well, in a manner of speaking…'

'What manner of speaking?' asked Sloan peremptorily. 'Come along, Tod…tell me in what way the body was or was not all right?'

Tod said awkwardly, 'It's like this, Inspector, the deceased had requested that she be buried still wearing her rings… nice rings, they were…very nice, actually…happens quite often, you know, in our way of business. Naturally we complied with her request. Sentimental, of course, but it sometimes stops the family fighting over them. We notice it particularly when there's more than one daughter or daughter-in-law—'

Detective Inspector Sloan looked quite dangerous. 'Tod, will you get to the point.'

'The rings had gone, Inspector. All three of them.' He pulled a notebook out of his pocket. 'Two on the ring finger and an eternity ring on the little finger. A diamond solitaire, a pale blue Sri Lankan sapphire and an eternity ring set with small stones – Victorian at a guess.'

'Whose grave was it, Tod? That's what I need to know. Now.'

'Oh, didn't I say? Sorry, Inspector, I thought I had. It was Josephine Eleanor Short's.'

CHAPTER FIFTEEN

William Wakefield stretched out on the double bed at The Old Post Office at Staple St James, consciously relishing a long lie-in. 'I don't know about the rough male kiss of blankets that that poet was always on about,' he said to Janet as she came into the bedroom. 'Give me the smooth female embrace of clean cotton sheets any day.'

'Nylon, actually,' she corrected him. She was standing by his bed, fully dressed, and bearing a cup of tea. 'Colour coordinated, you may have noticed, with the curtains.'

'Don't spoil the illusion,' he said, suddenly realising that it was the bright colours of both that were what he disliked about the bedroom. 'Or do I mean the allusion?'

'Don't ask me.'

He reached out an arm and pulled her towards him. 'Come here, my uxor…'

'What did you call me?'

'Wife. And don't distract me. Come here while I give you a kiss.'

'Bill,' she protested, wriggling free of his grasp, 'it's practically the middle of the morning.'

'What's the time of day got to do with it?' He gave a luxurious yawn. 'You know what that doctor said about a man's doing what a man's got to do when he felt like it, time being of the essence.'

'There's the washing-up from last night...'

He grabbed her by the arm and pulled her towards him more roughly than before. 'I'll tell you what you can do about the washing-up.'

'Don't do that, Bill,' she gasped. 'You're hurting me.'

'And I'll tell you when,' he said in a tone she had never heard before. 'Listen, sweetie, we're not talking about a bed of roses any more.'

'Have you taken leave of your senses, Bill?' she said, trying to shake him off. 'Let me go.'

'No,' he said swiftly. 'I've come to my senses at last. Now, you'll do what I say, Mrs Janet Wakefield, whether you like it or not. And me, I like it. Do you understand?'

'B-but...' she stammered.

'But nothing,' he said thickly. 'Now, get that frilly apron off pronto or I'll do it for you.'

'Bill, don't you remember that the doctor said—'

'Doctors don't know everything,' he interrupted her. 'They think they know all the answers. Well, they don't. I've found that out for myself. The hard way.'

'And what exactly do you mean by that?'

'Never you mind, my lady. Now get that blasted apron off this minute. It's putting me off.'

* * *

Detective Inspector Sloan hiked Crosby out of the police canteen without a moment's compunction.

'We need to get going, Crosby,' he said, jerking a finger in the direction of the door. 'Now.'

The constable pushed a plate to one side and scrambled hastily to his feet, always on the alert for a fast drive. 'Where to, sir?'

'Damory Regis,' said Sloan, adding neatly, 'And for your information Alice in Wonderland isn't the only one who found things getting curiouser and curiouser.'

The Reverend Derek Tompkinson was the first to agree with him. 'It's usually dead flowers that are the problem after an interment, Inspector. We leave them for a week or so and then the sexton clears them away, but I understand from Morton's that the deceased had particularly requested that there should be no flowers at her funeral.' He turned to the undertaker who was shadowing Sloan like a dog. 'That right, Tod?'

Tod Morton, standing one pace behind the police inspector, hastened to agree. 'That's right, Vicar.'

The clergyman nodded. 'It's quite common these days. It did, however, mean that the bare earth was more easily visible and that's what drew my attention to the grave in the first place. I wouldn't have noticed it at all if there wasn't going to be another funeral here next week and I walked over that way to check out where.'

Tod Morton nodded. 'That's right, Reverend Tompkinson. We've got the work.'

'It's an ill wind...' began Crosby.

Detective Inspector Sloan's only thought centred round the cliché about 'every man to his trade' or, in the case of the clergyman, his profession, but he did not voice it.

The vicar was going on, quite unperturbed. 'It looked remarkably untidy at a distance and so naturally I walked over to take a closer look. The undertakers usually make a better job of tidying things up and that's why I got in touch with them.'

'We like to leave things as we found them or even better,' put in Tod piously. 'Leave nothing behind but your thanks, as my dad always says.'

'Which I hope you have done,' said Sloan dryly, trusting that Tod on the other hand hadn't destroyed any evidence on his earlier visit. 'Now, which way is the grave?'

'Follow me,' said the undertaker, starting to lead the way across the grass. 'It's by the war memorial over there. The deceased had picked out the spot when she paid for her funeral plan.'

'But we still don't know why she had wanted to be buried here in this village, do we?' said Sloan.

Both the vicar and the undertaker shook their heads. 'No idea at all,' said Tod, 'and she didn't say. She just put her finger on the map of the churchyard and said that, when the day came, to put her in that particular spot. Quite cool and collected she was at the time, if I remember rightly.'

'We don't know either why she wanted to be buried in this exact plot,' said Derek Tompkinson, casting his eye round the rural scene that included his beautiful little Norman church.

'Who wouldn't?' said Sloan involuntarily, taking his mind off his work for a moment. 'It's a lovely spot.'

The vicar nodded and smiled. 'Isn't it? I did ask around, Inspector, but nobody in the parish knew Josephine Short's name or any reason why she should have wanted to come here.'

'Except for the view,' remarked Crosby, taking a passing interest in a table tomb with a dangerous list. He grinned. 'A tomb with a view.'

'Views are for the living, Crosby,' said Sloan austerely, 'and from the sound of it there aren't going to be many relatives visiting this one. Not if the grandson is going straight back to where he came from.' He reached the new grave and regarded the disturbed ground with misgiving.

'You can see what I meant, Inspector, can't you?' said Tod anxiously. 'And why I did what I did.'

Sloan nodded and said, 'You can tape all this off, Crosby. It's a crime scene now. I've alerted Forensics but you'd better whistle up the photographers first.'

Tod Morton, still in need of reassurance, said, 'I hope I did right but I just put the top board of the coffin back again, Inspector. That's all. Well, that and a bit of earth. I couldn't very well have left her lying in here with it open, could I?'

'No,' said Sloan. 'But what I want to know is, having spotted the loose coffin lid, what it was that then made you undo the shroud?'

'I didn't need to. Somebody else had done it first,' responded Tod with vigour. 'And then he'd just slid the coffin lid back afterwards and heaped some of the earth back on top of the grave. But not a lot.'

'And not very tidily,' observed the vicar, looking round.

'And not all the earth,' chimed in Crosby, waving a hand. 'It's all over the place.'

Detective Inspector Sloan cast his eye over the scene. Whoever had embarked on the grave-robbing certainly hadn't been too careful about covering up the intrusion.

Or, perhaps, had done it in the dark.

Or possibly had been disturbed in the act.

On the other hand, decided Sloan to himself, if the disturbance hadn't been spotted the ground would probably have settled back and levelled out, in time, of its own accord – certainly by the time a stone monument had been put in place. He was visited by another thought and turned to the undertaker. 'Tod, had the deceased arranged to have a memorial put here?'

'Oh, yes, Inspector. In due time, of course. We usually like to wait for six months or so for the ground to settle before we put any permanent marble down.'

'What sort of a memorial? I mean, what was to be put on it?' One thing that Sloan had learnt in the course of a working life in the police force was that the most arcane piece of information could constitute a valuable clue.

Tod Morton frowned. 'I'd have to go back to the office to be certain, Inspector, but I think Mr Puckle told us it was just her full name and dates – oh, and those of her son and daughter-in-law who had predeceased her.'

'No frills, then,' said Crosby, kicking at a loose stone.

'It's the Met,' said Detective Constable Crosby, hastily handing over the telephone to Sloan. They had only just got back to the police station at Berebury from Damory Regis. 'Coming back to us after my call.'

'That was quick,' said Sloan, putting the receiver to his ear. 'Good afternoon. DI Sloan, "F" Division, Calleshire, here.'

'In reply to your enquiry about a resident at the Erroll Garden Hotel, Inspector...' The voice sounded very young for his rank. A bright boy, decided Sloan automatically. Unless promotion came early in the Smoke. Or, an even unhappier thought, that they had no old men there.

'Yes?' he said.

'A male answering to the description you gave us booked in there last evening using what appeared to be his own name of William Wakefield, charging the account to his firm. Apparently this is quite usual as the firm in question use the hotel on a regular basis for their staff and business guests and raised no problems.'

'That helps,' said Sloan. In his view routine had a merit all of its own. Deviation from a known routine on the part of a suspect was from a police aspect often the icing on the cake.

'I can tell you one thing, Inspector, and that's that they don't stint themselves there. It's very plush.'

'Don't worry. I reckon it won't be long before we shake him out of his comfort zone,' said Sloan. Doing just that usually went with the territory, so to speak. Police territory, that is.

The man from the Met carried on. 'The subject of your enquiry registered on arrival at about seven o'clock and soon after that went down to dinner in the hotel dining room. He then went back to his room...'

'How on earth do you...or, rather they...know that?' asked Sloan spontaneously. Closed-circuit television was all very well in known trouble spots but not, surely, in the dining room of an upmarket London hotel.

The voice at the other end of the line chuckled. 'Ah, they've got some very sophisticated system attached to those computer cards they use to open the bedroom doors. Keeps a record.'

'I'm impressed,' said Sloan, and he was. Such supervisory instruments hadn't yet reached rural Calleshire. He for one didn't imagine any such system being obtained at the

Bellingham Hotel in Berebury. 'Tell me, do the guests know about it?'

'Couldn't say,' responded the other man airily. 'And I didn't ask.'

Detective Inspector Sloan could think of other places where such a system might come in handy: the homes of some of their own local troublemakers, for instance.

'Keeps a record of the cleaning staff, too, of course, remember,' observed the other man dryly. 'And room service.'

'Quite so,' said Sloan, wondering how soon a similar degree of surveillance would be in place to monitor police work. Perhaps things had gone too far, too soon. Why, his old sergeant used to reminisce about when he had to call in from a blue Dr Who-style police box on his beat at a certain time to prove he was where he should be at the right time. And safe. And if he didn't, then his pals would start looking for him, fearing that he had been attacked in a dark alley. Which he sometimes had been. Sloan brought his mind back to the present with a jerk. 'What was that you just said?'

'You're going to like this.'

'I am liking it,' said Sloan. 'Carry on.'

'That the man in question went back to his room just after nine o'clock...'

'Got that. Go on.'

'But at ten o'clock or thereabouts he went out again.'

'He did, did he?' Sloan pulled his notebook a little nearer and said, sounding, had he known it, remarkably like his own father years earlier when he, Christopher Dennis Sloan, had stayed out too late, 'And at what time exactly, may I ask, did he come in again?'

'He is recorded as re-entering his room just after half past three in the morning,' said the Metropolitan policeman, adding sedulously, 'that of interest to you people?'

'It is indeed. Tell me, did anyone in the hotel lobby see him come in?'

'Oh, yes. A place like that always has a night porter or two around then. Besides, they have cameras there, too.'

That was something else Sloan didn't suppose they would have at the Bellingham in Berebury. 'And did any of them notice anything about him at the time?'

The other policeman paused, torn between conveying an air of urban sophistication and accurate reportage. 'Oh, yes, Inspector. The porter said he looked like he'd had a real night out on the tiles. Knackered, in fact.' The voice added, man of the world, 'We do find this quite often, you know, in fellows who don't know their London nightlife.'

'Up from the country and let off the leash,' agreed Detective Inspector Sloan, a family man himself.

'The night porter said that he did wonder for a moment if the man had been mugged and he asked him if he was all right seeing as his clothes seemed all over the place and he had a bit of a bruise coming up on his right cheek. Apparently this William Wakefield said he was on top of the world, thank you, and staggered to the lift. Very much the worse for wear, was how the porter put it.'

'Thank you...'

'There's something else.'

'Yes?'

'When he had first checked in he had asked for an early call the next morning. When the automated one went off he didn't answer it so a chambermaid was sent up. Apparently he said something quite unprintable to her and then made an improper suggestion, which she reported to the housekeeper. It would seem that he then went back to sleep again. He didn't check out until nearly noon and that was after he'd been woken again and reminded that he had to vacate the room unless he was going to stay another night.'

Detective Inspector Sloan put on his provincial policeman hat and asked if the great expertise of the Met meant that it would be possible for the hire car companies to be checked for bookings by the man that night from London to Berebury.

'No problem,' he said cheerfully.

Chancing his luck, Sloan said, 'And for a man called Joseph Arden Short the night before?'

'Buy one, get one free,' said the man as he rang off.

CHAPTER SIXTEEN

'I don't like it, Sloan,' said Leeyes flatly. 'Any of it. Not one little bit.'

Detective Inspector Sloan hadn't supposed for one moment that he would. Come to that, he himself didn't like it either. A young woman had died in circumstances unhappy by any measure and now a grave had been opened. The case – or cases – were getting murkier and murkier.

'No, sir.' Altogether too much had been happening under cover of darkness for his peace of mind. 'And if someone could kill Lucy Lansdown at night without being missed, then they could desecrate a grave, too. Alibi or not.'

The superintendent sniffed. 'Grave robbery's not your usual sort of crime.'

'No,' agreed Sloan. 'I can't say it's exactly run-of-the-mill.' Actually, it was Sloan's first experience of...of what? He would have to look it up. Theft from the dead? From their heirs? Breaking and entering a coffin? Trespassing in a graveyard?

Robbery with violence? Robbery with violation, more like, he decided. Or would it be considered by the Criminal Prosecution Service as something totally mundane such as being contrary to the provisions of the Burial Act of 1852 or the 1897 one? As far as he was concerned it was good old-fashioned larceny; a policeman had known where he was with larceny, petty or otherwise.

Leeyes waved a hand. 'Not in Calleshire, anyway, Sloan. Ancient Eygpt, maybe. The Pyramids and that sort of thing, perhaps. Not here.'

'The churchyard at Damory Regis,' said Sloan, and not for the first time. 'St Nicholas's.'

'When?'

'The funeral was the day before yesterday so, assuming the deed was done in the hours of darkness, it would have been either last night or the night before.'

'And what have you done about it?'

'Alerted all local jewellers and pawnbrokers for starters,' said Sloan.

'Why not the London ones as well?' pounced Leeyes instantly. 'Didn't you tell me that the deceased's grandson was going to London today?'

Detective Inspector Sloan almost hung his head. 'Sorry, sir,' he said abjectly. The superintendent's capacity for wrong-footing his subordinates was legendary. 'That's right, so he was. To get a replacement passport for the stolen one so that he could go back to Lasserta as soon as possible.'

'Well, see that he doesn't go back anywhere until this case is cleared up,' commanded Leeyes.

Resisting a desire to say that might be mission impossible, since Sloan couldn't think of any statute under which he could do it, he forged on, 'We got a good description of the rings from the undertaker's. The nursing home knew all about them, too, of course, having seen them on the deceased for the last three years.'

'Then make sure that the grandson's not been in London trying to flog them off as well as pick up a new passport,' said Leeyes. 'Might as well give them a description of the man as well. And his name. Not that he'd use that if he was up to no good.'

'Yes, sir.' Circulating the jewellery trade was not difficult. Or an uncommon event.

'So we're back to Josephine Short again without knowing how or why Lucy Lansdown ended up in the river,' said Leeyes, drumming his fingers on his desk. 'All roads leading to Rome, you might say.'

'Quite so,' said Sloan. He, on his part, would be happy to settle for any of the roads he was working on leading somewhere. Anywhere. The connection between Lucy Lansdown and Josephine Short was one link he, too, would like to establish as soon as he could. Perhaps the hospital visit should come next, after all, court order or no.

'At least,' said the superintendent obscurely, 'we shouldn't ever have to worry about any roads not taken. Not in a criminal investigation department, anyway.'

'No, sir,' said Sloan, mystified. He took a deep breath and said, 'There is something else important, sir.'

'Go on.'

'The old lady's stated next of kin, William Wakefield, who was supposed to have spent the night of the funeral at the Erroll Garden Hotel in London on his return from South America, didn't spend all of it there and came home with a bruise on his face.'

'Ha! That's interesting. Are you trying to tell me, Sloan, that the man had time to hire a car, come down to Berebury, meet and half-strangle a girl on the bridge, chuck her in the river, drive back to London and go back again to the hotel?'

'It would seem so, sir.'

'Is that a yes or a no?'

'An affirmative, sir. At least, we're looking into it now but it's a distinct possibility.' He corrected himself. 'Well, feasible, anyway, so the Met are checking with the car hire people in case he did and on the grandson, too, in case he came down any time he hasn't told us about.'

'That's Joseph Short?'

'Yes, sir. Crosby's round at the Bellingham now seeing if any resident could come and go without being seen either night.'

'Or both,' said Superintendent Leeyes.

Detective Constable Crosby decided that in the circumstances the Bellingham Hotel was best approached by what he thought of as its soft underbelly – the kitchen door. He gave it a cautious push and found himself in a scullery stacked with crates of raw vegetables. He could hear the clatter of metal trays and the splashing of water beyond and advanced with considerable circumspection through another door.

He was greeted by a scene that – had he known it – could have come straight out of a painting by Pieter Breughel the Elder. There were signs of baking everywhere, and freshly cooked loaves, crusts still crackling, were giving off a delectable aroma, whilst a tray of round teacakes sat cooling on a wire rack. A man clothed in a white apron and checked trousers, his head surmounted by a chef's hat, soon spotted him.

'You can't come in here, mate,' he called out. 'Not

allowed. Health and safety and all that rubbish.'

'Sorry,' said Crosby untruthfully. 'I'm lost. I'm looking for the night porter.'

The man laughed. 'You'll be lucky. There isn't one.'

'What happens when people want to get in late, then?'

'If it's after midnight poor old Stanley – been here man and boy, he has; he started off as the boots – gets up and opens the door. And don't we know it – he moans about it all the next day.' The man rested a pair of floury arms on his hips. 'And the resident staff here all have their own keys to the back door if they're late back. That's what happens, since you want to know, but I can tell you that bit doesn't happen often, not with our working hours.'

'Unsocial, are they?' They were in the police force, too, but Crosby didn't say so.

'Tell me about it,' said the chef.

'Did he moan about having to get up last night or the night before?' asked Crosby.

'Not that registered on my radar,' said the chef, 'but we've been busy in here.'

'So where'll I find Stanley?' asked Crosby, averting his eyes from the teacakes.

'The cellar, most like.' The man suddenly started knocking up a lump of dough with notable vigour. 'But he'll be round here as soon as the smell of cooking gets to him. You can count on that.'

Murmuring his thanks, Crosby found his way to the open cellar door. Going down a wooden stairway that demanded care and attention – to say nothing of the attentions of the aforementioned health and safety executive – he found himself in the murky surroundings of the Bellingham's cellar. The smells that assailed his nostrils down here were very different from those filling the kitchen on the floor above. That coming from an open tub of stale beer predominated – although he wasn't entirely certain that some of them didn't emanate from the gnome-like Stanley who emerged from the shadows as he arrived.

'You from the brewery?' he asked Crosby, peering at him in the bad light.

Crosby shook his head. 'No.'

'Thought not. Then you can hop it,' he said. 'You're not supposed to be down here. Nobody is.'

'Except you,' pointed out Crosby, taking a quick look round. At the far end of the cellar a latticed metal grill led to the hotel's wine store.

'And it's no use your looking at the wine, either, mate,' said Stanley. 'It's locked and the manager keeps the key.'

'I'll bet he does,' said Crosby. He pointed at the heavy beer canisters on the floor. 'These metal kegs – how do they get down here?'

'How do you think?'

'Not by those rotten steps that I came down, anyway,' said Crosby.

'Course not.' Stanley jerked his shoulder towards a pair of trapdoors at one end of the cellar. A ladder with curved rungs and a hooked end stood to one side of them. 'They're rolled off the brewer's dray and come down the chute that way.'

'Ah,' said Crosby. 'And that'll give out onto Sheep Street, won't it?'

'Clever Dick, aren't we?' said Stanley.

'Kept locked, is it?'

'Not locked,' said Stanley. 'Barred from the inside.

Otherwise we'd have people falling through, wouldn't we?' He peered more closely at Crosby. 'What do you want to know for?'

'What I want to know is whether the door to the cellar is kept locked when you're not here,' said Crosby, not answering the question.

'I leaves the key in reception then, not that I need to. You couldn't get into one of these beer kegs if you wanted to – besides they need gas to pump them up to the bars. And, since you're so interested, the bottled beer's kept in with the wine and spirits.' He screwed his face up. 'I suppose you could draw off a cask if you put your mind to it.' He pointed to the open tub. 'Or drink the ullage in that firkin over there but you wouldn't like it.'

'Right.'

'Besides,' offered Stanley, 'seeing as how the beer has to be kept at a temperature between fifty-five and fifty-eight degrees I sometimes has to leave the cellar door open anyway to keep it cool nights.'

'So,' reasoned Crosby aloud, 'if you wanted to get out of the hotel in the middle of the night without paying your bill, you could come down here, swing that iron bar back and climb out onto the street.'

A look of great cunning came over Stanley's face. 'Not without my knowing, you couldn't. Because you couldn't close those doors behind you from the street, could you? And I'd know someone had been that way.' He gave a high cackle. 'He'd have to come back in again and close them behind him for me not to know.'

'So he would,' said Detective Constable Crosby, applauding this reasoning. 'You're quite right, Stanley. If he went out that way, then he'd have to come back that way.'

Stanley gave another high cackle. 'And make sure that nobody fell down the chute while he was out. It'd give way if it wasn't propped up from behind.'

'So it would,' said Detective Constable Crosby, not saying that it would be easy enough to hang a warning notice over the trapdoor to keep anyone off it for a little while in the night. 'By the way, why couldn't someone get out of the front door and leave that open behind them?'

'Because,' said Stanley with a look of great cunning, 'I takes that key to bed with me, that's why.'

'And has anyone got you up the last couple of nights?'

Stanley shook his head. 'Always quiet this time of year, but you wait until Christmas. It's different then.'

Crosby left by the Bellingham's front door but he soon turned right and right again and went down a lane beside the hotel until he found himself in Sheep Street at the back of the building. Seen from above, the two stout leaves of the trapdoor looked solid enough to take the weight of any number of pedestrians. And there was no visible way of opening them from the outside that he could see – unless, that is, you knew they were unlocked when it would have been easy.

He got out his notebook and wrote down what he had learnt before he forgot it.

Detective Inspector Sloan was on the point of leaving his office when a member of the civilian staff came in with a sheaf of papers.

'The report from the search team going over the house belonging to Lucy Lansdown, Inspector,' she said, handing it over. 'They've just done a first survey...they said to tell you that they've taken away all the correspondence they found for further examination but nothing interesting about her came up at first sight.'

Sloan cast his eye quickly over the report. It appeared that what had been found in the house was singularly unrevealing of the personality of the dead girl. If Lucy Lansdown had had a love life no sign of it had been found in her home. There were photographs of a late middle-aged couple and of a man and wife with two children – parents and the brother's family, the searchers had deduced – and a handful of what were clearly holiday snaps with mountain backgrounds. The presence of the brochures of several travel companies suggested another holiday abroad was being considered. Utility bills were neatly filed and had been paid.

The report ran on: 'Although the house was neat and clean, it did not show signs of being more than a place to eat and sleep. There were several nursing journals around and a study of the bookcase suggested escapist, romantic literature was favoured.'

Inspector Sloan turned the report over to see the name of its author and promptly dismissed him as an academic snob. The description of the house as unloved he could understand. People who worked for all-absorbing institutions such as hospitals and schools often had almost their whole being there, rather than in houses that weren't exactly homes. In those cases the danger came with retirement and with it the tendency to haunt the places where that working life had been played out. Or find long, dull days totally empty.

Mentally deciding that he wouldn't miss a working life spent in the police force as much as that, he went back to the body of the text and read on. 'There was no sign of a safe for valuables and nothing of really great monetary value was found. What little jewellery there was in the house was of no intrinsic value. The deceased's wardrobe was of no particular significance, clothes being off the peg and in subdued colours.'

Sloan grunted. Search teams weren't supposed to be fashionistas, either, just meticulous. He turned over the page. 'The refrigerator and freezer contained a number of ready meals for one person...'

He got the picture. A femme sole, a singleton, a spinster, a single woman, living alone – the condition could be described in a number of ways, all of them saying the same thing. A woman on her own. And, in police terms, therefore vulnerable. He sighed. Lucy Lansdown had been vulnerable, all right. And not from within herself either – that is if the pathologist was correct in his deductions. And he usually was.

The report had kept its bombshell until the last. Unless, it ran on in detached, professional prose, the officers who had first entered the house, whom they understood to have been Detective Inspector Sloan and Detective Constable Crosby, had run a very comprehensive search of every single cupboard and drawer, whilst wearing gloves, then someone else had.

Looking for what? Sloan asked himself at once but answer came there none. And when, exactly?

He scanned the report again looking for any mention of a handbag and found none. If Lucy Lansdown had taken it with her when she had gone out, then it had either been stolen or gone into the river with her. It certainly hadn't been found on the road anywhere near the bridge.

Reminding himself to alert the frogmen, he pushed the report away, rang for Crosby and picked up his coat. 'Calleford,' he said. 'The hospital there.'

'If we can get in their car park,' said that worthy gloomily.

'Even hospitals have tradesmen's entrances,' said Sloan. 'And, in a sense, Crosby, let me remind you that that's what we are. One of our jobs is keeping the streets clean, remember.'

The philosophy of policing did not interest Crosby. Driving fast cars fast did and they were soon speeding towards the county town and its big teaching hospital there.

The principal nursing officer there expressed her sadness at the death of Lucy Lansdown and saw no reason why the records of the nurse's time on the wards should not be made available in the circumstances. 'There should, of course, be a schedule of which wards she was on during her training because it is an important part of it, Inspector. We aim to make sure that every student nurse gains proper experience in every aspect of nursing.'

Detective Inspector Sloan explained that it would only have been any time spent in contact with female patients that were of interest to the police.

'Medical or surgical?' No one could have called the principal nursing officer slow on the uptake; indeed no one ever had.

'That we don't know,' admitted Sloan, adding half-apologetically, 'all we do know is the patient wasn't happy at the time and declined to go back into hospital some years later when she was dying.'

'Not uncommon,' she said briskly. 'Especially in the old. They don't want to die there. Quite understandable, of course. Most people naturally would wish to be with friends and family at the end.' She gave the policeman a very straight look. 'Although, I'm afraid that in our experience, gentlemen, that particular wish is not always reciprocated by their families.'

'Especially when the going gets hard,' put in Crosby
wittily.

The principal nursing officer ignored this and pressed a bell
on her desk. 'I'll get those records looked out for you now,
Inspector. It shouldn't take long. Perhaps you'd like to come
back after you've seen the chief executive?'

The chief executive exuded non-cooperation with anybody,
but especially the police. 'Certainly not, Inspector. I am not
prepared to make them available to you. Patients' notes are
sacrosanct. We have a legal duty to them, you understand.'

'This one is deceased,' said Sloan.

'And to their families,' swept on the administrator.

Detective Inspector Sloan had been schooled on the
aphorism that you caught more bees with honey than with
a stick. 'I quite understand your position, sir, and it's very
reassuring to know how careful you have to be.' He gave a
light laugh. 'I certainly wouldn't want the whole world to
know what I'd been treated for.'

'And you wouldn't find out from me,' said the man, still
firm.

'On the other hand,' said Sloan persuasively, 'I'm not
sure that just knowing which ward a patient had been in at
a particular time – we have the approximate dates from her
medical practitioner's records – is likely to be construed as
your being in breach of confidence.'

The man said nothing while he thought. Sloan said nothing
either. Short pauses – pig's whispers, they were called – could
be as loud as words.

After a moment or two Sloan went on, 'So you will
understand exactly why it is that the Calleford Police are
beginning the process of getting a court order in order to

resolve the situation. This, of course, will obviously absolve you and the hospital trust of any responsibility in the matter.'

The administrator visibly relaxed. 'That, Inspector, puts an entirely different complexion on things.'

'Of course, at the moment,' continued Sloan, 'the death about which we are making enquiries is in the hands of the coroner.'

'Of course,' murmured the administrator. 'Perhaps if I might just have a moment to consult with our legal people…'

Detective Constable Crosby was back at the wheel of the police car before Sloan looked up from comparing two lists of dates and said, 'Lucy Lansdown worked on Banting Ward for three months four years ago.'

Crosby braked hard very suddenly indeed, causing the papers on Sloan's lap to cascade to the floor. 'That was a near thing, sir,' he yelped. 'I nearly didn't spot that speed camera.'

'You nearly killed me,' said Sloan acidly. He retrieved his papers from the well of the car with difficulty, considerably hampered by a seat belt he had no intention whatsoever of removing until he was safely back at the police station and out of the car.

Crosby was unrepentant. 'Sneaky place to site it.'

'And as I was about to say, Crosby, these notes handed over with great reluctance by that jobsworth at the hospital confirm that Josephine Eleanor Short was a patient on Banting Ward at the same time.'

'Bingo,' said Detective Constable Crosby, picking up speed. 'Where to now, sir?'

'The churchyard at Damory Regis.' The forensic experts busily at work there had rigged up tenting all round the site of the disturbed grave, the canvas on one side brushing against the village war memorial.

Sorrow in stone, thought Detective Inspector Sloan to himself as he advanced towards the specialists, idly wondering the while whether anyone read the names on it these days. An A to Z of grief, you could call it. A to W, anyway, he decided, as the names only ran from Arden to Worrow. Soon, though, all would be forgot, just as Henry the Fifth had said in that glorious Agincourt speech of Shakespeare's that was drilled into all schoolboys. All forgot, that is, except the battle itself.

'This way, Inspector,' called out one of the white-clad figures. 'The tent flap's over here.'

Obediently Sloan picked his way over the grass, Crosby stumbling after him among the tussocks. Once inside the tent, his eyes took a moment or two to adjust to the muted light.

'Sorry if you two can't see very well. Got to have a roof over the top,' grumbled the bespectacled forensic scientist. 'Everyone seems to have a helicopter these days.'

'How are you getting on?' asked Sloan, not admitting to the police helicopter parked over at Calleford. Or how useful it and its infrared camera could be.

'It all seems to be fairly straightforward,' said the expert in the patronising way of all specialists. 'I should say that he, whoever he was—'

'Or she,' muttered Crosby, sotto voce.

The expert favoured the constable with a cold stare and repeated himself. 'He, whoever he was, tried to get in the head end of the coffin first and then found the job couldn't be done without clearing all the earth off.'

'Earth to earth,' said Crosby.

The expert pushed his glasses up on his nose and carried

on. 'He piled it to one side, just as the gravedigger had done, and then when he'd got what he wanted he pushed it all back again. Well, nearly all.'

'But not too carefully,' reasoned Sloan, 'otherwise the vicar wouldn't have noticed that the grave had been disturbed.'

The forensics man nodded. 'That's just what the archaeologist we had out here told us. Apparently it's very difficult to restore earth exactly as was. That's why they can find out so much about the ancient past.' He rolled his eyes. 'I must say the fellow did go on a bit about Anglo-Saxon postholes.'

It was the more immediate past that was engaging police attention at the moment and Sloan asked exactly what it was that the archaeologist had said.

'That it was a very recent disturbance, which we knew about anyway, and a thoroughly unskilled backfilling, which anyone could have worked out.' The forensics specialist added, 'Whoever it was, I have presumed that he'd have been working in the dark.'

'He's not the only one,' put in Crosby, kicking a nearby stone.

'Is there any hard evidence that it was a one-man job?' asked Sloan, reminding himself to have a word with Crosby later about the importance of professional solidarity.

'You never can tell that for sure, Inspector,' said the expert, pushing his glasses back again, 'but I would have thought so myself. After all, you halve your take if there're two of you, don't you?'

'True,' agreed Sloan. That was an old lesson. Even the three robbers in Geoffrey Chaucer's 'The Pardoner's Tale' had worked that out.

'To say nothing of the risk of your mate turning Queen's evidence.' The forensic man was clearly warming to his theme. 'And opening the grave up wouldn't have been all that hard work, not shifting freshly dug earth.'

Sloan brought him back to a matter more at hand. 'What about the coffin lid?'

'He didn't screw it back all that well, which is why your undertaker was able to slide it off again so easily. He got it back just well enough for the first thread on the screw to catch, in fact.' The man pushed his glasses back up his nose for the umpteenth time. 'Looked to us as if he'd brought the wrong size screwdriver with him, though. There's a few brass filings lying about.'

Wondering if carrying a screwdriver and spade after dark in a graveyard constituted 'going equipped' within the meaning of the Act, Detective Inspector Sloan said, 'Let us know when you've got everything you can from the site, will you, because we've got a post-mortem lined up for the deceased.'

And not before time, he added silently to himself.

It should have been done before.

CHAPTER SEVENTEEN

Detective Inspector Sloan had barely got back to his office when the telephone rang. He was aware that he really needed to get going with arranging another post-mortem but ingrained discipline made him – however reluctantly – pick up the receiver and say, 'Sloan here.'

'Charlie Marsden, SOCO, here, Inspector. About our examination of the Berebury Nursing Home in St Clement's Row after the break-in that you requested…'

'Ah, yes, of course, Charlie.' Since the finding of Lucy Lansdown's body the breaking and entering at the nursing home had receded in his consciousness. It shouldn't have done, he knew, because he was convinced that somehow it, too, must be a piece in the jigsaw. An important piece. 'Well, what have our Scene of Crime officers found?'

'Nothing retrievable, I'm afraid, in the way of useful marks from the carpet in the old lady's room. Too many people have tramped all over it since.'

'That figures,' said Sloan, sitting down and pulling his notebook towards him. 'What about the pantry window?'

'The intruder wore gloves, that's for sure.'

'Who doesn't these days?' asked Sloan rhetorically.

'So, Inspector, did whoever it was who got into that bedroom where the vase was broken. He wore gloves, too.'

'Ah, yes. The china. What did you find on that?' Sloan couldn't decide whether the SOCO was into sex discrimination or not. 'Anything?'

'We examined the pieces of the vase for fingerprints but there weren't any on any of them. It had been handled all right but with gloves on, too.'

'Which is odd,' said Sloan thoughtfully.

Marsden went on conversationally, 'Quite a nice one, it must have been. The wife's into porcelain and paste and all that jazz so I know that's all it was. Nice but not really valuable. Costs me a bomb, she does,' he added.

'I'm sure.' In spite of this promising opening Christopher Dennis Sloan wasn't going to say anything about what it was his wife, Margaret, the girl who had once worn the electric-blue dress at a dance at the Bellingham, had a penchant for. 'What about the break-in itself? Was it an amateur or a professional job?'

'Difficult to say, Inspector. A babe in arms could have got in that back window there,' said Charlie Marsden scornfully. 'All he needed would have been something to lever the window out. Any old pinch bar would have done the trick nicely. People put bolts and locks on their front doors and forget the back windows.'

'Until the horse has bolted,' agreed Sloan.

'We fingerprinted everyone in the building just to make

sure,' said Charlie Marsden. 'Had a bit of fun with some of the inmates, you won't be surprised to know. That Lady Alice gave us quite a runaround. Couldn't get away from her afterwards. Her good old days must have been something worth writing home about.'

'I'll bet.' Detective Inspector Sloan knew quite a lot about what happened when genteel young ladies from sheltered backgrounds cut loose, whether in wartime or not. And it wasn't always good news. 'And?'

'Ah, you're going to like this, Inspector.'

'I'm glad to hear it. Go on.'

'Obviously we took the prints of all the staff as well as the patients.'

'Obviously.'

'And all round the pantry and kitchen areas where whoever it was got in.'

'The intruder, Charlie. Let's settle for calling him that.'

'The intruder might have worn gloves that night but I can tell you someone who didn't at some time and whose prints shouldn't have been there anyway.'

'Who was that, then?'

'The Steele boy.'

'Not our Matthew?'

'None other than our own favourite young lag. We got several sets of his dabs in the pantry and the kitchen. His mother's are there, too, of course, because she works there. Not my province, of course, but she could have let him in.'

'Are you sure about his prints?' asked Sloan. He'd have Matthew Steele brought in for questioning, willy-nilly, and pronto.

'Matched perfectly with the records. I promise you.' The voice at the other end chuckled and added, 'Trust me, I'm not a doctor.'

'It's like a plaited cord, Crosby,' declared Sloan when he'd finally finished with Charlie Marsden. 'We've got these three strands all entwined together. The break-in at Josephine Short's nursing home is one of them for starters.' He paused for thought and then said, almost to himself, 'Yes, I think that did come first.'

The two detectives were sitting in Sloan's office at the police station. There had been a note on Sloan's desk from Superintendent Leeyes awaiting his return to it. The note demanded his report and his presence with it as soon as possible. Sloan was now engaged with Crosby in what he would have liked to think of as a mind-clearing exercise before this.

'With Matthew Steele on the premises anywhere anything could happen,' averred Detective Constable Crosby feelingly. 'He was the first bad 'un I ever nicked. Stole a bike down Railway Street and I got him for it.'

'No, I'm wrong,' murmured Sloan, half-aloud, following his own train of thought. 'The break-in mightn't have been the first thing that happened.'

'Sir?'

'Josephine Short was a patient in that big hospital in Calleford, remember, when Lucy Lansdown was a nurse on the ward at the same time as she was in there.'

'That was ages ago,' said Crosby.

'The seeds of crime,' pronounced Christopher Dennis Sloan, amateur gardener, 'can take as long to germinate as an orchid does.' Mixing his metaphors, he added grandly, 'It can have roots that go a very long way back, too.'

'All right, then, the girl and the old lady could have got together in hospital somewhere else a few years ago,' conceded Crosby, 'but it's not a lot to go on, sir, is it?'

'True.' Sloan nodded. 'So if that's the first thing that happens the break-in comes next.'

'Like I said, sir, with Matthew Steele around…'

'No, Crosby.'

'No?'

'Matthew Steele could have got into the nursing home at any time he wanted. Easily. His mother works there, remember.'

'I get it,' Crosby said. 'He could have lifted a key of the place – and the room – when he was in there anytime beforehand.'

'Or been let in by his mother,' pointed out Sloan.

'I'm still with you, sir. So he wouldn't really have needed to break into the nursing home.'

'Not so fast, Crosby, not so fast. Matthew might have taken the window out just to make it look as if he had.'

Detective Constable Crosby gave a deep sigh. 'It's very difficult, sir, isn't it?'

'It's called considering all the possibilities,' said Sloan tartly, a man now also soured by the thought of a bruising encounter with the gentlemen of the press, hastily arranged by the force's despised Press and Public Relations department. A note about that had been on his desk too. It was a toss-up whether it was a marginally less welcome prospect than an interview with the superintendent.

Crosby was clearly cogitating hard when he said, 'So either Matthew Steele could have pretended to come in through the window or someone else—'

'Person or persons unknown,' said Sloan, trying as

always to din 'policespeak' into the constable's head.

'Could have done it for real,' finished Crosby.

'And?'

Crosby's brow wrinkled. 'And what?'

'And entered Josephine Short's room and knocked over the vase in the process.'

'But we don't know why anyone went in there. That it?'

'Exactly, Crosby. I think if we did know we would be a lot further on. Then…'

The furrows on Crosby's brow deepened. 'Then somehow or other the girl goes in the river but we still don't know how or why.'

'There was something before that,' said Sloan, unsure now whether talking the case over with Crosby could really be said to constitute clearing the mind.

'What was that, then, sir?'

'There was the funeral.'

'What about it?'

'It happened the day before the girl went into the river and she had attended it.'

'How were they connected?'

'If we knew that, Crosby, we'd be a lot further along with this case than we are.' Exploring the ramifications of the break-in with Crosby was one thing. Doing it with Superintendent Leeyes later on was going to be much more difficult. He had another thought. 'That's assuming the whole scenario is one case. We don't even know that.'

'So then the girl goes into the river,' persisted Crosby. 'After being at the funeral, of course.'

'No, Crosby. You're going too fast.' Privately deciding that going too fast must be a first for the detective constable except in the matter of his driving, Sloan went on, 'The afternoon of the day of the funeral William Wakefield comes back from South America but does not come home that night. Instead he goes out somewhere in London...'

'A night on the tiles?' suggested the constable. He had never actually had one of these but liked the sound of it.

'Possibly, Crosby, quite possibly, but nevertheless I thought a check on hire cars was indicated and the Met are going to do that for us. With a good car he could have come down here, pushed the girl into the river, and got back to the Erroll Garden Hotel in the times that they have down for his coming and going there.'

Crosby nodded. 'And the other man – the grandson, Joe Short – could have got out of the Bellingham via the beer cellar and got back in again without anyone knowing. That's for sure.'

'Exactly so,' agreed Sloan. 'And if the River Board's calculations are correct Lucy Lansdown goes into the river – never mind how for the time being...'

'Dead or alive, you mean, sir,' put in Crosby.

'Not quite either but never mind,' said Sloan again, 'but at a time when either man could have done it.'

Detective Constable Crosby gave a deep sigh. 'And that only takes us up to the night before last and doesn't include Matthew Steele.'

'Moreover, today,' went on Sloan trenchantly, 'Lucy Lansdown's body is found and we learn that Josephine Short's grave has been desecrated although this was carried out at a time as yet unknown.'

'Since the funeral, though,' said Crosby brightly.

Detective Inspector Sloan gave his subordinate a pitying look. 'Well done.'

'And the funeral was only the day before yesterday, sir.'

'Thank you, Crosby, I am well aware of that.' He was still waiting for a written report from the forensics team presently examining the grave and permission from the Home Office and the coroner to exhume the body for a post-mortem. 'And nothing so far helps explain the break-in at the nursing home. Or its connection with the death of Lucy Lansdown, let alone the desecration of Josephine Short's grave.'

'Perhaps it's a case of multiple pathology, like the doctor said.' The constable hitched himself forward in his chair. 'So where do we go from here, sir?'

'Literally, as far as I am concerned, to face the press.' Detective Inspector Sloan got to his feet and said with tightened lips, 'Metaphorically I just don't know. And you, Crosby, you can go and bring Matthew Steele in for questioning.'

If there was one duty Detective Inspector Sloan liked least of all it was holding a press conference. No matter how well the force's press and public relations expert briefed him beforehand on how not to respond to snide questions, Sloan always felt his ire rise at the downright impertinent ones.

'I know you do, Inspector,' said that officer patiently. 'It is quite obvious to everyone present that you want to punch the reporter's nose at any such question, but if you do, I can promise you that you'll be the one to hit the headlines. And they won't help your career prospects.'

Sloan muttered something unintelligible in reply to the adviser, whose position in the force in any case he held to be a waste of space and public money.

'Moreover,' went on the man with professional suavity, 'it

should be remembered that press conferences quite often have a positive outcome.'

'Only when the villain's taking part,' retorted Sloan with some justification. 'The camera doesn't lie even if the suspect does.'

'True,' said the man, standing back a pace and regarding Sloan's appearance with a critical eye. 'Are you sure you couldn't be persuaded to go on camera in uniform, Inspector? It comes over so much better with the general public. They expect it, you know.'

'Quite sure,' said Sloan with unaccustomed surliness.

'What about wearing a raincoat, then?'

'It's not raining,' said Sloan stubbornly.

The man sighed. 'All right. Now can we please consider some of the awkward questions you might be asked?'

Sloan bristled. 'I shall just stick to the facts.'

The man sighed again. 'The press won't, of course. They'll try and jump you into saying something you don't want to.'

'Let them try,' he growled.

'I expect they will.' The press officer sounded resigned.

'I shall tell them simply and clearly about a woman being pulled out of the river – nothing more,' said Sloan with dignity.

'And who she is, of course…'

'No,' he said firmly, shaking his head. 'Not that yet.'

'Or that she was a nurse? They may have picked that up very quickly in any case. Nurses always make a good headline.'

'No.'

'Aren't you forgetting that they may have already talked to her next-door neighbour before coming here?'

'The name is not going to be released until the relatives

have been informed,' said Sloan with dignity, 'and I shall say so however many times they ask me.'

'And what are you going to say about the men diving in the river under the bridge?'

'They don't know about that.'

The man laughed outright. 'Don't you believe it, Inspector. Someone's seen them there and told the paper about it. And I've already been asked what they're looking for there.'

'Do I have to tell them?'

'They'll find out very quickly if you don't. Think ferrets – a sackful of the blighters – and you've got a press pack. So what's to do with the frogmen?'

'The girl's handbag. That's what we're looking for.'

'I can't see any harm in telling them so, then. After all,' said the man cunningly, 'it might lead you to it.'

'That would only be if it's not in the river.'

'Precisely. Now what about the break-in at the nursing home?'

'They might not have connected the two.'

The man gave a cynical laugh. 'Perhaps not, since I understand actually we haven't either, but it won't stop them asking you about it.'

Sloan wasn't sure whether to take the Press Relations Department man up on his use of the word 'we' or not but then decided it was an expression of professional solidarity and stayed silent.

'They'll say anything, Inspector, to bounce an unwary answer out of you.' He went on earnestly, 'They'll deliberately put two and two together to make five so that you automatically tell 'em how it really was in self-defence. It's human instinct.'

Detective Inspector Sloan ground his teeth: he was, after

all, supposed to be in charge of the Criminal Investigation Department. 'How do you people get to know all these things about the case?'

The man gave a tight little smile. 'We consider ourselves pretty well briefed. We have to be to field some of the questions that we get asked ourselves.'

'Well, I'm not happy about saying anything more than that,' said Sloan.

The man gave a deep sigh. 'I can well believe it but, Inspector, you should be aware that you are probably also going to be asked about some missing rings – valuable ones.'

Sloan started. 'But the grave robbery has been kept under wraps. Tod Morton promised and I'm sure the vicar wouldn't have—'

'Sure. But there's been nothing stopping any jeweller and pawnbroker in the town you care to mention having a friendly word with a reporter. You've circulated the details to them, remember? And those missing rings are very valuable – not paste. They'll want to know all right if there's any connection with the rings and the break-in at the Berebury Nursing Home, let alone what's going on at Damory Regis.'

'How did they know about the break-in anyway?' Sloan challenged immediately.

'No reason to keep it secret. That information will have been put out in a routine way. There's probably a paragraph about it already set up for tomorrow's paper.' He shrugged his shoulders. 'What goes on in nursing homes is always news, too, you know.'

'I wouldn't want the information about the grave robbery in the public domain yet,' said Sloan, suddenly serious. 'It won't help our enquiries.'

The man gave him a pitying look. 'If, Inspector, you imagine that the sight of white-coated police specialists working in the graveyard there hasn't alerted someone in Damory Regis to the fact that something interesting is going on behind those screens and in the tent they put up there, then I'm afraid you're living on another planet.'

It was therefore a considerably chastened detective inspector who submitted to an instant seminar on handling the press. His ultimate humiliation came as it was coming to an end when a minion entered the room with a message for him.

'Sorry interrupting, Inspector, but it's a message from your wife.'

'My wife?' he said, alarmed. Margaret Sloan never rang the police station save in dire emergency. 'What—?'

'She wants to know if you've got a clean shirt on for the press interview. She's heard it's going to be on local television.'

CHAPTER EIGHTEEN

'Ah, Miss Fennel, come in.' Simon Puckle sat back in his chair and looked hopefully at his secretary. 'How have you been getting on?'

'Quite well, really, Mr Puckle, all things considered.' She placed an orderly pile of papers down in front of him. 'I have been able to check all the relevant birth, marriage and death certificates – the registrar was most helpful.'

'Good going.'

'And,' Florence Fennel had never been one to need praise and so carried straight on, 'I have established that the late Josephine Eleanor Short was the daughter of a very wealthy family in West Calleshire. In her day they lived in great style in a big house called Blaxlandton Hall over there. I understand that the family fortunes had been based on some invention that they had made in the Crimean War.'

'The balaclava?'

Miss Fennel rose above frivolity. 'Something, I

understand, to do with cartridges for army rifles.'

'Where there's muck there's money,' said the solicitor ambiguously.

'The birth certificate of her son – that is George Peter Arden Short – doesn't show any name for the father and the place of birth is given as a home for unmarried mothers in Luston.' Florence Fennel, whose own personal life was a model of propriety, said indignantly, 'You'd have thought a family like that could have afforded to send her somewhere better, wouldn't you?'

'I would have thought that at that time it was more a question of morals than money,' mused Simon Puckle. 'They must have minded a great deal. Times change, you know.'

'They must have minded more than His Grace,' remarked Miss Fennel pertinently, the Duke of Calleshire's daughters having always been a notably lively lot. Puckle, Puckle & Nunnery had acted for the family for generations and she knew its history well.

'The aristocracy got its mind round illegitimate babies a very long time ago,' said Simon Puckle, privy to several *sub rosa* settlements concerning these. 'They tend to take them in their stride. The *haute bourgeoisie* have always found it more difficult. The purple of trade, as Oscar Wilde put it so well, doesn't take so well to scandal. Illegitimacy comes between them and respectability, you know. And the social climbing which seems to have been one of their chief objects in life.'

Miss Fennel was still indignant. 'There was, after all, a war on.'

Simon glanced at the date on the copy of the birth certificate. 'True. So this George marries in due course and has a son,

Joseph. And George and his wife lose their lives in an air crash and their son inherits. That right?'

'Yes, Mr Puckle.'

'So where does the Kemberland Trust come in? Have you been able to get on to that yet?'

'That proved a little bit more difficult, Mr Puckle, but I did find the case in the end. It would appear that the Kemberland Trust was set up for the benefit of the descendants of Josephine Short's great-great-grandmother on her mother's side.'

'Not the armaments people?'

'No. The other side of the family. They were successful manufacturers who had made a lot of money out of cotton. They would seem to have sold out when the going was good and well and truly tied the funds up for future generations.'

The solicitor nodded with professional approval, uninvested cash being the legal equivalent of the navy's loose cannon. 'Thus creating the Kemberland Trust, I take it?'

'That is so.' Miss Fennel consulted her notes. 'As far as I can establish the settlement came to an end with the death of Josephine Short's grandmother. This was the point that had been determined when the trust had been established when the capital had to be distributed to all her surviving grandchildren and the trust wound up.'

Simon Puckle nodded. 'Which is presumably when the family – or some of them, anyway—'

'Including her own mother,' said Miss Fennel, rigid with disapproval.

'...tried to stop Josephine getting her share.'

'Exactly, Mr Puckle.'

'They wouldn't have had a leg to stand on in law, of course,' said the solicitor thoughtfully. 'The provisions of the trust would be bound to be upheld by the court provided that it had been properly set up and administered by the trustees.'

'They had been, Mr Puckle, but it didn't stop the family trying to deprive Josephine of her rights.'

'Not nice.'

'Nasty,' said Miss Fennel militantly.

'It's my turn,' insisted Joe Short. He was on the telephone to The Old Post Office at Staple St James. 'After all, you fed me last time and it's only right that you should both come to the Bellingham tonight as my guests.'

'Well,' prevaricated William Wakefield, 'I'll have to ask Jan first. I don't know what she'd planned for this evening and we've got quite a busy time ahead of us today. I've got to get a lot done while I'm home. I'm due to go back to work quite soon.'

'I'm not going to be here all that long either,' said Joe. 'Now that I've got a new travel document or whatever they call it instead of my passport, I'm going to book my flight back to Lasserta for just as soon as I can get a seat. Cartwright's Carbons are benevolent enough but they're not silly.'

William Wakefield, who originally had had quite different plans for the evening, capitulated at this, and promised that they would be there at the Bellingham if Jan agreed.

Janet assented readily enough when he told her, her mind clearly elsewhere. 'Oh, all right, then. It'll be nice not to have to cook,' she said absently. 'Now, are you ready for the off? The receptionist said not to be late because she'd only just squeezed us in at short notice because you're at home. For once,' she added meaningfully.

'I bet he keeps us waiting, all the same,' forecast William Wakefield. 'He always does. Supercilious blighter. Besides,' he added half to himself, 'he hadn't told me the half of it. Not even for ready money.'

Janet's head came up. 'What was that, Bill?'

'Nothing, darling,' said Bill Wakefield. 'Just a quotation from Oscar Wilde, that's all.'

It was by no means the first time that Detective Constable Crosby – or, indeed, his uniformed companion – had visited the Steele household. Sometimes it had been in response to complaints about the drunken behaviour of Steele, *père*; more often than not in pursuit of his son, Matthew, for what might be said to be 'offences, various'.

The Steeles' house lay in a dingy street behind a deserted cinema, and although it was called Shepherd's Way, it was a very long time since anyone with a crook had lived there. That it was the home of crooks, though, was not, in the opinion of Detective Constable Crosby, in doubt. Indeed, at the police station it was known as Thieves' Way.

Crosby found number 5 and knocked on the door. There was no response at first and so he knocked again. Louder, this time.

'Shall I go round the back?' asked the uniformed police constable with him. 'There's an alley behind the houses and he's been known to scarper that way when he hears that we're here looking for him.'

'Hang on,' said Crosby, bending his ear to the letter box. 'I can hear someone coming.'

There was now an audible dragging of feet along the entrance hall behind the door. This was succeeded by the sound of bolts being drawn back and the appearance of a bleary-eyed Ellen Steele. She was wrapped around in a faded dressing gown and peered sleepily out at the two policemen. As soon as she saw the detective constable she asked, alarmed, 'What's wrong?'

'We want a word with Matthew,' said Crosby.

She relaxed a little. 'What's he been and gone and done now?' she asked wearily.

'Nothing that we know about exactly,' said Crosby, deliberately imprecise. 'We just want a word, that's all at the moment.'

'You'll be lucky,' she said. 'That's more than I've had with him for a couple of days.'

'Where is he, then?'

She shook her head, her hair still tousled with sleep. 'I don't know. He didn't tell me. Just took off and hasn't been back.'

'When?'

She screwed up her face. 'Must have been the day before yesterday. If you must know.'

'Yes,' said Detective Constable Crosby flatly. 'We must.'

'He wasn't here when I got back from work. That's all I know. And now I'm on nights I can't tell whether he's been back here or not.'

'Where does he usually go when he's not here?' he asked.

She gave him a bleak look. 'Prison.'

'And when he isn't in prison?'

'There's a girl...'

'Where?'

'He's not with her, I can tell you for sure, because she's been round looking for him, too. Little trollop,' pronounced Ellen Steele without rancour.

'Anyone else looking for him?' asked the uniformed policeman at Crosby's side.

Ellen Steele favoured him with a resigned look. 'You name it and they've been here after him. All of 'em.'

'Debt collectors?'

She sighed and said obliquely, 'He likes things, does our Matthew.'

'Drug dealers?'

She sighed again. 'Could be.' She gave a little shiver and said awkwardly, patently searching for the right words, 'They're not so nice.'

'No,' concurred the detective constable. That was his view, too, and he tried to steer clear of them when they came into the ambit of the police. Not that drug dealers took much interest in the police. Or much notice of them, either. They had their own way of meting out what they perceived as justice. Swift and sure it was, and no questions asked.

Belatedly Ellen Steele offered to let the police search the house. 'But Matthew's not here.'

Reckoning that she wouldn't have made the offer if he was, Detective Constable Crosby took his leave.

'And,' said Ellen Steele, as the two policemen turned to go, 'I didn't break that old vase at the home neither. Honest.'

'Well?' asked Superintendent Leeyes heavily when Sloan arrived in his room. 'How did it go?'

'Badly,' admitted Sloan. There was no need to ask what his superior officer was talking about. The press conference.

'How much did they know?' asked Leeyes.

'Nearly as much as we did.'

'Wouldn't surprise me if it wasn't a load more,' growled the superintendent.

Sloan hesitated. 'At least they hadn't cottoned on to William

Wakefield and the Erroll Gardens Hotel, which is one good thing, but someone at the Bellingham had talked to a reporter about a police constable having been sniffing around in the hotel.'

'I don't suppose the reporters are ever out of the bar there,' said Leeyes trenchantly.

'But the worst thing, sir, was the grave disturbance.'

'Robbery.'

'Robbery, then,' conceded Sloan. 'I had to skirt around that a bit.'

'Had they made the connection?'

'Not any more than we have,' said Sloan frankly. 'When they asked me about it, I just said that I understood that it was a disinterment being carried out in accordance with Home Office administrative procedures and no doubt an announcement would be made in due course and that we would be duly informed if it was for anything out of the ordinary. And so would they.'

This time Sloan wasn't criticised for sounding like a civil servant and stretching a point – or two. Instead Leeyes sniffed and said approvingly, 'That should have kicked it into touch if anything would.'

'Some bright spark wanted to know if the wrong body had been buried and I said not as far as I knew and that I had no reason to suppose otherwise. I bet they went straight off to Morton's after that.'

'That reminds me, Sloan. Tod Morton's been trying to get in touch with you. He wants you to go round there soonest. Deal with him, will you?'

'Yes, sir.' Sloan made a note before the matter got lost in the rest of a very busy day. 'Anyway, to date they didn't seem to know why an exhumation was in the process of being done and I didn't tell them.'

'Good,' said Leeyes absently.

'But they did want to know why the archaeologists had been brought in.'

Leeyes sat up. 'So do I, Sloan. Tell me...'

'Apparently they're the experts on disturbed ground.'

Leeyes, having a deeply ingrained mistrust of all experts, snorted, 'I don't know how that'll help.'

'Neither do I,' said Sloan wearily.

The superintendent changed tack. 'This William Wakefield – the man who went walkabout in the middle of the night in London the same night the girl went into the river – when are you going to question him?'

'When we can find him,' replied Sloan swiftly. 'He isn't around to be questioned – there's no one at his house. In the meantime the Met are checking up on whether or not he hired a car that night. We want to know the answer to that pretty quickly.' This was only partly true. He didn't suppose Crosby wanted to know the answer to that or to anything much else. 'We checked on the grandson, Joe Short, sir, while we were about it. He was on the flight he said he was, booked into an airport hotel on arrival and hired the car he's still using first thing the morning of the funeral.'

'Fair enough.' The superintendent scrabbled through some papers on his desk. 'So what's happening about the dead girl, Lucy Lansdown?'

'We're making enquiries now...'

'Anyone standing to gain from her death?' asked Leeyes trenchantly.

'That depends on whether it was murder or suicide and—'

'And?' Leeyes interrupted him.

'And if it was murder then presumably the murderer does,' responded Sloan, adding a rather belated, 'sir.'

'The old lady hadn't left her a load of money for nursing her or anything like that?' The superintendent leant back in his chair and pontificated in his usual authoritative manner, 'Some patients do, you know. The ill can be dangerously vulnerable. Open to persuasion, even.'

'No, sir. Josephine Short's estate goes – bar a few small legacies – to her grandson. There is no mention of Lucy Lansdown in her will.'

'And should he happen to step under a bus?' The superintendent paused and added thoughtfully, 'Or be pushed under one?'

'It goes to this William Wakefield of Staple St James.'

Leeyes sniffed. 'Who, I gather, is a relation of sorts. That right?'

'A second cousin. Next in line as a beneficiary, anyway, sir.'

'Ah.' Leeyes sat up.

'Simon Puckle has confirmed that for us.'

'Not fictive kin, then?'

'I couldn't say, sir.' There was no limit at all to the arcane information the superintendent picked up in his search for scholarship.

'It cropped up when we were studying the divine right of kings,' mused the superintendent.

'I'm afraid I'm not familiar with the term, sir,' murmured Sloan. It was the divine right of superintendents that held sway in 'F' Division.

'It's usually when the wife brings the money with her when

she marries and the husband adds her maiden name to his.'

Detective Inspector Sloan allowed his mind to wander briefly back to the girl in the electric-blue dress whom he had married. That she hadn't had any money to speak of on her wedding day had always been a source of some pride to her. Nobody, she had been heard to declare, could say she had been married for anything but herself: certainly not for anything she had brought with her, anyway. 'I don't think, sir,' he said austerely, 'that fictive kin is the case with William Wakefield. He appears to be a hard-working young man and the sole support of his wife rather than the other way round.'

'Then why isn't she working?' he asked truculently.

Sloan coughed. 'I was given to understand, sir, that it was on the advice of her doctors, but why that is the case, I don't know.'

'And why can't he be found? Or her?'

'That I don't know, either.'

Superintendent Leeyes changed tack once again. 'Any sign of Matthew Steele yet?'

'He hasn't been sighted anywhere that we've heard. He seems to have gone to ground completely. And unless his mother's lying through her teeth, he hasn't been home since the night after the funeral.'

'Put out a general call for him – and for this William Wakefield,' commanded the superintendent.

Wisely, Sloan forbore to say this was something that he had already done.

'And pull Joe Short in for questioning as soon as he gets back from London just to be on the safe side.'

Sloan thought it better not to say that this, too, had been on his agenda for action for some time now.

CHAPTER NINETEEN

'So what's to do, then, Tod?' Somehow Detective Inspector Sloan had fitted in a quick visit to the undertaker's premises before going on to Dr Dabbe at the mortuary. 'And why did you need to see me in person? Wouldn't a phone call have done? Or I could have rung you.'

Standing at his side, Crosby shook his head. 'Might have wakened the dead, though,' he muttered irrepressibly.

'It wasn't that, Inspector,' said Tod seriously. He ignored Crosby, gallows humour not going down very well in an undertaker's office. 'It was that I needed to see you here.'

'They say that a mobile phone can find you anywhere in the world,' went on Crosby, undeterred.

'Why here, Tod?' asked Sloan again. He wished he hadn't brought the detective constable with him now.

'This world, of course,' Crosby added a coda of his own.

'Come and have a look,' said Tod, leading the way through to the back premises. Their route lay through the firm's coffin store, rows of boards of varying heights being propped up against the walls. Crosby stepped aside and stood up in front of one of them.

'Too short,' called out Tod without looking round. 'Try the next one down. That would fit you better.'

Suppressing the temptation to add anything about the sooner the better, too, Sloan said, 'You must have to be quite good at estimating measurement, Tod, in your line.'

The young undertaker nodded. 'You learn early in this trade. Comes naturally after a bit. A man's height is seven times the length of his foot. Did you know that?'

Detective Constable Crosby had paused at the end of the row where the coffin lids had got smaller and smaller, the awareness that these were for children visibly dawning on him and reducing him to silence.

'And at two and half years old a lad is already half his adult height,' said Tod over his shoulder. 'Now, come out the back and take a look at something.'

He opened up a pair of double doors and led the way outside. The yard behind Messrs Morton & Son's premises was large enough for a stately hearse and two black limousines. Beyond it was a shed with an open side, shelved for flowers, with some wreaths already stacked there. Tod pointed. 'Here, Inspector, take a look at these marks. I'd only spotted them myself just before I rang the police station.'

Detective Inspector Sloan regarded a series of scratches on the outside woodwork of one of the windows with professional interest. 'Could be an attempted break-in, I suppose.'

'Thought it would be easy here, I expect,' observed Crosby.

Detective Inspector Sloan stood back and regarded the

damaged woodwork. 'I'm sorry, Tod, we should have checked on this as soon as the graveyard business cropped up. I reckon that whoever it was broke into the coffin at Damory Regis tried to get in here before the burial.'

'Nobody's perfect,' said the young undertaker philosophically. 'Until they die, of course. Makes you a bit cynical, do some eulogies.'

'I guess,' said Crosby.

'Now, gentlemen, like I said, take a look at the doors, too,' said Tod, getting back to business. 'See where someone's tried to lever them open?'

'I do.' Detective Inspector Sloan looked round. 'So how did whoever did this get into the yard? It looks pretty secure to me.'

'It is – up to a point, that is. It can be done, but that's why we've got those high railings on the walls over there. You'd be surprised how many youngsters try to get in here. Especially round about Hallowe'en.'

'For fun?' said Sloan. He didn't think the marks on the undertaker's door had been made for fun: they had a purposive look about them.

'For a bit of a dare, I guess,' said Tod, shrugging his shoulders. 'What they expect to see I don't know.'

'Bodies,' supplied Crosby lugubriously.

Detective Inspector Sloan snapped his notebook shut. 'We'll send the Scene of Crime people round soonest, Tod, so don't touch anything, but I don't think they're going to find much. Not now.' Once back in the police car he said to Crosby, 'I suppose it's a reasonable assumption that whoever broke into the nursing home and went through the matron's desk was after those same rings, too.'

'But the old bird must have flown by the time he got there,' said Detective Constable Crosby as the car picked up speed.

'Or she,' Sloan reminded him.

'But they did get them in the end, didn't they?' said the detective constable. 'The dead end, you could say, sir.'

'I shouldn't say it at all, Crosby, if I were you,' advised Sloan.

Miss Florence Fennel gave her customary light tap on the door of the room of her employer before entering, notebook in hand, ready to start work. 'I'm sorry for disturbing you, Mr Puckle, but I've just had Mrs Linda Luxton on the phone. If you remember, she's the matron of the Berebury Nursing Home...'

'Yes, yes,' he said, looking up. 'And what does she want?'

'Apparently they have a new patient – someone rather ill – whom they say needs to occupy Josephine Short's room as soon as possible. Rather urgently, in fact. And I gather you'd told young Mr Short that he could remove anything still there in his grandmother's room since it was of no intrinsic value.'

'I did indeed,' he concurred readily. 'I was assured it didn't amount to much and we have all the documentation we need for probate here already.'

'Well, apparently at first the police had said nothing was to be removed until they'd examined the room again after the break-in, but they have now and they're happy for anything still in there to be released.'

'Good, so...'

'Although why he didn't take everything before, I don't know. But I understand Mr Short can't be contacted by the matron.'

'So?'

'So Mrs Luxton wants to know if she can send anything there over to us.'

'I suppose so.' Simon Puckle sighed. The firm were still holding a pair of skis for a gunner officer posted to sub-Saharan Africa during the war and several sporting trophies from a big game shoot of yesteryear whose protagonists were now as dead as their victims.

'She says it's not a lot, but reading between the lines I'd say it's that she doesn't want Mrs Wakefield back there. All it amounts to are half a dozen books and a packet with old photographs and so forth in, some letters and a few personal belongings.'

'I suppose you'd better tell her to send them over here, then. Joseph Short can go through them before he goes back to Lasserta. He'll be coming in quite soon anyway to sign those papers for me.' He looked up and went through his customary ritual of saying – as they both knew – quite unnecessarily, 'They'll be ready for signature soon, I take it?'

'Of course, Mr Puckle,' she answered in the same spirit. 'Very soon.'

'Ah,' said Dr Dabbe pleasantly as the two policemen reached the pathologist's mortuary, 'Burke and Hare have arrived, I see.'

Detective Constable Crosby shook his head. 'No, Doctor,' he said, serious for once. 'The subject is an elderly woman called Josephine Eleanor Short.'

'So I am told,' said the doctor. 'And only lately buried, too, I hear.'

'The day before yesterday,' said Detective Inspector Sloan.

He found it difficult to believe that it had only been a matter of two days before, so much had happened since.

'Ah, too soon for adipocere, then,' said Dr Dabbe.

Crosby cocked his head enquiringly.

'Grave wax,' said the pathologist.

'In the churchyard of St Nicholas at Damory Regis,' went on Sloan, sticking to the point as best he could.

'A pair of resurrectionists,' said Dabbe, still jovial. 'That's what you two are.'

'Exhumed on the orders of the coroner, permission confirmed with the appropriate certificate from the Home Office,' said Sloan stolidly. Humour as a displacement activity he could understand; this was something else.

'And presumably,' went on the pathologist, 'you have your reasons for raising the dead, so to speak?'

'Yes, Doctor. The grave would appear to have been opened after the original burial and it is possible that some valuable rings that were said to have been buried with her have been removed.'

'And you two gentlemen want to know what she died from, I suppose?'

'Among other things, Doctor,' said Sloan.

'What did the *acte de décès* say?'

'Beg pardon, doctor?'

'The death certificate.'

'Left ventricular fibrillation.'

'The heart of the matter, you might say. And did her own doctor issue it?'

'Yes. Dr Angus Browne.'

The pathologist tilted his head forward the better to tie his facial mask on. 'Usually sound, although you can always have a good man on a bad day.'

That, as far as Sloan was concerned, was perfectly understandable in any doctor – except that he didn't want that bad day to be one on which he or his wife and son consulted him. Or her, he added automatically, even though Crosby couldn't read his thoughts.

'And what about the other things you want to know?' the pathologist asked in a now somewhat muffled voice.

'There are thought to be three rings missing from the body. We have been told that the deceased was wearing them at the time of her death, and this was confirmed by the nursing home in which she died and the undertakers, but it does matter whether they were removed before she was...' Sloan paused while he tried to think of the right word.

The pathologist supplied it. 'Encoffined.'

'Exactly. Thank you, Doctor,' said Sloan. 'Alternatively we need to know if they were removed before she was buried.'

'*A la* Hogarth,' said Dr Dabbe.

'Pardon, Doctor?'

'In his painting of *A Rake's Progress* they didn't wait for the undertaker. The midwife had the rings off the rake's wife's fingers the minute she died.'

'Not very nice,' said Crosby.

'We have, of course,' said Sloan austerely, 'also to make absolutely sure that the undertakers are not implicated.' The matching memory to the pathologist's Hogarth picture that came to Sloan's mind was the morbid vision that had so frightened Charles Dickens' character, the dying Ebeneezer Scrooge. It was when seeing in the vision of the Ghost of Christmas Yet to Come that all his worldly goods – even his bedclothes – were being stolen the minute he died. Or had it even been before he'd died? That morbid scenario was an ever-present worry for policemen.

'Your pigeon that, old chap,' said Dr Dabbe amiably. 'I only deal in what I can find.'

Detective Inspector Sloan, head of the Criminal Investigation Department of 'F' Division of the county force, would have liked to be able to say the same but detection wasn't like that. It was instead a mysterious compound of fact, speculation, good working practices, pure instinct and downright luck.

'And I can tell you one thing,' went on the pathologist, pulling down an overhead lamp, 'this isn't going to be anything like that painting Stanley Spencer did of the Resurrection at Cookham, when they all stand up out of their coffins as was.'

'No, Doctor,' agreed Sloan. He hadn't thought it would be.

'More "things ain't what they used to be",' murmured Crosby, beginning his customary withdrawal to the sidelines of any post-mortem.

It was very nearly an hour later before the pathologist straightened up and said, 'Angus Browne was quite right in what he certified. I can confirm that the subject died from heart failure and that the post-mortem lividity and the condition of the body is exactly what I would have expected in the circumstances that you have indicated to me. I can say that there is no reason for me to believe that death was other than from natural causes.'

'And?' said Detective Inspector Sloan. He had seen the pathologist examine all Josephine Short's fingers with great care.

'And that two digits on the left hand show signs of having had rings removed rather roughly. The skin under where they would have been is considerably whiter than on the other fingers and I would say that whoever removed them...'

'Yes, Doctor?'

'Did so after death.'

'And after burial?'

'That, Inspector, I cannot say.'

CHAPTER TWENTY

Detective Constable Crosby had visibly relaxed as soon as Sloan left the office. In theory he should have been drawing up a written list of what had happened in the case, setting out in neat parallel columns the movements of all the various participants. It was a theory in which he was well versed. What he wasn't so skilled at was the practice.

He had to remember, of course, that those he was writing about weren't to be called suspects, this being deemed politically incorrect at this stage of the investigation. Actually he wasn't absolutely sure which investigation he was supposed to be concentrating on at the moment.

He sighed and reluctantly started at the top of the page, as instructed, with the possible – no, probable – encounter between Lucy Lansdown and Josephine Short in the hospital over at Calleford when Lucy, the deceased, that is...he stopped and chewed the end of his pencil and reconsidered this. They were both deceased, weren't they? Lucy Lansdown and Josephine Short, a nurse and a patient, who might have – could possibly have – met when the nurse was still in training. If they had known each other then, this fact was something that mattered now. He was sure about that.

Then there seemed to have been a gap of three years in which nothing at all of any particular significance had happened – at least nothing that he, Crosby, knew about. He had a shot at writing the word 'hiatus' but soon gave up and wrote 'the death of Josephine Eleanor Short' down instead, now able to put 'from Natural Causes' after that. Somehow that fact had made the case even more confusing.

He searched his memory for something else he had been taught to consider. 'Events triggered by the death' – that was it. He gave this due consideration and a moment later wrote down 'funeral'. After a minute or two he crossed this out and wrote down 'return of Joseph Short from abroad'. 'Abroad' he considered a better word than Lasserta since he didn't know where that was exactly.

Then he crossed out the word 'funeral' once more and put down the break-in at the Berebury Nursing Home since that had happened sometime during the night before the funeral. The matron had seemed pretty sure about that. Someone looking for something. The rings perhaps. Perhaps not. He didn't know.

He next put down on his list the return of William Wakefield from South America. According to both his wife and the man himself, that hadn't been triggered by Josephine Short's death because he hadn't been intending to come home. Or had he? That wife of his would have let her husband's nearest workstation know for sure by email, even if she or they hadn't been able to get in touch with him. And had that really been the reason why he had come home? And why hadn't he come straight home the night he arrived in London?

Then he wrote down 'the funeral' again, this time more firmly.

What had happened after the funeral was easier to get in the right order. The wake at the Almstone Towers after the funeral – to which Lucy Lansdown hadn't gone. Why she had gone to the funeral in the first place was still a mystery. So was the reason why she hadn't put her name on one of those dinky little attendance cards the undertaker had been so pleased to hand over to Janet Wakefield afterwards. She hadn't done so, they knew now, because all the women who had been there and had filled in a card had been systematically eliminated from all police enquiries. He liked the phrase and wrote down that all the male attendees had been eliminated from their enquiries, too. Even that old schoolmaster, Sebastian Worthington, from out Kinnisport way, had been adamant that he hadn't ever set eyes on the girl with the auburn hair before the funeral.

Now, where was he? Crosby stared down at his notebook. Ah, yes. And then the very same night of the funeral the girl had been killed. Odd, that. And why she had been killed was an even greater mystery than why she had gone to the funeral. A worried brother in the North, even now making his way to Calleshire, hadn't been able to throw any light on this over the telephone. That there had been a love affair that had been broken off a couple of years ago at least, he knew, but in the way of brothers he was sure she'd got over that. In any event, he didn't know that she hadn't, since she had never been one to wear her heart on her sleeve. Perhaps the two events weren't connected. Perhaps they were.

Both William Wakefield and Joe Short could in theory

have slipped out of their respective hotels and met her at the bridge at Berebury, and Matthew Steele's movements were customarily so fluid he could have been anywhere and done anything without his mother or anyone else knowing.

And after that? After Lucy Lansdown's body had been found, that is.

Crosby frowned prodigiously. After that – or perhaps even the night before – some person or persons unknown had desecrated the old lady's grave and removed three rings from the body. If they were the same person or persons who had just murdered Lucy Lansdown and thrown her body into the river, then they had been working to a very tight timetable indeed. And they'd have been pretty tired by morning. Especially if they'd been busy breaking into the Berebury Nursing Home the night before. Crosby gave a yawn himself at the very idea.

Then, he decided, things had gone remarkably quiet. True, Joe Short had had his passport stolen, which was why he had gone to London, but he didn't think that particular event came into his schedule. Matthew Steele had gone missing, which Crosby was quite sure did. And both the Wakefields had left their home today and nobody knew where they had gone or why.

Then there was the question of motive. Nobody had come up with one for the killing of Lucy Lansdown yet, and the only motive he could attribute to William Wakefield was gain – and that was only if he were to kill Joe Short, which he didn't seem to have attempted to do. Joe Short didn't seem to have any motive for murdering anyone and Matthew Steele's motive led directly to pound signs.

It was all too difficult and Crosby gave up and went in search of a cup of tea.

* * *

There were parts of the police station in Berebury that the public saw and there were parts that they didn't. There were parts that the civilian staff worked in and never went beyond. There were, too, parts in the custody suite that those apprehended did see, albeit unwillingly. The part to which Detective Inspector Sloan had just been summoned was one not usually seen by anyone save those working from it. Lined with wet suits, it was the quarters of the underwater men.

'We got it, Inspector,' said one of them as Sloan entered. Even now he was unpeeling himself from his black rubber casing. 'It was a bit downstream of the bridge. Stuck in the mud. The bridge makes for little eddies there and it hadn't been carried far.'

'Good,' said Sloan, adding swiftly, 'was it open or closed?'

The frogman pointed to a bench on which lay a very wet black handbag. 'Closed.'

Feeling slightly foolish as he always did when he put them on, Sloan eased his hands into a pair of rubber gloves before he touched the handbag. It was still closed, a zip running all along the top.

'I reckon nothing can have spilt out,' said the frogman, peering over Sloan's shoulder at it.

'So do I,' said Sloan, 'which is quite important.'

The frogman moved away a little to give himself a shake very reminiscent of that of a long-haired dog coming in out of the rain. Meanwhile Sloan gently drew the zip back and opened up the handbag. Water had scarcely penetrated the leather and the contents were dry enough for him to make a careful examination of them. He methodically extracted all the items one by one and laid them out in a line along the bench.

'Pen, mobile phone, petty cash, handkerchief, pair of scissors,' enumerated the frogman, coming back to the bench a little drier. 'What did she want scissors for?'

'She was a nurse,' said Sloan as if that explained it.

The frogman shrugged and went back to listing everything aloud. 'Four ten-pound notes and one twenty. They're not well paid, are they? Hand mirror, comb, safety pin...I thought they'd gone out with the ark.'

'It's called being prepared,' said Sloan absently. 'But it's what *isn't* there that matters.'

'What's that, then?' The frogman was standing beside Sloan in his underclothes and socks now.

'The key of her front door,' said Sloan. 'It wasn't in her pocket.'

The frogman grimaced. 'No chance of our finding that, Inspector. Not in all that mud. Not if it went in separately.'

Detective Inspector Sloan straightened up from the bench on which the wet handbag lay. 'The key won't have gone in there. Not then and not there, anyway. He wouldn't have gone back to the river.' The question of gender didn't arise in his mind at all now. 'Too dangerous.'

Sloan headed for the nearest telephone and rang the SOCO in charge of the team who had searched Lucy Lansdown's house. 'I want you to go back there again,' he said, 'and look for any further evidence that someone else has been in there.' He looked down at his own hands. 'Especially someone wearing gloves,' he sighed and added under his breath, 'just like we did.'

'This other entry, Inspector, we're talking about,' the SOCO said, 'would that have been before or after you went over the house?'

'Before,' said Detective Inspector Sloan. That was something he was sure about now. In his book someone had removed Lucy Lansdown's key from her handbag before casting it in the river. And used it in all probability to get inside her house that same night.

'Though what he was looking for,' he said to Crosby as he arrived in his office a little later, 'I do not know. What everyone is looking for is a complete mystery to me.'

'Perhaps,' suggested the constable indifferently, 'they're all looking for different things.' He looked out through the window towards the police car park. 'Are you ready to go home now, sir? It's getting late.'

'Not while there's work to be done, Crosby, and there is.'

Sudden summonses – day and night – were part and parcel of the daily workings of funeral directors and usually gave rise to no surprises beyond what was expected in the everyday undertaking line of business. In the ordinary way this occasioned no more than a funeral conducted with decent expedition and the sympathetic handling of all concerned. More often than not, even warring, highly dysfunctional families succumbed to a skilled and orderly decision-making process that resolved such important matters as where and when the ceremony would be held and by whom conducted. The more delicate decisions such as who should pay tribute and whether children should be brought to the service were wisely left to the relatives to fight about.

Today was different.

'You there, Tod?' Charlie Morton was sitting in his office when Tod got back from burying a nonagenarian over at the village of Larking. He sounded disgruntled.

'Yes, Dad.'

'I want a word.' In his own domain Charlie Morton could be as autocratic as Superintendent Leeyes.

'Won't be a tick. I'm just changing.'

'Now!' The paterfamilias touch was well to the fore. 'This minute.'

Tod stood in the doorway in his shirtsleeves, his black frock coat dangling over his arm. 'What's up?'

'Those rings that have gone missing from Damory Regis...'

'I know, Dad. Awful, isn't it? I still can't—'

'It's more than awful,' interrupted the old man sternly.

Tod advanced into the office. 'It can't be—'

Charlie Morton said soberly, 'Oh, yes it is. I've had the police round here again.'

Tod said, 'About someone trying to break in here?'

'Not about someone trying to break in here,' thundered the old man. 'About us.'

'Us?' Tod sounded bewildered. 'What about us?'

'Those three rings,' he glowered at his son, 'they think we took them.'

'What!' Tod flushed a bright red.

'The police think we had them away on our toes.'

'Never!'

'Well, what else are they to think?' the old man demanded grumpily. 'It has been known in the trade. You can't say it hasn't.'

'I suppose,' said Tod slowly, 'you can't blame them for checking. It's their job to check everything out.'

'And I've had Chris Sloan, who I've known, man and boy, all his life, coming round here questioning me. Me, an honest businessman with a good name for over forty years!' Charlie Morton thumped the table. 'It's an outrage, that's what it is.

And to make matters worse he had that daft boy he calls his assistant with him.'

'Crosby,' said Tod dully.

'He was supposed to be writing down my answers. Did we keep the rings in the safe?' He sniffed. 'What do we need a safe for here? Do they think somebody's going to steal the stock? And what about our burglar alarm, they wanted to know. Our burglar alarm,' he repeated richly. 'What good do they think that would do? Wake the dead?'

Tod stood stock-still and silent in the middle of the room while his father continued his diatribe. 'Then they asked how could we be sure somebody else in the firm didn't pull them off the poor old lady's fingers just before we screwed the coffin down? And how could we be absolutely certain no one here unscrewed it again after that? Asking us that. Us. Morton's. The very idea!'

'But, Dad—'

'Especially when Bert and Fred and all the others have worked here since they were lads and I had to stop them waving at their friends from the hearse first time out.'

'Calm down, Dad. Calm down and take it easy.'

'Someone did try to get in,' insisted Morton *père*, unappeased. 'The police saw those marks outside. You showed them to them, didn't you?'

'I suppose anyone could have made them,' said Tod unhappily, realising now where the police were coming from on this.

'We didn't, though,' said the old man stubbornly. 'Nor anyone here, either.'

Tod's mind was still churning away. 'Remember, Dad, whoever it was, they didn't get in.'

'I know that,' he rasped.

'And don't forget, Dad, those rings are worth an arm and a leg. Even I know that. They were really lovely.'

'My reputation's more important than any number of rings,' he growled. 'However valuable. Rings belong by nature to the past. My name's my future and yours, too. Don't you ever forget it. I shouldn't have to remind you, Tod, that reputation's what counts in our line of work. If people think you're going in for funny business they won't come to you in the first place.' He grunted. 'That's not all. There's something else.'

'What's that, then?'

'I've had the chief reporter from *The Berebury Gazette* round – you remember, we buried his Aunt Mabel last year.'

'Don't say they've found out about the exhumation already?'

'You bet your sweet life they have but they don't know for why. Yet,' he added ominously. 'I didn't tell 'em and I'm not going to. And neither are you.'

'No, Dad.'

'I told them it was being done on the instructions of the Home Office and not a thing more. Got that?'

'Yes, Dad.'

'Sure?'

'Yes, Dad.'

The message came on the internal telephone from the desk sergeant at Berebury Police Station. 'There's a man here asking for you, Inspector Sloan.'

'Who?' asked Sloan warily. 'I'm very busy.' He wasn't sure if detectives were allowed to ignore any calls on their time at will. Probably not.

'He says he's called Short, Joseph Short.'

'I'll be right down.'

Joe Short was standing waiting by the counter when he got there. He looked older now and his lips were set in a firm line. 'I saw you on television, Inspector. That grave at Damory Regis that's been disturbed, which the reporter was asking about, is Granny's, isn't it? What on earth's going on over there? Tell me.'

'I am not in a position to say at this stage of our enquiries, sir.'

Joe Short's tanned complexion turned a darker hue and he growled, 'That's not good enough, Inspector. Surely I've got every right to know? I am her grandson.'

Detective Inspector Sloan, seasoned police officer that he was, contrived to invest his reply with sincere-sounding regret. 'I'm very sorry, sir, but further enquiries are pending and until then I can give you no further information on the matter.'

'But I've got a flight back to Lasserta arranged for the day after tomorrow. I can't change it now and I can't just go and leave something like that hanging in the air.'

Sloan was unbending. 'As soon as we have any more definite news, sir, we shall inform you and, of course, Mr Simon Puckle. In the meantime I'm afraid the matter is in the hands of Her Majesty's Coroner and the Home Office.'

'What has my poor grandmother done to deserve something like this to happen to her grave?' Joseph Short leant his elbows on the counter and sank his head in his hands. 'It's turning into an absolute nightmare.'

Detective Inspector Sloan did not attempt to disillusion him.

* * *

'You can keep your five-star hotels,' said William Wakefield
that evening, looking appreciatively round the comfortable
lounge of the Bellingham Hotel and sinking down into a
leather sofa. 'This is more like home, Joe, and I like it.'

'I don't know whether that's a compliment to my good
taste in interior design or not,' smiled Janet Wakefield, sitting
back in her chair in an unusually relaxed manner for her.

'If you could see some of the outstations up at Mathabo
where I'm living,' said Joe Short, 'you'd take it as a
compliment.'

'Tell me, Joe,' said Janet Wakefield, raising her glass in his
direction, 'what are you going to do now?'

'Fly back to Lasserta as soon as I can,' he said. 'Otherwise
I reckon Cartwright's Consolidated Carbons will soon be
wanting to know the reason why.'

'I meant,' she said bluntly, 'when you come into your
inheritance?'

'Oh, that. I don't really know. I'm on a two-year contract
with Cartwright's anyway and I'd want to finish that. Besides,
there's the matter of my parents' affairs out there. I can't just
leave Lasserta without winding them up – it's not the sort of
thing you can do at a distance – and heaven alone knows when
they'll be finally settled.' A shadow passed over his face. 'It's
been an absolute nightmare so far, I can tell you.'

'No throwing your cap over the windmill, then,' said
William Wakefield.

'Or hanging your hat in somebody's hall?' suggested Janet
mischievously.

'One day perhaps, but not quite yet,' he said, flushing a
little, 'but I reckon I won't be able to come back to Calleshire
for a bit.'

'Nothing to bring you back now, anyway,' said Janet. As her friend, Dawn, was wont to say, tact had never been Janet's strong suit.

'No.' He hesitated and then said diffidently, 'I suppose you wouldn't mind going over and making sure that Granny's grave's all right and that sort of thing? After I've gone, I mean. Could I ask you to do that? Once in a while, I mean, that's all.'

'Of course not,' said Janet immediately. 'I'd be happy to. Is there anything else we can do for you when you've gone back?'

'If anything more turns up in the local paper about that girl, Lucy, who was at the funeral, I'd obviously like to know – oh, and there'll be a gravestone put up in Damory Regis churchyard in due course, when the ground's ready, that is. The solicitor had a note of what Granny wanted put on it, all decided by her when she went into the nursing home, and he'll arrange it but I wouldn't mind a photograph of it sometime.'

'Of course,' she said, nodding.

'Actually,' continued Joe, 'I'm going over there again tomorrow morning. I've heard that there's been some sort of disturbance to the grave there and I'd like to take a look at it before I go back to Lasserta.'

William Wakefield said, 'Odd, that.'

'Isn't it?' agreed Joe eagerly. 'I don't quite understand what's been happening but I wouldn't want anything to have gone wrong with Granny's arrangements.'

'No. A really remarkable woman, your grandmother,' said Janet. She looked at the two men. 'I hope it's in the genes of both you two.'

'I realise that we have a lot to live up to,' said Joe lightly. 'All I can say is, for my part, that I'm doing my best.'

'So am I,' said William fervently, adding under his breath, 'and how!'

It was later that night that Janet Wakefield turned over in bed at The Old Post Office at Staple St James for the tenth time, punching her pillow quite strenuously as she did so.

'A bit restless, aren't you?' complained her husband drowsily.

'It's all right for you. I can't sleep.'

'Well, don't forget that I've got to be up early to catch the first train tomorrow morning.'

'I don't know why Head Office should want to talk to you again so soon,' she pouted. 'We've got so little time together as it is.'

'I've told you already it's for a briefing on the new job,' he said, pulling the bedclothes back into shape. 'Where's the end of this blanket got to?'

'Don't tell me that all those maidens you say you meet in the jungle aren't ever restless, too,' she said sweetly.

'Models of stillness, the lot of them.' He joined his hands together behind his head and rested them against the pillow. 'I will say one thing about the upriver maidens,' he murmured provocatively, 'and that's that they're a jolly sight more biddable than you are.'

'What was that you said?' She sat straight up in bed at once and glared at him.

He grinned back at her. 'I do like it when you get uptight. Do you realise that your face turns quite pink when that happens?'

'One day, William Wakefield, I shall hit you. I really will.'

'Actually, though, I'm afraid it's against company policy to take the maidens to bed.'

'I should hope so, too.'

'Only they put it a bit more obliquely in the contract.'

'I'll bet they do.'

'Wives aren't allowed to hit their husbands either so for goodness' sake stop wriggling around and go back to sleep.'

'I can't. Something's niggling me.'

'What?'

'If I knew that, then I could do something about it and get back to sleep, couldn't I?'

'Yes.' He turned over and shut his eyes. 'Go on thinking by all means but do it quietly.'

Janet was still sitting up in bed. 'You do realise, don't you, that we've only got one more night together after this before you go back to Brazil?'

'I do.'

'Those are the very same words that you used at our wedding, remember?' she stifled a sentimental sigh.

'I haven't forgotten,' he said wearily, turning his shoulder away.

'Bill?'

'What is it now?' he asked impatiently.

'That doctor we saw today...'

'What about him?'

'Is he any good, do you think?'

'I don't know but I can tell you he's the most pompous and mealy-mouthed man I've ever met. Anyway, time will tell, won't it?'

What Janet stifled now sounded suspiciously like a sob.

'Now,' he said firmly, 'if I'm not going to mess up tomorrow I must get some sleep. Goodnight!'

Janet Wakefield lay on her back, very still, for a long time, pursuing an elusive memory. It was a long time after that before she fell into an uneasy sleep.

CHAPTER TWENTY-ONE

Years of working in the law had taught Simon Puckle, country solicitor, the virtues of routine and punctuality. Thus he went through the same procedures every morning when he arrived for work. First on his agenda was what he had come to think of as a colloquy with Miss Florence Fennel. She would arrive armed with the morning post, each missive carefully annotated and awaiting his instructions. These duly given, talk would turn to ongoing matters.

'And Joseph Short,' finished Miss Fennel, who never used the diminutives of names as a matter of principle and never omitted a surname, 'has telephoned from the Bellingham to say that having now got his permit to travel he has fixed up a provisional return flight to Lasserta for late tomorrow afternoon. That is unless we require him to extend his stay for any reason.'

'I don't think we do, do we?' said Simon Puckle, frowning. 'We can send the probate papers and anything else that needs signing out to him.'

'In due course,' supplemented Miss Fennel automatically. 'We mustn't forget there are those letters and photographs that the nursing home sent round yesterday.'

'Get him to call round and pick them up before he goes, then. We don't really want them here. Now, what time do I have to be at the magistrates' court?'

Work relating to their activities at Berebury Police Station had begun in a rather less orderly fashion, the virtues of a daily routine only kicking in when everything was quiet in the town. Early as it had been when the police had called at The Old Post Office in Staple St James it was only to find that William Wakefield had already left for his firm's head office in London.

'His wife was still in bed, though, when we got there,' reported Detective Inspector Sloan to an acerbic Superintendent Leeyes.

'That's not my idea of a dawn raid,' observed Leeyes irascibly.

'We got her up,' offered Sloan, the only palliative that came to mind.

'It isn't his wife we wanted to talk to, Sloan,' rasped Leeyes. 'You know that. It wasn't the hen bird that had flown.'

Sloan acknowledged the witticism with a wintry smile. 'Janet Wakefield explained to us that they had both been at the Bellingham Hotel all the evening before with Joseph Short which is why we didn't find her husband at home then.'

'Wakefield sounds like that damned elusive pimpernel to me,' grumbled Leeyes. 'Has he gone straight to his office this morning like she said he had or is he going walkabout in London like the last time he was there? I hope you've checked on that?'

'Yes, sir,' said Sloan. 'Wakefield's at his office, all right. I've just checked that with them.'

'Well, I hope he stays there until he comes home and that you interview him as soon as he does.' Leeyes changed tack. 'Did you get anything out of your interview with the other fellow – Joe Short?'

'Not a lot. If he's a wrong 'un it doesn't show. And he did hire a car at the airport on the morning of the funeral, like he said, and not at any other time in his name that the Met can establish. And the photograph we've had back from his firm, Cartwright's Carbons, in Lasserta is definitely of him. He had all his answers off pat, too.'

'I don't like the sound of that, Sloan,' pounced the superintendent immediately. 'Not natural.'

'You could say he ticked all the right boxes when we talked to him, sir. And he insisted that he'd handed over to us all those funeral cards from the undertaker.'

'No way of telling, of course,' grunted Leeyes. 'Or even whether she filled one in.'

'No, sir, but we haven't established any connection between him and Lucy Lansdown, or come to that between the girl and William Wakefield either. Not yet, anyway. No one of his name seems to have hired a car the night that the girl went into the river. All her brother could tell us was that she'd had an unhappy love affair a few years ago but he didn't know who with and he'd definitely never met the man in question. He didn't know anything about him at all.'

'Brothers,' pronounced the Superintendent sagely, 'never understand their sisters' love lives and never will.'

'Quite so, sir. I'll talk to him properly as soon as he arrives in Berebury, of course.'

'And keep trying with both Wakefield and Short, Sloan. This is a murder case, remember, not petty theft.'

'I haven't forgotten, sir,' promised Sloan, making for his own office with a certain relief.

Some good news awaited him there.

'Cast your bread upon the waters, Crosby,' began Detective Inspector Sloan, a sheet of paper in his hands, as the constable entered with two steaming mugs of coffee.

'And it will be returned to you as sandwiches,' rejoined Crosby irreverently.

'Actually, Crosby, I had in mind a more general observation on the merits of following police procedure to the letter.'

'Sorry, sir.'

'And the importance of attention to detail.'

'Naturally, sir,' he said solemnly. 'It's worked, then, has it?'

Sloan smoothed out a message sheet lying on his desk. 'I am happy to say that the good practice of our routine general circulation of jewellers and pawnbrokers has paid off in spades.'

'The rings?' deduced Crosby.

Sloan read out aloud, 'An eternity ring, answering to the description of one of the three rings as outlined in your circular of yesterday's date, was offered for sale to Tatton's, the jewellers, in Luston High Street today for cash by an unknown young man.'

'Testing the market?' said Crosby.

'Just so,' said Sloan.

'A young man who happened to be too shy to leave his name and address?' enquired the detective constable.

'You've got it in one, Crosby. Moreover – surprise, surprise

– when pressed to write these details in their ledger, he took his departure with speed, and the ring, of course.'

Sloan's train of thought was interrupted by the latent memory of the unpopular pedant who had taught him English grammar at school. That he'd just committed a grammatical solecism, he knew, but what he couldn't remember was which one. There had been a phrase...recollection came flooding back after a moment: 'The man dropped a sigh and a sixpence' – that was it. The schoolmaster had called that a condensed sentence and quoted a famous playwright: 'Cut the second act and that child's throat.' In the playground afterwards he and his friends had dreamt up some more, schoolboy humour well to the fore, and better forgotten. He came back to the present with a jerk as Crosby spoke. 'What was that you said, Crosby?'

'Is there any description of the man, sir?' For once Crosby had his notebook at the ready.

'Some,' said Sloan, reading aloud from the message sheet. 'Medium height, brown hair and nondescript clothes. And hood, of course,' he added, since this item of apparel seemed to be de rigueur these days among the urban young of a law-breaking disposition. 'However, Crosby, fortunately Tatton's, who were not born yesterday in spite of the venerable age of their firm, possess a hidden camera with which they record a photographic image of all the customers who come into their shop.'

'Matthew Steele?' hazarded Crosby. He started to get to his feet. 'I could go over to Luston and get that picture, sir...it wouldn't take me long.'

'I'm sure it wouldn't,' said Sloan, 'but I'm happy to say that an image is on its way and will reach us even more quickly by computer.'

Crosby subsided back into his chair, a disappointed man. 'There's a general call out for Matthew Steele already so...'

'So there's nothing more to be done about him for the time being,' said Sloan.

'Except keep an eye open,' said Crosby.

'Except keep an eye on his home,' Sloan corrected him wearily. 'Bad boys always come home in the end.' That was something else he had learnt long ago on the beat.

'Those rings must be worth a real bomb or he's got a drug dealer putting on the frighteners in a big way.'

'Both, probably,' agreed Sloan sourly.

Detective Constable Crosby leant back in his chair and started to count off his fingers. 'So first he breaks into the nursing home and finds the body gone, and so he tries to get into the undertaker's next and can't, so then he goes for the grave.'

'No,' said Sloan.

'No?' Crosby looked puzzled.

'Well, yes and no,' said Sloan since he wasn't talking to the superintendent now. 'No, he doesn't break into the nursing home because in the first place he wouldn't need to, knowing where the keys are kept, and in the second place getting in there the night before the funeral would have been too late. The body wouldn't have been there by then.'

'So why didn't he break in there while it was?' asked Crosby simply.

'Probably because his mother didn't mention until after it had happened that the rings had gone with the body to the undertaker's. She knows him even better than we do, remember.'

'So somebody else broke in there,' concluded Crosby

slowly, 'someone who wasn't looking for the rings.'

'Exactly, Crosby.'

'So what were they looking for?'

'If, Crosby, we knew that I think we would know the answer to everything.' At this stage Sloan wasn't at all sure what the word 'everything' comprised. If he knew that, too, it would help. What he seemed to be investigating at the moment was a complicated melange of things that were not quite right. First and foremost of these was the death of a young woman called Lucy Lansdown. This had been about the time, not yet determined, of the disturbing of a grave contrary to the Burial Act of 1852, which forbade any such thing, thus leading to the theft of valuable property. He reminded himself that he must not forget a successful break-in at another place – the nursing home – and an attempted break-in at a quite different place – the undertaker's – to say nothing of the search of the dead young woman's house by person or persons unknown. It was, though, quite enough to be getting on with.

'They wouldn't have broken in to that nursing home for nothing, would they, sir? Without a reason, I mean. Whoever they are.'

'No.' That much was certain.

His brow furrowed, Crosby thought hard. 'If there was nothing valuable left in there…'

'Nothing intrinsically valuable,' amended Sloan.

'All right,' agreed Crosby, conceding this, 'then it must have been for something that someone didn't want found there.'

'Keep going, Crosby.'

'Like a photograph of Lucy Lansdown?'

'Could be. Too soon to say but that would be the sort of missing link between Josephine Short and Lucy Lansdown that we're looking for.' Detective Inspector Sloan turned his attention back to the message sheet from the jeweller's at Luston. 'There's something else interesting, Crosby. Tatton's, the jewellers, who are very experienced in these matters, had noticed the names inside the eternity ring before they handed them back to the customer. Indeed, they say they had actually pointed out to the customer that the names lowered the resale value.'

'Really?' The constable didn't sound too interested. 'I didn't know that they did.'

'Think, Crosby,' he said, exasperated now. 'Difficult, surely, to present it to the love of your life as new if it's got someone else's names engraved in it. Even you ought to be able to work that out.'

'Yes, sir.'

Sloan bent over the message sheet again. 'The names inscribed inside the eternity ring were Josephine and George, entwined.'

'Soppy,' said Crosby, unmarried and rather gauche.

'Sentimental,' said Sloan, married long since but still able to remember the uncertain swain he had been once upon a time. That girl in the blue dress had taken quite some winning.

'Same difference.' Crosby shrugged his shoulders indifferently.

'Josephine Short,' said Sloan, still a policeman, 'called her son George.'

'After his father, then, do you think?'

'I don't know. But George Peter Arden Short was certainly the name of Joseph Short's father,' said Sloan, stirred by a memory of something he couldn't quite place. 'And Joe's middle name is Arden, too.' Idly, Sloan wondered if both – if all three – had the family face, whatever that might have been. He'd been made to learn a poem called 'Heredity' by Thomas Hardy about that very thing, by that same schoolmaster. Since the penalty for failing to do so in those days involved the cane, the words easily came back to him now:

'*I am the family face; Flesh perishes, I live on, Projecting trait and trace Through time to times anon*

And leaping from place to place Over oblivion.'

Moreover, learning this for his English homework had not in his fourteen-year-old mind been something any self-respecting schoolboy should have had to do. He'd resented it, too, because in his opinion then Thomas Hardy was for girls. He sighed and said now, 'One more thing, Crosby, before we get going.'

'Sir?'

'William Wakefield. I still want a question and answer session with that man as soon as we can catch up with him and before he hoofs it back to Brazil. He must be interviewed the minute he gets back to Berebury. Do you understand?'

'Yes, sir.'

'And as for Joe Short...'

'Yes, sir?'

'We need to make quite sure that no ill befalls him before he goes back to his benighted island.'

The question of whether married subjects of either sex should be interviewed separately or in the presence of each other had always been a debatable one at the police station. Had he been asked, Detective Inspector Sloan would have taken a pragmatic view. Sometimes, he would have said, it helped to note the body language of one partner while the other one was being questioned, sometimes it was valuable for the one not to know what the other had said.

Much the same applied to encounters with the medical profession.

Which side of the debate succeeded with the police often depended on which member of the force was accompanying the interviewer. In the case of Detective Constable Crosby, Sloan was in no doubt. He was better without him. However, proper police procedure required that Sloan had someone with him when he questioned William Wakefield over the matter of his late return to the Erroll Garden Hotel the night after the funeral – or, rather, his failure to mention the fact when interviewed earlier.

And so it was with Crosby at his side that Sloan returned to The Old Post Office at Staple St James following at a discreet distance an unsuspecting William Wakefield back home after he came off the London train.

'We'd just like to run over a few things, sir,' said Sloan to William Wakefield overtaking the man as he walked up the garden path to his house. 'To make sure we've got it right.'

'Sure, Inspector.' The man seemed unalarmed. 'Come along in. I expect Jan's got the kettle on.'

Finding the door locked, Wakefield let them in with his own house key. Not only did Janet Wakefield not have the kettle on but she wasn't there.

'Funny,' said Bill Wakefield. 'I thought she'd guess I'd be on this train. I expect she's gone round to her friend, Dawn. Something must have cropped up because she didn't meet me at the station.' He led the way to the kitchen and put the kettle on himself.

'What we are investigating, sir,' said Sloan, 'are your

movements the night you got back from Brazil.'

He turned to face him. 'I told you, Inspector. I checked in to the Erroll Garden Hotel.'

'What you didn't tell us, sir, is that you went out again after that. Would you like to tell us where you went?'

William Wakefield glanced round the room as if to make sure that the three of them were alone. He took a deep breath and said, 'Only if you promise not to tell my wife.'

'I can't give you any specific undertaking of any sort,' said Sloan steadily, 'and I would remind you that we are investigating a matter of the utmost seriousness.'

The man wasn't really listening. 'You could say,' he said slowly, 'that I was being taught a lesson. Well, having one anyway.'

'Sir?'

'My wife and I have been trying to start a family. Having fertility treatment and all that.'

'Brazil's a long way away,' observed Crosby in a detached manner.

'When I'm at home,' he said with dignity.

'And?' said Sloan.

'And the doctor johnnies always try to pin the blame on the wife, willy-nilly. Or so they say. But they shouldn't. Not always.'

'The male ego being a tender plant?' suggested Sloan. This was something no policeman needed to be told: it was demonstrated most Saturday nights by alcohol-fuelled punch-ups in the town centre.

'I thought perhaps someone else might be able to help,' said William Wakefield simply.

'Someone with very wide experience?' suggested Sloan expressionlessly.

'All right, then, Inspector.' He opened his hands in a gesture of defeat. 'Have it your way. A lady of the night.'

'And did she?' enquired Crosby with interest.

William Wakefield favoured him with a long look and then his face suddenly burst into a grin and he yelped, 'And how!' He gave Sloan a playful dig in the ribs. 'I'm going to tell that supercilious medic that he only told me the half of it.'

'Not a *mariage blanc,* surely?' said the superintendent, pursing his lips.

'Not exactly,' said Sloan ambiguously. 'That's his story, anyway,' he added, deliberately vague.

'It's new, I will say that,' commented Leeyes. 'And what, might I ask,' he went on, rolling his eyes, 'did his wife have to say about that?'

'She wasn't there.' Sloan didn't suppose they would have heard about the matter at all – or was it an alibi? – if she had been. That she hadn't been present in the house was something he was beginning to find a little disturbing.

'It takes two to tango,' remarked Leeyes obscurely.

'Her husband told us that he didn't know where she was, either,' Sloan reported to the superintendent. The policeman in him wondered whether this, too, was something else he should worry about.

'Wakefield's London story isn't provable, of course,' Leeyes went on, pursuing his own train of thought. 'That he was with a lady of the night when he says he was, I mean, or exactly where.'

'No, sir.' Those of the red-light district never gave their names and address to the gentlemen from the blue-lamp police station if they could avoid it. Or to anyone else, come to that.

He coughed. 'If he wasn't with anyone like her, of course, he would have had time to come down to Berebury. All he had to do was arrange to meet Lucy Lansdown on the bridge or anywhere else and he could still get back to his hotel in the early hours. 'Joseph Short,' he added fairly, 'would have had even more time because he was on the spot here in the town and he could have got in and out of the Bellingham very easily.'

'Out and back in, you mean, Sloan.'

'Yes, sir, of course. Sorry, sir.'

'And I take it we still don't know who gains from Lucy Lansdown's death?'

'Not yet. We're working on it.' Other minions were indeed going through every piece of paper that had been found in Lucy Lansdown's house – so far without finding anything that might lead anywhere at all.

'Or what Matthew Steele was really up to?'

'We're working on that, too, sir.' Even to Sloan's own ears that sounded lame. Nobody knew what Matthew Steele might have been up to: a man who could rob a grave – if he had – was doubtless capable of anything at all. 'He hasn't been near his home yet. We do know that.' That it was all they knew, Sloan decided it was prudent not to add.

Leeyes drummed his fingers on the table in a peremptory way. 'How long have we got, Sloan?'

'Sir?'

'Before two of the three men connected with Josephine Short and thus presumably with Lucy Lansdown leave the country,' Leeyes said impatiently. 'She didn't go to that funeral for fun, you know.'

'Twenty-four hours,' said Sloan bleakly. He was tempted

to add *One Fine Day* but thought better of it just in time. 'I'm told Joseph Short has a flight back to Lasserta booked for late this afternoon and William Wakefield one first thing tomorrow morning.' He didn't hazard a guess as to what Matthew Steele's intentions might be or where he might have got to; perhaps he ought to be as concerned about his being missing as he was about Janet Wakefield not being around but he wasn't. The devil usually looked after his own.

The superintendent leant back in his chair. 'Have we got any grounds for detaining either of them? Or, better still, both?' Leeyes, too, seemed to have forgotten about Matthew Steele for the time being.

'None whatsoever, sir. Any half-awake solicitor would get them released in minutes.' Habeas corpus might be one of the oldest statutes in the book but it could still be invoked.

Leeyes sighed but said nothing.

'Quite so,' said Sloan, responding to the sigh not the silence. Having egg on his face was something that never had appealed to the police superintendent.

'And you're quite sure, Sloan, there's nothing we can get either of them on as of the present?' Leeyes sounded quite wistful now. 'Or Matthew Steele for anything at all yet?'

'Not unless Wakefield attempts to kill Short,' said Sloan succintly. 'Joseph Short dead would be worth a great deal to William Wakefield and his family and old Josephine Short was worth a lot to Matthew Steele dead – at least her rings were. We know that now but as to who benefits from Lucy Lansdown being dead, we still don't know.'

'And what has the man Short got to do wrong to give us some leverage? He seems to me to be sitting pretty if he does nothing at all.'

'Attempt to kill somebody,' said Sloan uneasily, 'although I can't for the life of me see why he should. The same goes for Matthew Steele. He's connected with Josephine Short, too, even if it's only after death.'

'Well, Sloan,' commanded Superintendent Leeyes at his most authoritative, 'just you make sure that nobody kills anybody else. And report back to me soonest.'

Suppressing any retort that included references to Merlin and sundry other wizards, Sloan made for the door. As he neared it Leeyes called out to his departing back, 'Think off-piste, Inspector.'

There was nothing for it, decided Detective Inspector Sloan, but to start at the very beginning of the case all over again – and not a lot of time left now in which to do it. 'It's back to the drawing board, I'm afraid, Crosby,' he said as the constable entered his office with two steaming mugs of tea. This wasn't the place for exotic skiing parallels.

'Calleford Hospital, you mean?' said that worthy readily. 'When Josephine Short was an inpatient and Lucy Lansdown was a nurse over there on the same ward and where Joe Short last saw his grandmother alive…'

Sloan stared at him. 'Say that again, Crosby.'

Obedient as ever, Crosby repeated the sentence.

'That's what I thought you said.' Sloan hunched his shoulders forward. 'Joe Short told us that he visited his grandmother there when she was ill there, didn't he?'

'That's right, sir. Something like three or four years ago. Before she went into the nursing home and before her son and daughter-in-law were killed in that accident. She was living over in Calleford then. I've got the dates in my notebook.'

Sloan wasn't listening. 'The stars in their courses...' he murmured softly.

'Pardon, sir?'

Sloan hit his palm hard with his other fist. 'What fools we've been, Crosby. Utter fools.'

'Sorry, sir, did I give you the one with sugar in?'

'In that hospital and then was one time that those three people could possibly all have met, although we don't know for sure that they did and might not be able to prove it.'

'That's right, sir. When the old lady was a patient there and the grandson was visiting her the last time he was back in England and Lucy Lansdown was nursing at the hospital,' repeated the detective constable. He took a sip of his own tea and screwed up his face. 'Ugh. No sugar.'

'But don't you see, Crosby?' Sloan said urgently, 'Lucy Lansdown was at that funeral at Damory Regis and as far as we know didn't recognise Joe Short then. At least, she didn't attempt to speak to him there. Janet Wakefield told us that and so did Joe Short himself and nobody else saw her approach Joe Short either. It was the first thing we checked. Short said that he picked up her handbag when she dropped it and handed it back to her but that was all. Or so he told us,' added Sloan, a new thought to do with fingerprints on the handbag retrieved from the river coming to him. He stored it away at the back of his mind for further consideration.

'And,' said the detective constable, suddenly tumbling to the meaning of what Sloan had said, 'that Mrs Wakefield confirmed that Joe Short didn't appear to recognise Lucy Lansdown either.' He screwed up his face in a prodigious frown and then went on, 'Or if he did, he didn't let it show.'

'But he might just have guessed who she was,' reasoned

Sloan slowly. 'And why she'd come to the funeral. She seems to have been the only young woman there, anyway.'

'To meet Joe Short again?' hazarded Crosby.

'If so, then perhaps he isn't Joe Short,' concluded Sloan, starting to get to his feet. 'And that might be why she had to be killed. If she knew he wasn't who everyone else thought he was, then she would have been undoubtedly in danger.'

'Was in danger,' pointed out Crosby.

'From someone,' said Sloan, the image of the dead girl on the riverbank rising unbidden in his mind.

'Everyone else does say he is Joe Short, sir,' pointed out Crosby, pushing his mug in Sloan's direction and taking the other one for himself. 'His firm emailed us his photograph, remember, and that was definitely of him.'

Sloan sat down again. 'True.'

'And his photograph was in the old lady's drawer with the other ones. That was of him, too.'

'So it was,' conceded Sloan. 'And since he handled it there, his fingerprints will be all over it. His photo'll have been in his passport, of course. Simon Puckle said he had looked at that before it was stolen.'

'It mightn't have been stolen, sir,' offered Crosby. 'He could have lost it on purpose.'

'No point doing that, though, if the photograph had already passed muster, was there?' said Sloan. He frowned. 'Handwriting?'

'There weren't any letters from him at the nursing home, remember.' Crosby stirred his tea with vigour and took a sip, smacking his lips with relish. 'That's better. I like it sweet.'

'He said that the old lady was practically blind, of course, and so he'd given up writing,' said Sloan automatically. 'They said that at the nursing home, too.'

'And deaf.'

'Suppose,' said Sloan, thinking aloud, 'that the nursing home was broken into not to take something away but to put something there...'

'Like a photograph?' suggested Crosby.

'Exactly... but it doesn't get round the fact that his firm sent us one of him which matched.'

'Perhaps he isn't Joseph Short there,' said Crosby idly. 'More tea, sir?'

Sloan reached for the telephone. 'I think, Crosby, we'll check with the nursing home all the same.'

'The room's occupied again,' the matron answered his call crisply. 'And all the contents have gone to the solicitors.'

When applied to, Simon Puckle said that they were indeed holding the contents of the drawers in Josephine Short's room. And that Joseph Short had arranged to call in to collect them before he went back to Lasserta since there seemed to be nothing of relevance in them to the winding up of their client's estate. 'That will be in due course,' added the solicitor automatically.

'Don't give them to him,' ordered Sloan. 'Stall.' He replaced the telephone and turned to Crosby. 'Simon Puckle shouldn't find that too difficult. Solicitors do it all the time.'

'Surely if Joe Short was the one who broke into the nursing home he could have taken away any picture he wanted so those can't matter all that much,' reasoned Crosby.

'That's true,' admitted Sloan. 'But we can't afford to leave any stone unturned.' That might not have been the equivalent of thinking off-piste but it was what he had been taught.

'More tea, sir?'

'Certainly not. Let's go.'

'Damory Regis?' suggested Crosby hopefully.

'Puckle, Puckle & Nunnery,' countered Sloan.

Miss Florence Fennel handed over a packet of old photographs without hesitation. 'Would one of our interview rooms be a help, Inspector?'

Seated and gloved, Detective Inspector Sloan went through a little pile of photographs one by one for the second time. He put aside the up-to-date one of Joseph Short and then turned his attention to the others. They were black and white and obviously older and much handled. Some even had the deckled edge of an earlier photographic era. They included several of a young couple outside a little house labelled on the back 'Us at Number 29'. Then one of the same young couple with a small baby on a rug in front of them in the garden of the house, 'Us with Joe at six months', then that baby, a small child now, standing uncertainly beside a dining room table set for a meal, his head exactly level with the tabletop. Written on the back was 'Joe at 2 years, six months'. The rest of the pile comprised a series of pictures of foreign parts – Africa, the Middle East and presumably Lasserta.

'We've seen them all before,' complained Crosby, looking over Sloan's shoulder.

'They haven't changed,' said Sloan quietly, 'but we have.'

Crosby straightened up. 'I don't get it, sir.'

'To put it the modern way, Crosby, our knowledge base has been increased.'

'I still don't get it.'

'By Tod Morton.'

'Tod? The undertaker? What's he got to do with—?'

'Something he told us.'

'Not that bit about a man's height being seven times the length of his foot?'

'You're getting warm, Crosby. Try again.'

'A piece of string is twice as long as half its length?'

'Not that. Got a measure on you?'

Crosby wriggled his hand through several pockets before producing one. 'Here, sir.'

'No, you do it.'

'What?'

'Measure the height of this table.'

'This one here?'

'Go on. They're pretty standard.'

Detective Constable Crosby pushed his chair back and measured the height of the table from the floor. 'I've done that, sir. Now what?'

'Double it.'

'What, like doubling the number you first thought of?' asked the constable.

'No...yes.' Sloan stood up. 'Hold the measure up to twice the height of the table.'

Crosby stood up, too, and raised the measure in his hand. 'Like this, sir.'

'Just like that, Crosby.' Sloan stood back. 'Would you say that Joe Short was taller than where the end of your measure is now?'

'A lot taller. He's a big man.'

'That's what I thought, too,' said Sloan softly.

'Taller than you, sir, anyway.' Crosby drew himself up to his full height and said, 'But not as tall as I am.'

'All right, Crosby. I get the message.' There was no use telling the constable that shorter policemen reflected full employment and taller ones unemployment and thus more tall candidates to choose from. 'You can put that measure away now, thank you.'

They were interrupted by a call on Crosby's mobile telephone. 'For you, sir,' said Crosby, handing it over. 'William Wakefield's getting worried about his wife. She hasn't come home yet.'

'She's not with her friend, Dawn, Inspector,' said Wakefield down the telephone, and sounding quite agitated. 'I've just checked and Dawn hasn't heard from her at all today.'

'What about her mobile phone?'

'Not switched on and she hasn't responded to my voicemail message to ring me back.'

'Have another look around for any written message she might have left you saying where she might have gone,' ordered Sloan.

'There's nothing here, Inspector, I'm sure,' said Wakefield. 'She must have gone out earlier thinking she'd be back before I got home.'

'Keep looking,' said Sloan. He was beginning to agree with William Wakefield that his wife might very well have expected to be back before her husband returned from Head Office. 'And we'll keep in touch.'

'I know she had something on her mind,' went on William Wakefield, 'because she slept so badly last night. She was worried, I could tell, but she couldn't remember exactly what about – just that something didn't quite add up – and anyway I had an early train to catch.'

Detective Inspector Sloan had never been a believer in

false reassurance and he didn't offer any now. Instead he told Crosby to get an unmarked car ready and put out a general call for Joseph Short's hire car.

'Quietly does it, Crosby,' said Sloan not very long afterwards. 'No blues and twos. I may be wrong but the grave at Damory Regis is the only place that I can think of that Janet Wakefield would willingly have agreed to go to at short notice with Joseph Short. She'd have been suspicious of any other destination being mentioned but visiting the graveyard there would be logical enough after they'd heard what had happened to the coffin. They'd naturally both want to take a look at the ground again – and Short would have the excuse that he's going back home soon.'

'He only thinks he's going back, sir.' Crosby dropped the car to the speed he considered proper for the reeling, rolling roads of rural England. The poet might have loved them but he didn't. 'He isn't.'

Detective Inspector Sloan spotted the couple walking away from Josephine Short's grave as the police car slid to a quiet stop alongside the churchyard wall at Damory Regis. As the two policemen advanced towards them over the uneven ground the pair paused just short of the war memorial and awaited their approach. A name on the memorial caught Sloan's eye as he stepped past it: Arden, GP. He'd seen it before but it hadn't made sense then. It did now.

Janet Wakefield was the first to speak. 'Oh, Inspector, there's nothing wrong, is there? Joe saw you talking on television about the grave and he's just brought me over here for a last look at it before he went back to Lasserta. Isn't it all a mess now?'

Joe Short nodded composedly. 'I could have wished that there hadn't been those tarpaulins everywhere, that's all, Inspector. I'd have liked to take a better memory back overseas and all that.'

'It's not quite all,' said Detective Inspector Sloan at his most professional. 'Joseph Short, I am arresting you for the murder of Lucy Eileen Lansdown. You don't have to—'

The man, still quite composed, interrupted Sloan with a smile. 'You haven't turned over two pages or something, have you, Inspector?'

The memory that was to stay with the police inspector, though, was quite a different one. It was of blood draining rapidly from the face of Janet Wakefield. She pointed a finger at Joe Short and said in a trembling voice, 'You told me you knew that poor dead girl was called Lucy, although nobody else did, because the dim constable had let it out by accident.'

'I never,' began a highly indignant Crosby.

Janet Wakefield started to cry. 'And I believed you!' she quavered, now shaking an unsteady fist in Joe Short's direction. 'You...you...you're so plausible, you...that's what you are... just horribly plausible.' Her eyes widened as the realisation dawned on her. 'You killed that poor girl, didn't you?' She didn't stop talking even as Detective Constable Crosby slipped a pair of handcuffs over Joseph Short's wrists. She went on in an ever-rising crescendo 'You knew all along that she was called Lucy, so don't you try to tell me that you didn't.'

'Janet Wakefield might have gone on a bit, sir, but Short didn't say a thing. He kept his nerve up all along,' reported Sloan to Superintendent Leeyes later. 'Very cool, calm and collected, he was. And charming with it, still, even with the cuffs on.

Kept smiling and insisted that there must be some mistake somewhere.'

Leeyes didn't go for charm. 'What I don't get, Sloan, is why he came back to England in the first place. Couldn't he have stayed over in Lasserta and done everything – claimed the inheritance and all that – by post?'

'He didn't know what was still here in the way of incriminating evidence and couldn't be sure without checking,' explained Sloan. 'And he needed to put his photograph into his grandmother's room and take away any of the real Joseph Short that there were as well as see what was in Lucy Lansdown's house. She'd been very friendly with the real Joe Short – they had first met at the hospital when his grandmother was in there – until the engagement was broken off, you know.'

'By Brian Brenton?' The telephone wires between Lasserta and Calleshire had been very busy. Brian Brenton was the name of the employee of United Mellemetics who was said to have gone missing, just as the man calling himself Joseph Short had reported for his new job at Cartwright's Consolidated Carbons in his stead.

'Yes, sir. Brian Brenton couldn't risk keeping up the link with Lucy Lansdown after he'd killed the real Joe Short so he broke off the connection. That's what brought about the end of her love affair and made her so unhappy.'

'That's definite, is it?' asked Leeyes. 'That Brenton'd killed Joseph Short, I mean?'

'The two men had worked together at United Mellemetics and Brenton had picked up a lot of the history of the Short family there from Joe. Certainly enough to get by, anyway. Then, after the aircraft accident, he saw his chance. After all, he knew then that there was no one around in England any more after that to contradict what he had learnt. Don't forget that the Short boy had been educated all over the place – not in England at all – and so there wasn't anyone around here likely to remember him well. Brenton'd altered the photograph in Short's passport...well, fudged it a bit, anyway. That's not too difficult and most people don't look at passport photographs too closely.'

'Passport photographs don't tell you a lot,' pronounced Leeyes sagely, 'but I suppose it was better lost.'

'Not for that reason, sir,' said Sloan, sticking to his narrative. 'He lost the passport because it had Joseph Short's height in it. Brian Brenton is much taller.'

'So that's what all that business with the table was about, Sloan.'

'Yes, sir. That was the proof positive. The clincher, you might say. That's why he had to lose the passport – after Simon Puckle had seen it but before anyone cottoned on to the height difference.'

'Go on.'

'Joe Short had applied to Cartwright's after he lost his parents and got the job there. Brenton killed him when they went on a trek in the jungle the weekend Short was supposed to leave United Mellemetics and go to Cartwright's. The body's never been found, and according to the ambassador there, isn't likely to be, the jungle being what it is. Then all Brenton had to do was turn up at Cartwright's as Joe Short. It's a big island, you know, and the two places are a long way apart and in a slightly different way of business.'

In the maelstrom of investigations, Sloan had found an atlas and turned up the island of Lasserta.

'Then,' he carried on, 'when Brian Brenton didn't turn

up for work at United Mellemetics as usual and the false Joe Short turned up at Cartwright's Consolidated Carbons as planned, everyone out there thought it was Brenton who had gone missing.'

'Malice much aforethought,' observed the superintendent judicially.

'Very well planned indeed by a very cool customer,' agreed Sloan. 'All he had to do was wait until the old lady died and then come back and claim the inheritance. A big one, mind you, that he must have known all about. Don't forget that she was blind and deaf by then and wasn't alive anyway when he did turn up.'

'There being nobody still around here in Calleshire to say he wasn't the real McCoy,' Leeyes played with a pencil, 'since nearly all Josephine's family had fallen out with her in the past and weren't in touch now anyway.'

'Nobody around except Lucy Lansdown, that is. Don't forget, sir, as far as she was concerned the Brian Brenton whom she saw at the funeral could have been any member of the family. She didn't know – had no reason to know – that he was there masquerading as Joe Short. He came in late, remember, and she didn't go to the wake. All she was supposed to think was that Joe Short hadn't come back from Lasserta for it, which wouldn't have been unreasonable considering the distance.'

'And he finds out where she was living these days from those little cards the undertaker gave Janet Wakefield?'

'Yes, sir. He might have known it already but Lucy Lansdown had moved from Calleford so he mightn't have done.' He coughed. 'I'm afraid Mrs Wakefield feels very guilty about passing them on as she did. Naturally he would have destroyed that one straightaway.'

'I think she should feel very lucky that Brenton didn't kill her as well,' said the superintendent robustly. 'You got there just in time, Sloan.'

A noticeably shaken Janet Wakefield had explained to Sloan that she had been about to ring the police and tell them that she had noticed the slip the so-called Joe Short had made by mentioning Lucy Lansdown's name when no one was supposed to know this. Then, before she could do anything about it, the man himself – as amiable and plausible as ever – had turned up on her doorstep suggesting a farewell visit to the grave on his part.

'Then,' she had told Sloan, 'while we were driving there he actually led the conversation round to that very thing. He asked me if I'd noticed and I said yes.'

'Did you indeed?' said Sloan, glad to be interviewing her in her own home and not looking down at her dead body in the morgue. 'And what did he say?'

She had given a shaky little laugh. 'He made me promise not to say anything about it because that dim young constable of yours had let it out by accident but he didn't want him to get into any trouble.'

'Plausible,' said Detective Inspector Sloan, but not unkindly. 'I understand Crosby feels the slur deeply.'

This was, in fact, an understatement. The detective constable was still muttering about it when Sloan finally reached his own office.

'Hanging's too good for some people,' declared Crosby. 'He shouldn't be allowed to get away with it.'

'I don't think he will, Crosby. The evidence against him is pretty conclusive, although that slip over the girl's name was the only one he seems to have made.'

'That's good, sir.' He pushed a report under Sloan's nose. 'This'll help, too. The Met confirm that, although a man calling himself Short arrived from Lasserta when he said he did, and booked into the airport hotel for the night, he actually hired a car later that same night – a quite different one from the one he collected the next morning. He used Brian Brenton's passport and driving licence the first time...'

'His own, actually,' Sloan corrected him mildly. 'I expect he posted them straight back to Lasserta first thing the next day.'

'To come down to Berebury and break into the nursing home to plant that photograph there,' carried on Crosby who, once started, was difficult to deflect. 'Pretty silly that, if you ask me, to use his own passport and driving licence.'

'Not really,' mused Sloan. 'If anyone had got as far as finding that much out, he knew he'd be sunk anyway. And the first hire company would have wanted some evidence of identity and a driving licence before they let him take one of their cars away so he would have had to use Brian Brenton's for those. He couldn't very well use Short's passport then, now could he?'

'It'll all take a bit of explaining away, anyway,' observed the constable with some satisfaction.

'There'll be fingerprints and so forth coming from Lasserta now that the cat's out of the bag,' said Sloan, who had been busy with the assembling of evidence for the Crown Prosecution Service. 'He's still keeping his cool, though.'

'Even he can't pretend he's six inches shorter than he is,' said Detective Constable Crosby incontrovertibly.

'And even a defence counsel shouldn't be able to talk his

way out of that,' said Detective Inspector Sloan. 'At least, I hope not,' he added, a man given to hedging his bets as far as the Crown Prosecution Service was concerned.

It was some time later before the reinterment of the body of Josephine Eleanor Short took place in the churchyard of Damory Regis. Janet Wakefield had had no hand in making the arrangements this time. Instead the formalities had been accomplished by Simon Puckle in his capacity of sole executor and trustee of the deceased's estate. He stood beside the coffin now, solemn and respectful.

The Reverend Derek Tompkinson, the vicar, was there, murmuring that canon law didn't really cover reinterments but that he would be saying a few suitable prayers. It was he who had told them that people called Arden had lived in the village for a long time, although there were none of them now there. 'The last one – that is George Peter Arden – was killed flying over France in the war,' he had explained. 'Dangerous, hectic days...'

Tod Morton was there in his best frock coat, and supervising the lowering of the coffin back in its place. 'No dummy screws this time, Inspector, I promise,' he whispered in Sloan's ear as he led the way past him. He had pointed to the war memorial nearby and said, 'At least we know now why the old lady chose to be buried just here in the churchyard.'

The police had come there dressed in uniform for reasons too indefinable to put into words. Detective Inspector Sloan and Detective Constable Crosby were solemn and respectful, too. And silent on the matter of a recent raid by 'F' Division's Drugs Squad that had discovered a Sri Lankan sapphire ring in the home of a notorious drug dealer. And equally silent on the matter of a proposed raid on the home of Matthew Steele, scheduled for dawn the next morning, although as Crosby had said, 'I don't know why we should bother, sir. The diamond ring must have gone ages ago and he still hasn't been back home.'

'It's a loose end,' said Sloan.

Superintendent Leeyes had expressed himself forcefully on the matter of loose ends. 'I don't like them, Sloan. You tell me that you think Steele had tried to break into the undertaker's first.'

'That's right, sir. And when he couldn't get in there he went for the grave.' Sloan had told him that the young man was in dead trouble with a dealer at the time, as if that completely explained his behaviour – which perhaps it did. 'We'll get him in the end, sir,' promised the inspector. 'He hasn't got any brains.'

'See that you do,' ordered Leeyes grandly.

Janet Wakefield was there. She had dressed with great care for Josephine Short's first interment at Damory Regis. She had dressed with equal – if not, greater – care, too, for Josephine Short's reinterment in the churchyard there.

But differently.

'I'm going to be wearing my black,' she had informed her friend, Dawn, at one of their coffee sessions.

'But, Jan, I thought you—'

'I feel I really know Josephine now,' Janet insisted, 'and that even though she's dead she's still part of our family.'

'If you ask me,' said Dawn frankly, 'I should have said it was more of a case of your being part of her family.'

'Yes, well, maybe… Anyway, I wished I'd known her when she was alive.' Janet went on earnestly, 'She must have been… well, very feisty in her day.'

'In spite of losing everything,' Dawn reminded her. 'And I don't mean just her faculties.'

'She had lost everybody who was anything to her,' said Janet sadly. 'How she stayed sane, I don't know.'

'At least she was spared knowing that her grandson had been murdered,' said Dawn, metaphorically looking for crumbs of comfort in a notably bare larder.

Janet kept her head turned away towards the coffee pot, not meeting Dawn's eye, while she said, 'Bill and I have decided that if we have – if we were ever to have – a girl, that we'd call her Josephine.'

Dawn looked up sharply enough to catch sight of a blush creeping up her friend's cheek. True friend that she was, she merely said diplomatically, 'What a nice idea. How long now before Bill comes home again?'

'He's working his notice out now and then he's coming back for good. Not,' she added hastily, 'that Simon Puckle says we can assume anything on timing as far as inheriting the estate is concerned. Not yet, anyway.'

'Not until it can be proved that the real Joe Short is dead, I suppose?' said Dawn, who had been briefed on the matter by her husband, an insurance man. 'Don't you have to wait for seven years or something awful like that without him being found?'

'We understand from Simon Puckle that it may not be necessary,' said Janet, pushing a coffee cup towards Dawn.

Dawn sat up. 'How does he work that out?'

'Actually...I know this sounds silly...but Brian Brenton is being very helpful.'

'I can't believe that, Jan. Surely not?'

'He is. He's told the police exactly where in the jungle to look for the body.'

'You're joking!'

'No, I'm not.' She frowned. 'It seemed very odd at first and I didn't understand, but they told me he's hoping to be charged with murdering Lucy Lansdown and to go to prison for that here in England.'

'Hoping? He must be mad.'

'They have the death penalty for murder in Lasserta,' Janet explained simply.

Lucy Lansdown's brother was also there at the interment, soberly dressed and still sad. 'It's nice of you to come,' Janet said to him.

'It doesn't do to think of what might have been, does it?' he said, shaking his head. 'Poor Lucy.'

Janet shuddered and nearly lost her composure. 'No.'

'Poor Lucy,' he said again.

'Poor everybody,' said Janet.

Matthew Steele wasn't there. He was in custody on charges, various, carefully drawn up under the Theft Act.

Mrs Linda Luxton wasn't there either. As she had explained to Simon Puckle, there was someone else in room 18 now and she was very busy. 'And one has to move on, hasn't one?'